PENGUIN BO(

SALVAGED FROM 1. ._ rALL

Dawn is a feminist academic researcher and writer who strives to bring the stories of erased or forgotten women and their role in history to centre stage. She called Singapore home for twelve years during which time she made lasting friendships, was a volunteer guide for the city's museums, began her fiction-writing career and found publication. She has a PhD in Creative Writing from Edith Cowan University in Western Australia and now lives in Perth. She misses many things about the vibrancy of multicultural Singapore, especially the food.

She has published five novels, including *The Straits Quartet*, four novels set in nineteenth century colonial Singapore (2007–2013); and *Finding Maria*, a mystery set during Singapore's post-war race riots (2017) which was shortlisted for the Penang Monthly Literary Prize (2018). Her short stories have featured in anthologies in Southeast Asia and Australia. In 2013 she won the Melbourne Athenaeum Library Short Story Prize. She also writes for stage and screen and won the NexGen Short Film Festival Prize in Perth for her screenplay *The Wallpaper*.

Amongst other things, she is currently writing a crime/detective series set during the Japanese Occupation of Singapore. She is passionate about history and heritage conservation and volunteers with the National Trust of WA.

Website: www.dawnfarnham.com
Facebook: dawnfarnhamauthor
Instagram: @farnhamauthor

ADVANCE PRAISE FOR *SALVAGED FROM THE FALL*

'This is an excellent novel . . . compelling, with rounded and engaging characters. A wealth of sensory detail brings the world of 1940s occupied Singapore to vivid life.'

—Professor Diana Wallace, author of
The Women's Historical Novel 1900-2000 (2004)

'A wonderful piece of writing . . . evoking place and time . . . saying something about the human experience that conventional histories struggle to do.'

—Christine de Matos, author of
Japan as the Occupier and the Occupied (2015)

'The novel skilfully integrates wartime Singapore and Malaya's historical, social and physical settings with the seven main female characters' actions and interior realities. Perceptive authorial insights give her novel a balanced moral authority.'

—Dr Simone Lazaroo, author of
The World Waiting to be Made (1994)

Salvaged From The Fall

Dawn Farnham

PENGUIN BOOKS

An imprint of Penguin Random House

PENGUIN BOOKS

USA | Canada | UK | Ireland | Australia
New Zealand | India | South Africa | China | Southeast Asia

Penguin Books is part of the Penguin Random House group of companies
whose addresses can be found at global.penguinrandomhouse.com

Published by Penguin Random House SEA Pte Ltd
9, Changi South Street 3, Level 08-01,
Singapore 486361

First published in Penguin Books by Penguin Random House India 2023

Copyright © Dawn Farnham 2023

ISBN 9789815058765

Typeset in Garamond by MAP Systems, Bengaluru, India

www.penguin.sg

There must be those among whom we can sit down and weep and still be counted as warriors

—Adrienne Rich, *Sources*

'Each time a girl reads a womanless history, she learns she is worthless.'
—Myra Pollack Sadker
Still failing at fairness: how gender bias
cheats girls and boys in schools and
what we can do about it (2009)

'The truth has never been told about women in history: that everywhere man has gone woman has gone too, and what he has done she has done also. Women are ignorant of their own past and ignorant of their own importance in that past.' *Of Men and Women* (1941)
—Pearl S. Buck,
Nobel Prize for Literature, 1938

'Everything we know about war we know with a man's voice. Women are silent. Only at home or among their combat girlfriends do they begin to talk about their war, the war unknown to me. Not only to me, to all of us.' *The Unwomanly Face of War: An Oral History of Women in World War II* (1985)
—Svetlana Alexievich,
Nobel Prize for Literature, 2015

SYONAN

Koki 2605
Showa 21
1945

Simone

Queen Victoria has lost her nose. A sooty crack threatens her orb. A pitted grey rash crawls from her gown to her tiny, chipped crown. Heavy to move perhaps, but heavy on symbolism. Her Majesty's reduced state might appeal to the Exhibition Committee.

Simone writes this on a sheet of shiny toilet paper and savours, for an instant, the faint olfactory evocations of carbolic. The stash of Jeyes bum wiper has become too valuable for its former uses. For that there is their shitty newspaper.

Her wooden sandals make a click clack on the tiled floor. Click clack. Other shoes. Green snakeskin platforms with peep toes and ankle straps. Dancing at the Sea View. *Blue moon, the only one I could care for.* What happened to them? What does it matter?

She steps over the ant army relentlessly crossing the gallery with a booty of dead moths, cockroaches, and cicadas and clicks down the gloomy alley of snakes and lizards. Sagging stuffed tigers, tapirs, boars and monkeys, moth-eaten buffalo heads, the Sultan of Johor's rickety elephant skeleton. She avoids the lifeless staring eyes. Natural history museums: a miserable hecatomb of dead animals. The heat is heavy and damp. The smell is mould, mothballs, paraffin, and neglect. She catches her image in a flyblown glass case of marine molluscs. Scrawny. The twice-patched armpits on her blouse threaten to let her down. And what a fright, the hair. She turns away.

In the old taxidermy room are the portraits of colonial big wigs. An unconsciously ironical choice was it? She pulls open the shutters. The room floods with light. Mrs Sugiyama, secretary to the Exhibition Committee, has asked for Shenton Thomas and the degenerate King Edward VIII. Hensei. The word is new to her but it's fitting and she likes the way it rolls in her mouth. Strange. Degenerate. Bizarre. The whole damn thing is bloody *hensei*.

A faint bumblebee drone. B-29s glint silver as they sail towards Nippon. She understands the tactics. The Allies have to destroy the hive. Until the Emperor Bee is dead, the workers will never stop. The flyspecks below must wait.

All the world's a stage. Singapore, once the Old Vic, is now a theatre of the Noh where masked faces of ghosts and spirits play out their part in the agonisingly slow, tedious drama of survival or death. Where the actors, at any moment, drift unnoticed off the edge.

Outside, a Periplaneta americana smacks into the window pane. She watches its wings flutter and picks idly at the scabs on her arm. Another hour to lunch. Because the Marquis is coming today it should be copious. A big dollop of soft white rice with soupy chicken curry and crispy fried kankong. Oozy sago pudding with palm sugar. Her stomach gripes. Hunger is the one true thing. Don't grumble, Simone, she says to the one inside her head who wants to scream. Keep your head down. You haven't got boils or bloody beriberi.

She shuffles paintings, searching for Shenton Thomas's fatuous phyzog and the hensei ex-King, one eye on the stunned cockroach which, recovered, flies away. Mounds of paper begin to pile against the windowpane like sand.

The museum garden is ankle-deep in leaflets, doing a fox trot with the wind. They swirl into eddies, skip, trip and tumble between the serried rows of tapioca and sweet potato and cling thickly to the hairy red fruit of the rambutan trees. Hundreds of thousands of others dance and flutter on the streets and rooftops of the town.

Germany has surrendered unconditionally to the Allies, she reads. *Japan now stands alone.*

JOHOR

Kay

Three tiny Chinese men are on their knees, hands bound. Two miniature Japanese officers roll up their sleeves. The third, perched on the steps of a flimsy hut, harangues the villagers knotted together in fear.

Kay can't hear the words. It doesn't matter. It's always the same. There is only guilty and only one punishment.

The Chinese say *sha yi jing bai*, kill one, warn a hundred. Chinese idioms are short, brutal, direct. The English use a more subtle French expression, *pour encourager les autres*. It comes to the same thing.

With a flourish two officers draw their swords. Children hug their mothers' knees. A woman flings herself at the feet of the third. Kay flinches. Don't beg. They like it when you beg. The officer kicks the woman in the head. She slides to the bottom of the steps and lies still. A crushing wave of memory moves Kay's hand to her breast. The children's mouths open in silent screams.

The swords rise. The two young Malay sisters at Kay's side draw breath and turn away.

'Look,' Kay says. The girls slide their eyes. She can't let them not see. To endure you must nurture hate. And ruthlessness. You must above all cultivate ruthlessness.

4

The downward stroke. The blades cut clean. Tiny, red spurting fountains. The headless bodies slowly tilt and droop like rice stalks under heavy rain. The villagers collapse in a heap. When it's safe, they will bury their dead, gather all their belongings, their tools, their chickens, goats and children and join the communist camps. They have been punished for the crime—rightly or wrongly—of supplying food and information to the guerrillas. All the Japanese have achieved is an abandoned village, abandoned plantations and a fanatical allegiance to the communists for whom they will now clear land and grow food on the slopes of the mountain valleys. The communists turn no one away. They are the legions of the last recourse.

'Let's go,' Kay says.

They follow the tree line on the ridge. The descent is gradual, a muddy, slippery trudge. The hill people's meandering path to the road is overgrown. Invisible to eyes other than theirs.

The police station is a planter's house on the edge of the run-down rubber estate, abandoned as the Japs swept down Malaya. Bamboo staves bar the windows. Isolated. Insecure. Kay frowns and looks along the road. Deserted in the late morning heat. Cicadas drone. She knows this place. There are three Malay policemen in the station. No Jap soldiers.

'Why here?' she whispers to Ravi at her side. 'This place is too easy to attack.'

Ravi, her most trusted Sikh lieutenant, stretches his neck. 'They captured him last night at the bookshop the commies use as a meeting place.'

'Feels like a trap.'

Ravi shrugs. That is the information. Lao Wu, head of the communist anti-Japanese forces in southern Johor, was captured last night. He is being brought here. Contacts are the intimate concern of their Chinese radio operator, Yuan, who has a network of Malay, Indian and Chinese fishermen, shopkeepers and farmers from Senai to Johor Bahru. Kay never asks. If she's captured she doesn't want to have anyone's name on her lips. Not ever again.

The sound of a car and they ebb into the forest. Kay raises her shiny new Lee-Enfield. The Japs found a stash of British weapons hidden on a beach. That information had zinged along the jungle telegraph. Poorly guarded by the Malay heiho auxiliaries, it had been easy to steal it.

The fact is that the Japs know way too much about the Chinese communist-led forces and their contacts with the British infiltration Force 136. There's a traitor in their midst and, astonishingly, she knows it is the communist leader Lai Tek, whom they've observed coming and going on the roads of southern Johor, seemingly untouchable in a Morris 8 HP saloon, number plate S4678, property of the Singapore Kempeitai. He's a double agent. It's so damn obvious. How can those fools not suspect him?

Her unit has limited contact with the reds. As far as Kay knows, the existence of this little force is unknown to the Japanese, the vast mishmash of communist and KMT guerrillas, bandits, criminals and the generally furious and dispossessed, all loosely gathered under the heading of the Malayan People's Anti-Japanese Army. She intends to keep it that way.

The rifle is shiny. A dream. At night she sleeps alongside it, laying her scarred cheek against its smooth, wooden stock. She locks a bullet into the bolt head, aims towards the car and scopes the men who get out. One Jap officer. A captain. She draws a sharp breath.

Tsuji.

Shock, fear and hate burst like a grenade. She gets the back of his head in the crosshairs of the rifle and wraps her finger on the trigger. One second, and he'll be dead. But her hand shakes. Sweat swamps her body and her head swims. Miss and they'll all be dead. Kill and they'll all be dead. The Jap by Tsuji's side carries a 99 Arisaka light machine gun. Reliable and deadly. She hasn't prepared the others to spread out and ready themselves for combat. She wipes her hand on her thigh and stretches her fingers.

A second Jap soldier half-drags a hooded man from the car. 'That must be him,' Ravi whispers. 'Lao Wu.'

She hears the drone of the American planes, a reminder of the wider war. Nothing to them down here. This Lao Wu is a prize for the Japs. They should rescue him if they can. If not, they should kill him. But right now, in this instant, the sight of Tsuji has set a drumbeat in her head. Kill him. Kill him. Kill him. She puts her finger to the trigger.

The sound comes first like the whoosh of wind before rain. A storm of paper blots out the sun.

SYONAN

Zahra

The leaflets drift and flutter in the courtyard. Zahra gathers them, glancing at their words before bundling them into a basket, signalling with her hands to Noor, her young sister, to help.

Together they clear the courtyard but there is little they can do about the piles on the roof tiles and ledges. Or those stuck on the bamboo washing pole jutting from the front of the house, its Japanese flag sticky with soot from the recently bombed oil depots on the outlying islands.

She feels the usual sudden burst of soul-shivering shame at this slavish, craven act. Unmade, worthless. What actual difference does the surrender of Germany make to them?

If life is a house then what is she to make of living in this one? On shelves and in cupboards she bumps into remnants of the family that lived here: a Chinese almanac, a child's hairbrush; scattered pictures in a drawer—grandmothers, fathers, uncles, aunts, children; a woman's shoe abandoned on the top stairs. She knows they're all dead. The cracks radiating from the bullet hole in the hall mirror are words. Ghosts everywhere.

She goes to the mirror and stares at her distorted image. Each crack reminds her of the things she had chosen not to see. Her eyes, a thousand shards, look back. She's a ghost too, a transparent, shameful parody.

She tries not to think about any of this. The sharp cutting edge of the shattered glass might be a way out but like thinking, no damn good if, despite all the shame or perhaps because of it, you have to last. She begins to cover the bruises on her neck with powder.

SINGAPORE

8 December 1941

By the grace of Heaven, Emperor of Japan, Emperor Syowa, seated on the throne occupied by the same dynasty from time immemorial, enjoin on ye, Our loyal and brave subjects.

The pilots of seventeen Mitsubishi G3M Nell bombers of the Mihoro Air Group of the Imperial Japanese Navy look down through light cloud on the distant but brilliant lights of Singapore. It is 4 a.m. The Emperor's call to duty is fixed in their hearts. The seven-man crew in each of the planes is buoyant with confidence. The planes carry a 1800-pound payload and have a range of 2400 nautical miles, a feat no other aircraft in the world can match.

Seven of the bombers stay at 12,000 feet to draw any searchlight or anti-aircraft fire. The attack formation languorously sheds 8000 feet. The sea races below the bombing windows. The harbour is lit. The streets of the city are lit. The lead bomber drops his bombs into the light. The others follow. The bombardiers watch the flashes and puffs of smoke below. The Nells fold unharmed into the night.

Banzai! The call echoes on their radios.

SYONAN

1945

Katsu-san

A smart cat in bad times keeps to the roofs and trees. The occupation and its privations have taught the cats of Syonan to be skittish and wary of the sibilant overtures of hungry humans. But this cat's tail curls around Simone's ankle in greeting. They're old friends. Survivors. In Syonan, the greatest of all skills is to learn to live with their contempt and your degradation. The price, if you let it, is dissolution. Shells, bones, silence. Once she had been unsure of life but perfectly sure of herself. To contemplate either, now, is pointless.

The cat has no concept of price. She has odd-coloured eyes, one blue, the other green, as if born into ambivalence and reared in scepticism. Though Simone cares little for cats—the stealthy assassins of the wild world—she sees in this one an example and an odd sort of comfort. Be the cat, Simone. In the early days she said it often. To stop feeling like a worm, cravenly wriggling in front of them. To understand the limits. To stop going mad. To endure the void.

It has not eluded Simone that the various incarnations of the cat reflect, like some feline chameleon, the personalities and social standing of her various guardians.

When Simone first saw her, she was flabby and dozing in front of a blazing fire in the air-conditioned study of Shenton Thomas, the Governor of Singapore, inevitably and unimaginatively named Winnie in some sort of awkward cross-gender adulation of Winston Churchill. Simone had learned, not entirely to her surprise, that the Governor always kept a fire in the grate, even in steamy Singapore. It reminded him of Surrey.

She'd been ordered into Government House to be verbally rebuked for a little article she'd written about his shabby and spineless leadership, the indefensible paucity of air raid shelters, the thousands of deaths a day, and the collapsing defence of his city. A week later the British had surrendered.

Winnie had been called simply Neko-chan, Little Cat, by common and ordinary vulcanologist Professor Tanaka, the first Japanese director of the museum and botanical gardens. Neko-chan had gone almost bald and appeared dazed and confused by the fall from colonial privilege. Tanaka, his research fatally hampered by the lack of volcanoes in Singapore, had busied himself instead in his self-congratulatory role as sainted scientist and saviour of the museum. Six months later, he'd been unceremoniously yanked back to Tokyo for his perceived pro-English bias. A liking for Worcestershire Sauce, Earl Grey tea and Robertson's Golliwog marmalade had been his downfall.

Now, after her adoption by the Marquis, a person of appropriate rank, the cat is sleek and glossy, and her name is Katsu-san—Miss Victory. Katsu-san wipes her whiskers at the foot of the statue of Raffles. Removed from his position on a plinth outside the Victoria Theatre and brought here, Raffles has, ever since, occupied a lowly position on the floor, diminished, as intended, by the size and majesty of the great rotunda, hopefully but not always successfully ensuring his head is never higher than any of the visiting Japanese dignitaries who occasionally pop in to gloat and take a few snaps.

Chaplinesque dictator, General Tojo, short and slight, made sure of his superior position by viewing the statue from the balcony above. Beneath the portrait of the weasel-faced Emperor, a photograph memorializing this visit stares down on Raffles alongside the band of Tojo's Keystone Kops: Wang, Zhang, Bose, Ba, Laurel, and Hardy, the Siamese one whose name she can never recall. Somehow, right from the beginning, she's been unable to stop herself using figures of American cinema as avatars of the conquering nationals.

Katsu-san signals the presence of her current guardian, the Marquis Fujimoto, Honorary President of the Holy Trinity, Chief Advisor of Malay Affairs and Civilian Governor of Malaya, handily related by marriage to the Emperor of Japan, their patron and protector. Katsu-san sprays a sharp stream of urine on Raffles' leg then pads quietly away, tail swaying, aloof and alone to hunt the rats and mice which infest the building.

Mrs Sugiyama erupts from the ethnographic room, carrying a tray of shrunken heads. Simone bows to fifteen degrees, an informal bow. Mrs Sugiyama has perfected the art of the bow on the run, especially to an inferior like Simone. To the Japanese scientists, The Three Stooges, it is thirty degrees; to the Marquis the formal bow of forty-five degrees held for a full three seconds. Like every hapless citizen of Singapore it has taken time and countless verbal humiliations, slaps, beatings, slow crucifixions and bloody beheadings to fully understand the enormous importance of O-jigi. But they'd got there.

'O-hayo gozaimasu,' she calls but Mrs Sugiyama, her ample grey and maroon kimono flapping, her geta clacking like gunshot, has disappeared. She is flustered because of the Marquis. The minute he arrives, never on time, he wants a pot of green tea and a tray of shrunken heads.

The Marquis had carried out some sort of ethnographic research amongst the Dayaks in Sarawak in the Thirties and fancies himself an expert on shrunken heads. It is rumoured he had cut off a few himself and shrunk them as a gift to the Emperor. Simone tries to imagine him crouched in the steamy jungle peeling the hair and skin from some bloody, recently removed head, sewing the eyelids shut, sticking a peg through the lips, boiling the lot over a lonely fire. She cannot. Shrinking heads is far too time-consuming and frankly icky.

Nevertheless, a visit by the Marquis is an occasion for joy. A bon viveur and man-about-town, he usually orders a proper lunch for his loyal minions, thus ensuring a warm and vibrant welcome. The rumour today is that this is goodbye. The Marquis has seen the kanji on the shoji screen and is flying away. If Katsu-san stays they will know. Rats desert the sinking ship. The biggest rats get out first. And they don't take the cat with them.

JOHOR

Java

The leaflets are a nuisance, inches of rustle underfoot. But gradually the paper is becoming mush, sucking up the moisture from the forest floor. An hour searching, spread out. Soft as mice. They find nothing. No Japs. No machine gun nests under palm fronds. One of the Malay policemen sits outside on the veranda, smoking. When the end comes, the policemen will be the first to die. They give names.

The heavy, shrill song of the cicadas drowns out any sound inside the house. The policeman flicks his cigarette butt and goes inside. They wait. Nothing moves. As if everyone's sleeping in the damp, oppressive heat. Or half-dead. Tsuji's car is still there. Kay can't shake the idea of a trap.

They settle down and share food. Spam, cold rice and tinned fruit dropped at night by the Brits. The Japs have no planes and the hills belong to the Orang Bukit—the hill people—and the guerrillas. The drops mean there's no shortage of food anymore; after three long years, no shortage of rifles, ammo, or radios either.

'Who told you Lao Wu was being brought here?' Kay says to Yuan.

'Malay heiho. Saw it. Told one of my informants.'

'You trust this information?'

He shrugs. What is trust? Who is trustworthy? The man had been thrashed and press-ganged into the Heiho, the unarmed Japanese auxiliary army. His sister had been raped and murdered, his family ruined. Hate is the primal motivation. 'The information is that this captive is Lao Wu. There are no soldiers around. We've looked everywhere.'

Her mind goes over and over it, like waves battering the shore. Lao Wu is valuable. Why don't they take him straight away to Johor or even Syonan? Do they really believe this information hasn't been spread on the jungle telegraph? Are they that arrogant? Or careless? Is this hooded man even him?

The sound of an engine echoes on the deserted road. Kay crouches, binoculars ready. Watson-Baker RAF issue. Crisp. Came with the last drop. In battle your equipment is everything. Everything.

From the car a woman is dragged, hauled between the soldiers. Kay, eyes pressed to the binoculars, is shocked. She lets this information digest. The woman is a friend. No. More than that. And because she recognizes the woman, she knows now who is this Lao Wu. He is Harold Cheng and the woman being hauled into the jail is his wife, Teresa.

Now Kay understands. They've brought her here to torture her, beat her, shoot her, behead her. Or threaten to. To make Harold talk. To make them both talk. When beatings, water boards and electric shocks don't work, they search for wives, husbands, sons, fathers, mothers. Tsuji has no time to waste with official paperwork or long journeys. He'll be here one day and no more. This station has been chosen because of its proximity to Harold's capture but also its isolation. Harold will talk or he will not. Either way neither of them will make it out alive.

'We have to attack,' she says to Ravi. 'I know that woman. She is Lao Wu's wife. They'll torture them to death. And Lao Wu may reveal names, places. Anything.'

Ravi is strong and loyal, her friend and bulwark against the long loneliness of the nights. Yuan and four other Chinese men, now hard, experienced, solid. The Malay sisters, hiding in terror, who watched their entire family massacred and ran into the jungle. Crazy now with youthful bravery, but trained and ready for anything. In camp there are six more. One Gurkha, down with blackwater fever. Two young, wounded Chinese men. Uma Nair, their Indian doctor. A middle-aged Chinese man with his Jakun wife who had lived and worked in the tin mines but fled to the hills when the Japanese came. This is Java Force. A motley crew forged from misery and necessity.

She signals to Yuan and the sisters. 'Spread out.' Yuan is really too important for combat. He's their radio operator and knows too much. But he never wants to stay behind. They all nod, obedient, and move out. They've become tight. They gelled to her because she knew the jungle better than they did. Where to rest. What to eat. They survived on her skill at trapping small animals and knowledge of jungle plants. And later, when it became a hell, they survived because of her understanding and closeness to the hill people. They trust her. So they follow her. Everything, she now knows, is a choice made from circumstance. There is no absolute morality—that is a lie. Everything really is a lie. Once she had believed everything. Now she believes nothing.

'One officer,' Kay says. 'Four Jap soldiers, three rifles, one 99 machinegun. Three unarmed Malay policemen. Two hostages, plus unknown prisoners inside. The Malay policemen will get out when they see us.' Kay looks at the group. 'Face covers. Close quarters. Throats. Chests. Clean. Take out your knives.'

They pull on the modified hijabs they use as face coverings and draw the slender razor-sharp fighting knife which can slit an artery and penetrate the ribcage. She settles the Enfield into a tree. The Chinese guerrillas carry theirs strapped to their backs, but it is too bulky on her small frame and no use in close fighting.

She touches the mask, the knife, the Webley sidearm at her waist, the reassuring motions like the protective sign of the cross. They all have their rituals and superstitions.

'Decide amongst yourselves who to target,' she says, 'don't forget the machine gun. The officer is mine.'

SYONAN

Kingfishers

Zahra watches Samad depart. He's had a bad night. Ulcers. He makes them all pay, including his sister Fatima flitting up and down the stairs at his whim. He only trusts Fatima to bring him medicines. But he loves sambal. Chillies. Pepper. Spice. The result is suffering. For them all. Zahra recognizes the defective intellect and utter irrationality but is powerless to combat it. He does not blame the ulcer, only the women who must cater to his demands which, of course, gives him the justification for punishment. His hatred of women makes no discrimination or concession to family. Fatima has her share of blows and humiliations.

But he's puffed with pride. The first native Deputy Director of the Syonan Kao Kunrenjo—the political training school for those deemed suitable to assist the Japanese in the regulation of the southern empire. The Jap Director recently scuttled off to Saigon. That's the only reason Samad's in charge. It's surprising they haven't closed it down. The Nippon language schools have turned into storehouses for artillery and heavy ammo. Every day the trucks unload. Reinforcing the centre. Ready for the siege.

The training school is in the north of the island. No cars, no petrol. The bicycle ride is two hours. Samad will live there. The work, he announced with a long look down his sharp nose, will take up every minute of his day and night. He will return on

Sunday. His absence is a glimmer of relief amidst the relentless violence and fear of the house.

Samad was the son of their servants. Before the war he'd worked for the Japanese Consulate as a clerk, learned to speak the language, and absorb their martial philosophy. She'd had no idea how ardently he wished for a Japanese victory. No idea that he'd applied to the Kao Kunrenjo the moment it opened in May of 1942. His parents continued to serve her father like the faithful retainers they were. She hadn't realized how much Samad hated that and them. She, who'd barely registered his existence, could have no idea that he never forgot her.

She'd imagined herself free. Her father, a widower, was a modern man. He took no other wife for it was a marriage of mutual love. He was a teacher of Malay language and literature. A poet. A believer in education and devoted to his daughters. He got her the job at the Malayan Broadcasting Company. The English bosses wanted a woman. She was the voice of the Malayan-language service, free to come and go as she pleased. She revelled in it. Believed it. Even after the Japanese took over she continued to work in the Cathay Building for Radio Syonan. The Japanese boss, soft-spoken and hapless Yoshida, liked her. She liked him. The Malay language propaganda was important to them to appease the Sultans and win over the people. Her voice was gentle and pleasing. Engaging and trustworthy. She translated and read out a lot of rubbish, but she didn't care.

Her father's sudden death had quickly shown her the truth. Amidst the arid pain of her grief, she came to understand that her freedoms were because of his power and protection. They evaporated overnight. Women were never free. It was an illusion. An uncle, a man she barely knew, emerged to bully her. Resign and get married, he ordered.

Yoshida wouldn't hear of it, so another man's protection saved her. The uncle had no power over him and the propaganda needs of Radio Syonan. But when Samad returned from a year studying in Japan, a favoured son of Nippon, a man she did not even know, her life became a wreck. He spoke to the uncle. It was impolitic to recall that Samad was a son of servants. He was now a man to be reckoned with and in the trust of the masters. Samad's gifts to the uncle were generous. Yoshida didn't care about forced marriage so long as she continued to work. Raising the whole sordid issue would have embarrassed him. Yoshida avoided all unpleasant subjects—torture, starvation, degradation—with an anxious sniff and a turn of his head. It had all been agreed between men. The first she knew was when the Imam turned up. She had never given her acceptance. Never said the words. By their own laws she isn't married and Samad is a rapist.

Samad had moved them all into this house of death. His parents live in her father's house now and have servants of their own. Zahra is scared for her sister, Noor. Thirteen years old, profoundly deaf, Noor has no one but Zahra. She is certain that one day Samad will take Noor as well. At first Zahra recoiled in disgust but also out of anger and hurt pride. How dare he touch her? Screaming at him until his fists struck arms and back and his boot kicked the air out of her lungs. Now she plays the submissive slave, stepping, when he comes, out of her body into the dark stream where she is carried into oblivion. It is, mercifully, brief. He has no interest in pleasure, merely power and control. His lack of stamina, his tiny penis and his pointless ejaculation, once endured and understood, permit her to live beyond the physical assault and bury herself within her mind. So she tells herself, but, sometimes, she isn't sure whether she is just playing at submission. Who is she now? She tries not to think about this. Why think about this?

Fatima, their gaoler, talks in phrases parroted from her brother. Words she barely understands. Kodo Seishin, Hakko Ichiu, Dai Toa Kyoeiken, Amaterasu Omikami. Every time she passes it, she bows to the Emperor's portrait. She does it out of fear of Samad's violent temper, as they all do. Once he would not have dared. Now he can crush her like a bug. All is circumstance. All is circumstance. Nothing else has changed but the power and morality of this moment in time which has turned everyone's world topsy-turvy. Sometimes Zahra feels like she's passed like Alice through a looking glass. Perhaps they all have.

She thought she was love and kindness and discovered that she was also hate and cruelty. A charmed, careless life had been ripped away and she had found aspects of her nature which had simply, perhaps, not been required. She was not resentful, she was glad. War, such a cataclysm, needed to make you something else, didn't it? She'd tried not to think about it, but now she fed on it. Hate of Samad gave her substance and the ability to endure. Love of Noor kept her sane.

Fatima, even controlled by Samad, cannot be with her every minute of the day. She has her own work at the Ministry of Information and Propaganda. Noor is the hostage, locked in the house forever in the charge of a simple-minded guard, ensuring Zahra's return. Where on earth, in any case, would they go? She has no one she can trust.

She parks her bicycle and joins the press corps. They have been summoned to the Museum. The Marquis is here to talk about the Great Yamato-Damashii Exhibition and always makes press announcements in his elegant, fluent Malay.

Dressed in impeccable grey hakama, the black haori carrying the crest of the Fujimoto clan, he walks the exhibition halls like a sleek goose, honking, followed by his gaggle of compliant goslings. He halts before a fragment of stone. She knows he will give a lecture on this ancient slab with its undecipherable markings relating it in his warped imagination to the Japanese concept of Hakko Ichiu—all the world under one Japanese roof. He is unflagging on the topic and adores a captive audience.

She hasn't set foot inside this place since before the war. She looks around and her eyes stop on the kingfisher exhibit. Memories of other times slide into her mind. She does not like to think of the past, unhinged as it is from the present. Dreams of superfluity—of food, of space, of privacy, of love—what good are these? Dreams of a future—that way madness lay. There is only the moment to moment.

Movement in the distance draws her eye and she sees, through the glass of the exhibit and with a jolt of recognition, a woman's face. But she cannot call or move. The grey goose is flapping his wings. The goslings must follow.

JOHOR

Teresa

The two Japanese soldiers smoking in the garden die instantly, their mouths smothered, the knives driven silently under the rib cage. Ravi takes up the machine gun. Two of the Malay policemen, as soon as they lay eyes on the masked heads of the guerrillas, fade into the darkness of the surrounding rubber trees. The third screams, perhaps involuntarily, surprised and afraid, raising the alarm.

They walk into the station. The third Jap soldier is scrabbling for his rifle. Two shots from her companions finish him. All her attention is fixed on finding Tsuji. She runs down the corridor towards the cells. The rattle of the machine gun and screams behind her tell her that the fourth Japanese soldier is dead and perhaps the Malay policeman too.

Kay sees Tsuji at the end of the corridor. Their eyes cross like swords. She raises the Webley. Only then does she see the grenade in his hand. It seems to absorb all the light. He slams the door as she fires. The explosion rocks the house. The door flies towards her like a steam train, hurling her to the floor, but saving her from the blast and the shrapnel. As the dust settles, ears ringing, she pushes the door off herself and scrambles to her feet.

She picks her way across the debris and sees the car screech away. She fires two shots at the tail lights and screams into the night. Tsuji has got away. Why didn't Yuan shoot him? Where is the watch? Her fury boils up but there is no time for that now. Tsuji will raise the alarm. She turns back into the house and picks her way to the cells.

He didn't throw the grenade at her or she would have been dead. He wanted to get rid of Harold. The grenade has collapsed the inner wall of the cell and blown a hole in the outer. Harold is in the middle somewhere, blown to bits, stuck to the debris in bloody chunks.

'Teresa,' she calls. The next cell is damaged but empty. She crosses the corridor to the office. Here the damage is less but part of the ceiling has collapsed. She sees a foot and moves chunks of wood. Teresa is bloody but breathing.

Ravi is at her side. 'Get her,' she says. 'On your back. We have to get out of here. The officer escaped. Where was the watch?'

She doesn't wait for an answer. She knows most of them would put a bullet in this woman and move on. The KMT men have no love for the communists. But they don't question. They tie Teresa to Ravi's back. She weighs nothing, a bag of bones.

They set the planter's house alight, gather all the weapons and ammunition they can carry, chuck the rest into the fire, and regroup. She grabs her rifle and they melt away, heading for the safety of the hills.

SYONAN

The Blue Feather

The two English scientists, Bertie Bradshaw and John Hatter, are muttering as she joins them in Bertie's room. 'Move the exhibits to the seed house. Why would the allies bomb the seed house?' Sandbags have appeared at the museum doors.

For most of the Occupation, these two Englishmen rarely knew where they would lay their heads at night. Hatter has been billeted in a room in the headmaster's house in nearby St Andrew's School for the past six months. That has now been turned into a military encampment. Bertie's been in an old storeroom in the Museum for that time. Katsu-san is curled sleeping in one of his old felt hats. When Tanaka was hauled back to Tokyo, Bertie took Katsu-san under his wing and nursed her, bald and pregnant, back to health. To Bertie's chagrin, the Marquis took mother and all six kittens to his own house. But it seems that Katsu-san's fondness for Bertie never disappeared. When it comes time for the Marquis to leave, this is where they always find her.

'I've been quite happy here,' Bertie says with a grin. Simone looks around the storeroom filled with unwanted specimens, boxes, and broken furniture. A pile of stuffed animals had been parted like the Red Sea to make a place for a camp bed surrounded by lumps of coral and earthenware jars and presided over by a Burmese Buddha in bronze. The corners of his mosquito net are tied to the leg of a mangy bear, the long tooth of a tiger's head, the arm of the Goddess Kuanyin and the handle of a pile of suitcases. She sees his point. The room was an expression of the man himself, scruffy, comfortable and quiet. Today both men are taking up residence in Hatter's old house in the Gardens. 'Do you need any help?' she asks but the men shake their heads.

Simone strolls back to Raffles and comes to a stop. A flash of brilliant blue against the alabaster white. A distinctive and beautiful feather lies at Raffles' feet. It is the plumage of the Javan kingfisher. She looks around. The halls are empty and silent except for the faint clacking of shoes on the marble floor in the distance. The museum has just closed its doors to the public for the day.

She walks quickly to the bird gallery. Along with the shrunken heads, the bird and butterfly galleries are the most popular with the Japanese public.

The stuffed kingfishers are perched on branches arranged by Mrs Sugiyama in an artful display of avian ikebana. The Javan kingfisher is in central position, given pride of place for its brilliant, deep-blue plumage and sharp bright-red beak.

She reads the exhibit plaque of faded typed lettering. Family: Alcedinidae, Subfamily: Halcyonidae. Above it, stuck onto the cabinet door with flaky yellowing scotch tape is the Japanese name: Kawasemi—River Cicada—poetic and pretty. Unscientific of course, but Mrs Sugiyama does not strive for science. She has put a poem alongside it written in hiragana in her elegant hand.

In the cicada's cry
There is no sign that can foretell
How soon it must die.

Most of Mrs Sugiyama's two sons lie on the icy ground of Northern China but the bones of their hands repose in the identical white boxes she keeps on her desk. They were cut off by a comrade and charred to bone for return to Japan, a grisly reminder of the supreme sacrifice. The shells of the two cicadas sit in a small bowl nearby, the ghostly shape of the insects retained in the minutest detail; as fine as gossamer when the light catches them in the morning. The white boxes of Mrs Sugiyama's sons are sealed with a carved jade cicada. The cicada and its ghostly shell. Symbols of fragility and brevity but also immortal regeneration.

Together Mr and Mrs Sugiyama have the flora and fauna of noble grief—the only sort permitted by the empire—covered. Mr Sugiyama is the titular head gardener in the Botanic Gardens, clipping order and silent emotion into the manicured bonsai. Mrs Sugiyama creates and recreates ikebana out of birds and insects, making dead things artful and beautiful.

Simone opens the cabinet and examines the Javan kingfisher closely. Is it missing a feather? She can hardly say. Mrs Sugiyama likes to dust and rearrange the birds regularly and, through over-handling, they are looking vaguely battered. But the feather did not find itself by chance at Raffles' feet. The blue feather is a signal from the old days. A call to arms, to a secret rendezvous. It is always to the same place and at the same time. After so many years it is not only astonishing but also deeply unsettling.

She is annoyed at the leaflets. Annoyed at the feather. For the three years and four months of this occupation, she has let herself go limp like a rabbit when the jaws of a fox clamp on its neck. Thanatosis. Self-mimosis. Feigning death in order to be spared it. Like the ghostly cicada shells on Mrs Sugiyama's desk, the old life shucked off, safely hidden in the trees and spaces of what she calls the Trinity: Father Library, Museum Son, and the Holy Gardens. They are the blessed haven, the perfect hideaway. And hunting for fatuous exhibits of British folly and colonial misdeeds, dusting shrunken heads and making tea for the Stooges, walking in the gardens in the moonlight, watching fireflies, sorting seeds, filling forms, reading and writing in a vast library untroubled by patrons is the perfect life in this hensei world made by vicious men.

But an ending trembles just over the horizon. What must we endure in this new eruption? It feels too much to bear. The Japanese won't surrender. The streets will be rivers of blood. The Great Exhibition is about this: Seishin, the Japanese spirit. Death before *their* dishonour includes all the inhabitants of the island. The newspapers din this in with headlines: *Those Who Do Not Fight, Do Not Eat. Those Who Do Not Win, Shall Not Survive.*

But there is hope, just a little bit of hope, for Bertie, Hatter, herself, and all the others there in that little sanctuary under the protection of the Emperor of Japan. All they have to do is sit still. Play dead.

She goes to the window. She feels as far from them as if she was at the North Pole but also, simultaneously, flushed with a longing to hear their voices. A tall rain tree stands outside the window, the sinewy fingers of the late sun striking the inner heart of it turning leaves and branches to amber and gold. A single leaf detaches itself and rests on the air, suspended it seems for a very long time before it falls.

A guttural shout startles her and a breeze snatches the feather. She gasps and leans out. Below a squad of sprawled, half-naked Japanese soldiers leer up.

SINGAPORE

1934

The Crocodile

'We are going to retrace the journey of Ponompuan,' Kay Chan said to the group of eleven-year-old girls seated cross-legged around her, 'the only daughter of the Great Creator Kinoingan, who climbed Kinabalu to make offerings to the spirits of the dead and then walked into the jungle wilderness to sacrifice herself for the good of the people. Also to honour Miss Lilian Gibbs, our Captain's aunt, who was the first woman and first botanist to climb Mount Kinabalu and discover thousands of plants new to science.'

Kay was twelve, only one year older than them, but a natural and articulate teller of tales. In the wavering light of the low campfire her face looked like an ancient seer, her voice sombre.

'It will take one afternoon, one night, and one morning. At the end you will be transformed, filled with the unselfish spirit of Ponompuan and the unflagging courage of Miss Lilian Gibbs, and we shall be as one.'

'How?' said Simone.

Kay smiled. 'Magic.'

'Ooh, magic,' said Molly and gazed at the stars.

'You are joking. A night? In the jungle?' Anita drawled, mouth turned down. 'What about the mosquitoes? I'm quite sure mummy won't approve.'

Kay sighed. 'Your father has given his permission. Your parents or guardians have all given permission. Captain McKenna has arranged everything. At the end of the trail on Sime Road she will be waiting at the King George Curry Cafe.'

Zahra clapped. 'Wonderful. Can we catch a monkey and cook it?'

'Oh, oh, my goodness. You can't eat a monkey, can you?' said Molly wrinkling her nose. 'I'm not eating a monkey. It's cruel.'

'You eat chicken don't you?' Zahra said. 'What's the difference?'

Molly made a face at Zahra. 'We're Buddhists. We don't eat animals.'

'No, yes, right, we're Buddhist,' Jenny said. 'Oh and Christian too. Anyway, the monkey king will punish us.'

'Really? A monkey king?' Zahra laughed.

'Actually we Hindus have a monkey *god*.' Anita looked condescendingly at Jenny. 'We're vegetarian. Pretty sure I shouldn't go.'

'I'm not sacrificing myself for anyone,' Simone muttered. 'But I'll keep notes for the newsletter. I don't particularly want to eat monkey but if needs must.'

'What about snakes?' Teresa said. 'Are there snakes? I'm scared of snakes.'

'You're scared of everything,' Zahra said.

'*Sangti Maria, nopuno' de graasia.*' Kay clapped her hands sharply. 'That's enough. No one is eating monkey. You will bring water and whatever food you eat with you, enough for two meals. There is a Scout hut on the trail. We will stay there.'

'There won't be boys, will there?' Molly said and Zahra turned her eyes heavenwards.

'When you say mountain do you mean Bukit Timah Hill? Let's get this straight,' Simone said. 'This spirit worship thing. I'd like more details.'

'It's a legend,' Kay said. 'We're not worshipping anything. We are taking a journey. Buck up your ideas.'

She tossed a small log on the fire sending sparks shooting into the night. They all sensed Kay's annoyance. Silence fell.

'Will there really be the spirits of the dead?' said Teresa finally, drawing closer to Kay and looking into the darkness.

'Only if we find some boys,' Zahra said and the others howled.

They were seven. Halcyon Patrol was an English-speaking mixed Girl Guide troop and Miss McKenna's pride and joy, the tangible expression of her absolute belief in internationalism and the sisterhood of women. Jean McKenna was Australian, fifty, unmarried, a life-long Guide, a teacher at the Zenana Missionary School and the Captain of the 5th Singapore Company of Girl Guides. She'd lived half her life in Malaya and arrived in Singapore bouncing with enthusiasm and generosity only a few months ago and begun the 5th Company. Currently the 5th Company consisted only of Halcyon Patrol.

'The parents take the girls out as puberty approaches,' Jean told them with a sigh. 'So you, my brave and wonderful girls, must carry the colours for the whole company for now. Whatever our station, whatever our differences, here they are as nothing. In the Guides there is no shall not and no cannot. We come together as equals in courage and resolution. Remember girls, it matters not how strait the gate, you are the master of your fate, you are the captain of your soul'.

She'd wrapped them all in her embrace. They had no idea what puberty was but they asked Kay. 'A damn nuisance,' she'd said. 'I'll tell you about it later.'

Kay, Chinese, was from Sabah, tall, dark-haired and dark eyed. She wore a raft of badges on her uniform, a band of kingfisher feathers on her hat, a bracelet of shells and animal teeth and a short-handled curved kris in her belt. She'd been raised by her Kadazan nanny. None of them knew the first thing about Kadazans. They'd never seen anything like her.

Their badge was the Javan kingfisher, *halcyon cyanoventris*, and Kay chose Java as her guide name. The others had taken the names of the other tree kingfishers. Zahra Zamroud—Blue—was Patrol Second. Anita Shah was White. Molly Salgado was Woody. Teresa Wong was Gray. Simone Martel was Red and Jenny Tan was Blackie.

The day of the trek they had been together in their soft brown dresses, scarves, and hats, occasionally fractious and sullen, for two months, practising knots and Morse Code, lighting fires, learning to cook things on sticks and forming tentative but disparate friendships. Simone and Zahra hit it off instantly, both tomboys, both frisky with legs that couldn't keep still, in love with hiking and dancing. Molly babied Teresa, who was small and shy, and was friendly and loving to everyone. Anita and Jenny couldn't stand each other because Zahra confided to Simone they were both spoiled rotten by their rich parents and anyway the Indians and the Chinese couldn't get along. They all liked Miss McKenna but were wary of Kay's fierce temper.

The climb and descent of Bukit Timah Hill and the trek along Rifle Range Road to Kampong Chantek was uneventful. The track to the Scout hut was muddy and the night spent there amongst general grumbling eventually passed, drowned out by a deluge of rain. The next morning, they plunged into the jungle following the trail alongside the sinuous west bank of MacRitchie Reservoir, now fed by overflowing and muddy waterways.

Until they reached Batu Creek. Where the crocodile changed everything.

Perhaps Kay knew that the crocodile was there, hiding in the murky shadows of the lagoon. She and Miss McKenna had walked that trail a dozen times. None of them asked. In the end it didn't matter. That journey and the crocodile became their creation myth.

Batu Creek was the final hurdle on their trail from Bukit Timah Hill to Sime Road. Normally a wide shallow stream of gently rilling water with a bridge of bamboo and rope, the deluge overnight had transformed it into an Amazonian artery four times its size, or so it seemed to their anxious eyes. The bridge lay broken and trailing in the rushing waters. There was no way to get across here and Kay turned them all upriver where the creek was higher and level, a wider and more placid lagoon filled with boulders. There, she told them, they would straddle the water and get safely to the other side.

It would take each of them helping the other to get across the causeway of six great stony giant's teeth between which rushed a series of teeming waterfalls filled with macerated leaves, sticks and branches. No one could do it alone without the risk of falling in and being crushed by the force of the debris. They must make a chain.

The six girls looked in dismay at the task which confronted them. Kay knew the signs of revolt. Molly was biting her lip and Anita's face would make a bear blink and tugged at her ear. Kay took a rope from her pack.

'We'll tie this around our waists and move forward one at a time. You are Guides remember. A Guide is a sister who has courage and is cheerful in all difficulties. We confront problems and solve them. After this it is only fifteen minutes to Sime Road.'

Perhaps the thought of a difficult return journey in sweltering humidity made up their minds? Perhaps it was the thought of ice-cold mango lassi and the taste of crispy roti prata at the King George Curry Café? They all nodded, even Anita who, with bad grace, agreed she didn't want to turn back.

Kay designated the order of their passage. Kay was first. Teresa was second. She was the smallest girl. She lacked physical strength but she would do anything for Kay so stepped forward with determination. With her right hand in Kay's and her left in Simone's, the rope locked securely around her tiny waist, she stepped onto the first rock. Simone joined her and sent out her hand for Jenny. Molly followed, then Anita and finally, drawing up the rear, Zahra. After Kay, she was the strongest of them all.

When Kay reached the bank on the other side and Teresa joined her, she quickly released them both, tied off the rope to the stout trunk of a coconut palm and shouted encouragement to the others. They were almost across. Simone and Jenny had just gained the bank, Molly was on the last rock, Anita was on the second to last rock and Zahra was behind her. Anita had been told to put her water canteen inside her pack but, as usual, she'd disobeyed and it now swung loosely around her neck. She stumbled and slipped as she stepped onto the final rock and went to her knees almost dragging Molly and Zahra into the lagoon. The canteen smacked the water as it landed, and the crocodile emerged like a spear from the depths and caught the canteen in its teeth, pulling Anita into the lagoon. Molly screamed as Anita's head disappeared and Zahra slipped into the seething water.

The rope was all that held them together and only the fact of Molly wedging her back and feet instantly into a crevice of the rock face stopped Zahra going further into the water. By now Anita was invisible. Zahra grabbed the rope around Anita's waist, pulling with all her strength. There was nothing she could do against the fearsome might of the crocodile but she drew near Anita, knife in hand and swiftly cut the leather strap on the canteen. The release caused Anita to bob to the surface and for both of them to fall back into the water.

Molly held firm but by now Anita was gasping for air, hysterical, and with each panicked scream and throw of her arms her head went below the water and she pulled Zahra with her. Jenny and Simone, both still attached to the rope, planted their feet against the rock and leaned back supporting Molly who, hand over hand, was desperately trying to reel in the other two. Kay plunged into the water and grabbed Zahra, pulling her towards the bank and Zahra grabbed the rope around Anita's waist with one hand and her long plait with the other, bringing her to the surface. Anita gasped and coughed but found ground and staggered up the bank. Zahra followed.

Kay was about to join them until she heard Molly's scream and turned back. The crocodile emerged, tail lashing, and sped towards Kay. And this was the part that no girl would ever forget. Kay did not give an inch but gathered up a thick branch which lay wedged between the rocks, steadied herself against the bank of the creek and waited. As the crocodile approached with open jaws, she side-stepped, thrust the branch into its maw and with a fierce cry punched it hard in the eye. The creature retreated below the water.

'Let's go,' Kay said, grabbing a terrified and paralysed Teresa, and they all turned and bolted away from the creek. After two minutes, Kay pulled them up and they collapsed into a heap and allowed all the tension to escape by laughing and crying hysterically.

In the fifteen minutes between the creek and Sime Road, they gathered themselves together, held hands and raised their voices in a spirited rendition of Comin' Round the Mountain.

When they met Miss McKenna at the King George Curry Cafe, they were filthy, scratched, bleeding, and bedraggled but also calm, uncomplaining, and magically filled with the unselfish spirit of Ponompuan and the unflagging courage of Miss Lilian Gibbs.

JOHOR

The Hill Camp

Teresa's breath is short and laboured. The journey to their camp was too hard. She lies on a bed of fronds. Kay wipes her face erasing the sweat and grime. They have medicine. They have morphine. She has given a shot, watching the liquid slowly enter Teresa's veins. Teresa opens her eyes. Her teeth are broken, her lips split and fissured. The frame of Teresa's body is cracked. Kay puts a cup of water to the ruined lips. Teresa drinks and recognizes Kay. She offers a smile.

Kay wants to sob but clenches her teeth together.

'You,' Teresa wheezes. The word holds a wealth of memory as it crawls feebly, croakily out of her. You and Me. Us. There had been a moment when, for each, nothing but the other mattered. Teresa's arm moves and she extends a hand. Kay puts it to her cheek.

'Yes, darling. Oh, my sweet girl. It's Kay. You're safe.'

'Harold?'

'Dead. It was quick.'

'A daughter. We have a baby daughter.'

Kay frowns.

'Zejian. Her name is Zejian.' Teresa coughs. Kay lifts her and blood spurts. 'With the nuns at Kampong Laut,' Teresa spits out the words between coughs. Blood pools in her lap, covers her chest. Gobs cling to her lips. Teresa grips Kay's hand. 'Get her. Save her. Promise.'

A baby. There is a baby. Thoughts crowd Kay's mind. She cradles Teresa's destroyed body. How can she be responsible for a child after what she did? But how can she refuse?

'Yes, I promise.'

Teresa's eyes close and Kay holds her.

'I don't mind dying, Kay,' Teresa whispers. 'Not now. Don't cry. I love you.'

'I love you, my darling. Sleep now.'

A promise. But how to keep that promise? Kampong Laut is a fishing village on the straits near Johor Bahru, the heart of the enemy, bristling with Japanese army camps.

SYONAN

Birds of a Feather

Simone organizes her bicycle under the verandah of the old black and white bungalow on Cluny Road that she shares with six other people. Three bungalows occupy this compound and are for the use of those working in the Trinity. The second bungalow houses Mr and Mrs Sugiyama and their servants. The third bungalow has accommodated various tenants over the years, usually lower-order visitors from Japan or its occupied territories. The compound, its vegetable gardens, and all the people in it are cared for by Jumairah, a Malay widow who lost a mother, father, husband, and four children in the bombing and seems to find a silent solace in her tasks.

Once the Gardens had a Korean food controller, but the Marquis had not liked him, and the business of the gardens and its produce has, for almost the entire occupation, been the responsibility of Mr Guan who is guardian and steward of the produce of the gardens to the benefit of the large staff and their families. He is scrupulously fair and, though many here have succumbed to disease, no one in these Gardens has died of starvation.

The Guans have two girls aged seven and five. They speak Japanese and know scads of Japanese songs, though their arithmetic is hazy. They speak no English, though both Mr and

Mrs Guan—Straits Chinese—speak it fluently. The Guans know the Japanese will punish them if the children speak English. The girls don't remember that this was once Singapore. They think that Bertie and Hatter are pale-skinned slaves like the POWs they've seen working in the streets and in the vegetable gardens. On occasion they are presented to visitors to the Gardens as perfect examples of the Emperor's loyal little subjects and give a concert to Japanese delight. Mrs Guan long ago learned that such displays mean increased rations and the gift of milk from the strictly sequestered herds of goats and buffaloes kept in the Gardens.

Simone eats her tasteless meal of tapioca cake and palm-oiled fried vegetables. It is Saturday. Tomorrow is a day of rest. Usually she sleeps, reads, goes for a walk in the Gardens, weeds the vegetable patch, practises Malay with Jumairah, or helps Mrs Guan make the spicy fig or mango chutney she sells to the top-end Japanese-only hotels to supplement their income. The war, of necessity, has improved her poor cooking skills simply by avoiding the confusion regarding more than three ingredients.

In her room Simone takes from under her bed Isabel von Hoff's suitcase. It contains the last of Isabel's dresses, white silk with pearl buttons, which she is saving for 'The Victory'. An empty bottle of lavender water still sends out a whiff of memory. Under the suitcase, below the floorboards in a tin box, are her old notebooks. She takes one out.

George Baker, the chief editor at the *Singapore Tribune,* had said to her one day as the town was bombed to ruination and the dead lay stinking in the streets: 'Forsan et haec olim meminisse juvabit. It's Virgil. Aeneas to the demoralized troops at the destruction of Troy. Perhaps someday we shall like to remember even these things. If the worst happens, Simone, write it down. Write it all down.'

She hadn't understood then. He was the editor. Why didn't he write it down? She soon found out.

The Japanese are fanatically opposed to the keeping of any kinds of diaries or records. At the beginning there were regular sweeps, the soldiers bursting in and throwing things around; over time, with their victories assured in their own minds, all that stopped. But it can begin again. She doesn't care anymore. Stories that start must run their course. It is no longer a choice. This story has become the teller of her. Of them all.

She opens the notebook at the first entry.

10 December 1941:

Saw Jenny today. At the big ARP post in the Chinese Secretariat building, which is used by the MAS as a first-aid station. Writing a story on the local efforts for civil defence. The bulk of the volunteers are Chinese but everyone gives a hand. Wardens telephone in telling the drivers where the ambulances are needed. The stretcher-bearers search for victims on the bombsites and bring the wounded back. The worst cases are taken to the hospital. Others are patched up and sent home. Jenny is working alongside the Eurasian and Chinese nurses in their starched white uniforms. She's radiant, smiling. Doing good. It's important, she said, excited.

Sixty camp beds were in rows in one of the rooms, filled with wounded. Chinese and Malay Girl Guide troops run the canteen, serving tea, coffee and biscuits all night. Proud of them. The post never closes. It is all run efficiently by the skinny young Chinese school teacher and his enormously fat number two, a dealer in goldfish. There's not a European in sight.

Everybody filled with zeal and gusto, giving their all.

Hardly inspiring stuff. All a bit Girl's Own. Still it was the first entry. She'd clipped the first article she'd written in this heady new role of war correspondent and stuck it under her entry. It was better.

Taking whatever is coming.

> Chow Hin Wah, age sixteen, is a St John's Ambulance Brigade
> nurse. She lives opposite her first aid post. She was wearing her
> white nurse uniform when I saw her and was on duty in spite of
> a bandaged head and badly shaken nerves the moment her house
> was razed to the ground. Hers is the spirit of the women and
> children of Singapore's diverse population which proved last night
> that it could take whatever was coming.

And to the end they'd stood, those young local nurses. When the
European nurses were ordered away, there they stood, the only
succour to soldiers and civilians right to the end.

She closes the notebook and takes out three photographs,
all the visual evidence she has of her past existence. The first
is a stiff traditional portrait. Her mother is seated with Simone
in her arms, her father standing behind. They are expressionless.
Were they pleased? It hardly mattered. By the time she was two, they
were both dead of influenza. The second is a class photograph
at the mission school when she was seven, thin, eyes cast down,
sitting alongside Teresa Wong, suffering from the chronic disease
of mixed blood, which caused shameful shyness. The third is the
day of Teresa's marriage to Harold. She touches Teresa's thin face
with the tip of her finger. They are standing outside a Chinese
restaurant. Above the door is a banner of Churchill alongside
Chiang Kai Shek. *Unity is Strength* it shrieks, the Chinese characters
marching alongside the combined troops of nationalist China
and Great Britain. All over the town, posters had mushroomed
showing vicious, short-sighted, buck-toothed Japs drooling over
a map of Asia.

She hadn't recorded this meeting but that day comes back
to her now, vivid and clear. The last time they were all together.
Nineteen years old. That day in December. Two days earlier Santa
had been blasted off the façade of Robinson's Department store
by Japanese bombs and the tenements of Chinatown obliterated.
Sixty men, women and children had died. They were at war.

So it was a surprise when Teresa asked them to attend her wedding reception and not just because they had all thought that communists didn't believe in marriage but because the husband, they all thought, was locked up in Changi.

Of course, Jenny said with a dismissive wave, Teresa had only become a communist because of Harold Cheng. Jenny's family were KMT, supporters of the China Fund and Chiang Kai Shek, as zealous as the Reds. To be here, Jenny had to believe that Teresa wasn't really a commie, just a pawn for Harold's ambition. But Simone knew that wasn't true. Teresa had joined the Communist Party at sixteen, a fact the others didn't know.

In 1938, the British had first locked Harold up for organizing strikes in the coalmines in Selangor. After his release he'd gone into hiding only to be arrested again, along with dozens of other young communists in 1941 and stuck in jail.

What a difference a few Jap bombs could make. With the crumbling of Malaya Command's northern defences, the communists had gone from terrorists to desirable recruits for the new British guerrilla forces being organized to fight against the common enemy. Harold, currently in the uniform of the Straits Chinese volunteer force, was about to embark on some hush-hush jungle training.

Jenny was in her second year of medical school. 'They've closed the place down,' she said. 'I'm working at a MAS unit at Havelock Road.' She spoke brightly, Simone recalled. Filled with a strange light of optimism. 'It's not just up to the British doctors any more. We have to prove our mettle.'

'They'll live in some hole on noodles and the communist manifesto,' Anita said, 'but perhaps they'll have each other.' Anita was glum. An arranged marriage was on the horizon. The man had been chosen. She loves another. Wrong caste. Wrong family. Not enough money. Not for the first time since growing up, Simone notes what a relief it is not to have parents bossing her about.

'Don't marry this man,' Molly said with romantic fervour and Anita shook her head.

'You don't understand.' And of course she was right. Molly couldn't understand. Beautiful Molly was carefree. She and her brother, Charles, lived with a dotty aunt on the generous allowance of their wealthy Ceylonese grandparents. Good-looking Charlie made Malayan movies and Molly lived in a world of song. That day, unusually, she was not in the company of her lugubrious middle-aged Austrian music master, whose breath, like his intentions, was murky, but a slender English pilot in uniform. He was ill-at-ease and perhaps wishing he were in a club somewhere having a gin pahit with fellow pilots rather than stuck in this dreadful mix of Reds and oriental misfits. Only his inbred politeness and perhaps a lusty desire for Molly appeared to keep him in the restaurant.

'Harold wants to make sure Teresa is taken care of by his parents, do you think?' Molly said, 'because he has to go off and fight. It's very brave, don't you think? And romantic.'

Simone didn't think it was romantic. Harold's parents were not present. If they'd known about this marriage they'd have been horrified. Harold's communist beliefs, his stand for a cause, despite or perhaps because of his parents' sugar fortune, gave him a certain curiosity value. He was ten years older than Teresa, good-looking in a deadly serious sort of way. Why did communists lack a sense of humour?

They'd been married in some tawdry civil ceremony. In the beginning Simone had believed that Harold was taken with Teresa because she represented the downtrodden proletariat. Love too, perhaps, but she could not quite shake off the idea that Harold had chosen to marry a woman who had shock value and was guaranteed to make his father die of shame. 'Harold had a sister,' Simone said. 'She led a guide troop to China to fight the Japanese. She died. Actually, I think they all died.'

'Oh, yes,' Molly said. 'I read about her. Celia Cheng. It was in the papers. His sister.' She turned her eyes to Harold with a renewed admiration. 'God, how brave.'

'Foolish,' Anita said. 'What good did it do?' She looked around. 'Where's Kay? Is she coming?' Anita pulled at her uniform. They'd all agreed to come in their guide outfits, to present a solid front for Teresa. All for one and one for all with no distinction as to class. A suitable decision for a communist wedding, Jean had insisted. The idea of Anita turning up in some splendid sari had made the decision easy.

'Kay will be here. There's Jean and Zahra.' Simone moved toward the new arrivals, trailed by Molly and Anita, both horrified at the thought of talking to the grim-faced Reds gathered in one corner of the restaurant.

Anita's words had stayed with Simone. 'What good did Celia Cheng's sacrifice do?' Was an article in the newspaper enough to lose your life? Perhaps Harold and Teresa thought so. Did a desire for noble death give meaning to life?

There are watchers and doers. The guides had made Simone take action but it was always, despite her energy, with a restless reluctance and more as a witness than participant. Her curse perhaps was that she could see issues from more than one angle. A watcher. A reporter. Teresa, despite her shyness, was a doer. She'd found a meaning and purpose to her life in Harold, the communist party, the struggle against British colonialism and female disempowerment. Simone knew what the others did not. Because of her awful past Teresa was filled with the joys of freedom, the spurting love of life. Her freedom was the engagement with and for others, for her sisters in struggle.

The girls hugged. They thought of themselves as girls, perhaps because Jean was there. As Jean moved to greet Teresa, Jenny whispered: 'Jean doesn't look well, does she?'

'She looks a bit too thin,' Molly said. 'Perhaps she's worried about her family in England with all that blitz thingy.'

'That's in London, silly, not Australia.' Zahra made a face. Molly turned pink.

'Well, I don't know,' Molly said, shaking her head. 'I wasn't any good at geography. I don't even know where these Japs come from. Or why they want to bomb us.'

'Oh, that'll all be over in no time. The British will knock them off soon enough,' Anita drawled.

The town was awash with men: Australian, British, Indian, foot soldiers, flyers, sailors. The streets and beaches, the cafes and restaurants, clubs and hotels were bursting. Like all the other newspapers and radio stations the *Tribune* trumpeted that the British will boot the Japs up the backside. The little half-blind yellow men. 'And the Indian Army will sort them out,' Anita said. 'There's this one man…,' Anita looked up and blushed.

'What about Asia for the Asians?' Jenny said, seeing Anita's face and changing the subject.

'Are you a Red, too?' Molly said with a frown.

'No.' Jenny sounded fierce. 'Of course not, but it's no secret that Kay, Jean, and I think that Malaya should be for Malayans. Have you seen what the Japs are doing in China? Haven't you seen the photographs? Jean gave a talk on the atrocities last week. It makes her frightfully unpopular with the English, you know. They want to ignore it all for the peace of the colony.'

Jenny sounded pompous, kitted out with self-importance. What had been on at the pictures recently? Joan of Arc? The Straits Chinese liked to think of themselves as the keepers of some ancient heritage yet, at the same time, defenders of a modernizing China. Sun Yat Sen's portrait certainly occupied the hall of Jenny's house as it did almost every Straits Chinese house in Singapore.

'Now that the Japs have attacked us,' Jenny said, 'the British need every able body they can get. Women should be involved

in the fight like Yang Hui Min and the Shanghainese girl guides.'
For a woman who wanted to minister to the sick, Simone noted,
this was a strange position to take. But this entry into war had
revealed sides to each of their natures she had not expected. Her
own included.

'I agree. We should be doing our bit,' Zahra said. 'We are not
caged, like birds.' Simone wasn't sure this interest in a noble war
wasn't linked to Zahra's growing infatuation with an Australian
journalist, one of a dozen who'd landed in Singapore after the
first bombing raid.

Molly's mouth gaped. 'Really, you two. How you talk. What do
you think, Simone?'

'If you wear khaki, you'll never see red. Isn't that what they
say? Guides don't turn into communists.' Simone smiled.

'Alamak!' Zahra said. 'Guides are girls of action, girls who
think. More likely to turn red than not.'

'Are you a follower, Blue?' Simone said. 'How does
communism work with Islam?'

Zahra shrugged. 'I'm not anything. Down with all ideologies.
Belief blinds you, reduces all difference to a crippling conformity.
Faith is for fools. Communism is a religion as much as Islam or
Buddhism.'

The conversation came to a slightly embarrassing halt at this
utterance. They stayed away from religious discussion. Anita's
face looked like a monkey had bitten her and Molly turned away.
Zahra shrugged. Simone knew she didn't care what the others
thought. In a way Zahra was the most radical of them all. She
refused anything that stood in the way of her will, her freedom.
She kicked anything in her path.

'Well,' Simone said, not minding the quandary Zahra had just
put the others in but intent on breaking the silence, 'actually I've
got a bit of news. Since all the men have rushed off to join the
Volunteers, my editor wants me to step in and cover the conflict.
I'm off the women's page and on the war.'

Simone spoke calmly but could hardly contain her pleasure, and trepidation, at this instant promotion to war correspondent. Her ambition had burst into flower. This was her chance to turn herself into a real journalist.

Anita stared and Molly clapped her hands. 'That's marvellous, Red,' Jenny said and grinned.

At that moment Teresa left Harold's side and came towards them, arm in arm with Jean. She looks sweet, Simone thought, in her simple red cotton dress. How fortunate that red was not only the colour of communists but of Chinese marriage. Young and vulnerable. It belied her inner toughness but Simone was glad Teresa had married Harold. The two of them had taken a stand. They suited each other and Simone felt a pang of envy at such clear affection and moral certainty.

'Hello,' a voice said and they all turned. Kay glided towards them. She was like a panther, light of step. She had a handful of kingfisher feathers.

'Put them in your hats, ladies,' she said and rattled the tiger teeth bracelet at her wrist. 'Birds of a feather stick together,' she said and laughed. Like glass shattering on stone.

When they sat down for the spartan meal, Harold called them comrades and gave a little speech about Marxist theory, social responsibility, and the struggle for the end of colonial rule. Anita and Molly scowled. Harold held Teresa's hand and called her his comrade and helpmate. It was all said in a tone of conspiratorial yet pompous condescension that set Simone's teeth on edge, and she was appalled at the low-eyed soft gaze that Teresa cast at Harold. But then to Harold, his wife wasn't their friend and companion. She wasn't Teresa and certainly not Gray. He called her Ying, her Chinese name, as if he wished to throw off her past associations and subsume her into this new 'Red Chinese world'.

Molly whispered that she'd gone off Harold, and Simone had to agree. But there was no denying the excited sense of pride and hope that buzzed around the room. When this was over, Harold said, the British would see what they had done and foster a new Malayan Union. Merdeka! Freedom! A world worth fighting for—a world of liberty, equality, fraternity. Onward to victory, shouted Harold, and the room erupted in cheers.

Jean gave Teresa the money they'd all put in for a present. Simone hardly remembered anything else of that day. She gazed at the photograph. What she didn't know then in her immaturity but realized now was that, though they were all so very different in temperament, Jean had chosen them expressly because she recognized their inner natures, a natural non-conformism, an inability somehow to fit into the narrative of colonial female life. A bunch of outsiders. 'You will need each other,' she'd said, 'in ways more mysterious than you can imagine.'

Then Joseph Chee, the *Tribune*'s photographer and newly revealed patriot, also in the uniform of the Chinese Volunteers, had called them all together and Kay had said: 'You must promise me that come what may you will always care for and help Gray. That we will always care for and help each other. Sisters in blood. Sisters under the skin. The promise and the law. Swear it. Remember Ponompuan and Miss Lilian Gibbs.'

Jean was their glue but Kay—Java—was their spiritual and physical guide: the one who showed them the possibility of a different sort of life. Anxious and ignorant girls on the cusp of womanhood, Kay had been the moon pulling them together in the fearful gushing of their pubescent blood. They loved her because she was the centre of truth. They had all sworn—of course they had—and Joseph's camera had flashed.

JOURNAL

18 December 1941

I started this journal again today. Not only because it is my opinion that, as George Baker once said, the worst is coming but also because we are all standing in the midst of history. It is not just a solemn duty. I also realize that I can write here what I cannot write in the newspapers. Censorship is damning. Official communiqués are a pack of lies.

A reminder for me and for posterity, I suppose. The first attack on 8 December took everyone, including the damn High Command, by surprise. But we were not to worry. Everything was under control. Up to then the official line had been that the Japs were busily tied up in China, had no ships or planes to speak of, and were generally not equipped for long-range fighting. Now just ten days later, the Japanese have naval bases in Indochina, a non-aggression pact with the Thais and far more and better planes than the aged Brewster Buffaloes and Hurricanes of the RAF. All the airfields are bomb craters. And, the greatest blow of all, the only two British battleships in the entire Indian and Pacific Oceans are at the bottom of the sea. American survivors of Pearl Harbour have steamed off to California. Across the vastness of those waters the Japanese are now supreme.

Europeans from Penang have begun flooding off the trains. Penang is lost apparently. No official response. Rumours run wild. The Japanese have gone from ridiculous to monstrous and inhuman.

* * *

20 December 1941

Finally the government admitted the surrender of Penang. Duff Cooper, the abrasive special envoy, came on the radio and made a speech. 'It has been necessary to evacuate many of the civilian population. We can only be thankful that so many people have been safely removed.' What he meant was Europeans have been safely removed and of course all the Asians know it. The local population was left to face the Japanese alone.

This is a disgrace which George reports on with a great deal of pomposity. What happened to the white man's burden, he cries. So do the Chinese, Indian, and Malay press. Rumours that the Governor of Penang kicked a large family of Chinese off a boat in order to bring his car with him are not entirely unbelievable.

It is clear that the government is shaken up. They have refused to encourage the European evacuation of Singapore, even of the 'useless mouths', women and children. No man under forty may leave. Still, all will be well.

JOHOR

Golden Slumbers

What do Communists say over their dead? What is a funeral service for a Red Chinese warrior?

Kay places the last stone on Teresa's grave. She wants to be consumed by her grief. To give herself wholly to misery. Beat the grave and wail into the sky like the Arab women. Unjust God. Unjust World. She cannot. She glances at others as they wander back to camp.

She remembers a song. The anthem of the young Chinese communists in Dalforce that tugs at communist hearts as strongly as the Marseillaise of the French Revolution. *Yiyongjun Jinxingfu:* The March of the Volunteers.

> *Arise, arise, those who would not be slaves.*
> *With our flesh and blood let us build a new Great Wall!*

She can't say those words, even if Teresa believed them. There is another song. One they sang at the end of every meeting of the Patrol.

> *Golden slumbers kiss your eyes*
> *Smiles await you when you rise*
> *Sleep pretty baby …*

She sways. A long cloud, burnt orange, sits in the sky, quivering and dissolving as she tries to blink it into stillness. The twilight throws gold haze over the view from the hillside and the last rays of the sun illuminate the jungle below. The dark shapes of birds like flights of angels hover against the sky.

It isn't bad to be here, is it? If you had to die? We all have to die, don't we? You died for something, didn't you? Flew away in the loving arms of Kay. Knowing peace. Knowing Java will save your child. Knowing that. It must have given peace. And so it gives a fleeting comfort to her.

Peace. Will there ever be peace? And what will it mean? At this moment she has no idea what she would be if she were not Java. Who is she crying for?

JOURNAL

25 December 1941

Christmas is cancelled. The only Christmas lights are searchlights. Beams criss-cross the darkness until they fix suddenly on a plane that cannot be stopped. What is the point? I hoped to have Christmas lunch or at least a drink with one of the girls. But neither Kay nor Jean are to be found. Molly is in Ceylon with her grandparents. Jenny's too busy with the MAS crowd. Zahra, Teresa and Anita don't bother with Christmas anyway. So I was happy to go with the correspondents to the Coconut Grove. A cynical and hard-drinking lot, but great fun. They are my kind of tribe. I've taken up smoking. Does that mean I'm grown up?

Not only do the Japanese drop bombs, they drop leaflets, thousands and thousands of leaflets in every language spoken on the peninsula exhorting the local people to rise up against the colonial oppressors.

Asia for the Asiatics! Their leaflets are crude caricatures. Fat white man with a whisky glass in his hand, his feet resting on the back of a crouching and crushed Malay. The peninsula surrounded by Rising Sun flags. Burn all the white devils in the bright flame of victory! Why do you work to fatten the British high-hats? We fight only the white men!

Viewed with amusement by the Brits. But a lot of the locals are drawn to this message. Especially given the rapidity with which the Japs are gaining victory after victory. The white man's time has come. Murmurs. Yet most carry on regardless in the face of death, destruction, a lack of shelters and a lot of lies from the colonial government.

Indian train drivers walked off the job. What inducement to stay? Meagre wages. Danger of death. White tuans heading south. Who can blame them? Europeans driving the trains now.

SYONAN

Seishin

The B-29 Superfortress lies in front of the museum. Missing its wings and part of its tail, but the cockpit and most of the fuselage are intact. Here and there, in between the streaked scorch marks spread along its sides, it glints silver in the sun. A tattered, soiled American flag is displayed on its side. The stricken bomber marks the entrance to the Great Yamato-Damashii Exhibition.

The banner hanging in front of Raffles has been prepared in five languages: Japanese, Chinese, Malay, Tamil, and English. The Japanese have long ago abandoned the hopeless desire for the linguistically disparate civilians of Singapore to instantly abandon their mother tongue, as well as English, and embrace Nihongo. Both, despite the most strenuous efforts, remain. By and large, English continues to be the language of administrative communication with the population. No one could quite figure out how to abandon it. Japanese, it became common knowledge, was too difficult to learn beyond the most banal expressions. The Japanese themselves often took up English in order to be understood.

Above the text is the image of a samurai warrior in full armour, sword raised, astride the oceans, ships and lands of South-east Asia. *'Yamato-Damashii,'* it reads, *'is the soul of Japan. It comprises seishin—spirit; kakan—courage and daring; yūmō—valour; seijo—purity; and jiko gisei—self-sacrifice.'*

Visitors are directed to the left—the American exhibit. The Yanks are the foe that the Japanese fear. The battering ram beating against the shores of the homeland. The first image is a montage, on a loop, of film of a Japanese plane shooting down a B-29.

'It's been doctored', Guy Medoc says, 'the plane got engine trouble and had to be abandoned. Japs have no air power here. The B-29s are meant to be massed and visible, glinting in the sun, with those long vapour trails. We're coming, we're here, invincible. Tremendous. It gives us hope.'

Guy's voice trembles. He was an Australian soldier. Now Simone wonders if he will be able to survive the next weeks or even months of uncertainty. He, alongside others, had been sent to scrape an aerodrome out of a coral outcrop on some far-flung island. Day after day, under the tropical sun, beaten and starved, they died and were fed to the sharks. He had not expected to live and had returned a ghost, filled with dysentery and malaria. He speaks of this to her from time to time. He had been quick to pick up enough of the lingo, he says, and he thinks that it is this slender knowledge which saved him, for he received a sliver of rations greater than the others when it served their purpose. But that fact, too, haunts him, causes him such shame that he abruptly falls into silence.

Guy loves birds and to his observation of them, attributes his mental survival. When he was back in Changi prison, he'd asked permission to write a small book on island birds. This had been brought to the attention of the Marquis and he'd ordered Dr Ueno to print it and move Guy out of prison and into the more agreeable surroundings of Maxwell Road Internment Camp where the various Allied prisoners who are needed in the town by the Japanese civil authorities live: doctors, engineers, scientists, and interpreters mostly. Guy's health has benefited from the extra rations, better accommodation, and an escape from the monotony of imprisonment.

But this, too, causes him shame. Simone is beginning to understand that unspoken sense of confusion and guilt. Privileged to survive when all around others are dying. The blue feather springs to mind. Was it a call for help? Is this refusal a betrayal of them and of herself? Increasingly she feels agitated and wretched.

She and Mrs Sugiyama have been choosing photographs for the walls, which are now decorated with paintings of cherry blossom, the Japanese metaphor for the beautiful death and sacrifice of the warrior. A carpenter in civilian life, Guy's duties include mounting the photographs.

There is the poem by Motoori Norinaga, 'The Spirit of the Japanese'. 'Mountain cherry blossoms glowing in the sun,' Guy snorts. 'Arseholes.'

Next to the poem is a photograph of three Japanese boys, no older than sixteen, their heads wrapped in the Rising Sun bandeau, bowing to the portrait of the Emperor. The children of the Special Attack Unit throwing planes against the decks of American ships. Photograph after photograph of proud, smiling teenage boys being farewelled by proud, smiling, teenage girls. Then paintings and posters of those planes in flames, whirling and plunging into destroyers and battleships. The kamikaze, the suicide pilots of the Divine Wind.

The lyrics of the pilots' song are on the wall. *Umi Yukaba.* A sad, mournful tune played as often on the radio as *Kimigayo*, it is virtually Japan's second national anthem. The anthem of death.

If I go away to the sea,
I shall be a corpse washed up.
If I go away to the mountain,
I shall be a corpse in the grass

But if I die for the Emperor,
There will be no regret.

Her job, over the last few days, is to cut out the articles in the newspaper, listing the immense successes of the Special Attack Units in order to mount them next to the photographs.

Special Attack Forces wreak havoc on Foe.
Ten Army Special Attack Planes take out Ten Enemy Ships.
In death-defying body-crashing attacks against the enemy forces …

On and on. The closer the Americans get to Japan, the more outlandish and hysterical the articles have become.

'Can this all be true?' she asks Guy. 'Are they ready to kill even their own young so nothing will remain.'

'Where have you been, Simone?' Guy says, and she flushes. 'They worship death.'

As their workday ends, Simone stands with Guy waiting for the truck which makes the rounds to pick up POWs and take them back to Maxwell Road.

Lieutenant Uehara approaches. He is willowy and elegant, impeccable in his pressed and perfect army uniform. He bows to them both. She senses Guy stiffen as they return the bow. Lieutenant Uehara ignores Guy.

'Simone-san, I have Dr Ueno's car today. I am taking Sugiyama-san back to the Gardens. Perhaps you would like to accompany us?'

'Thank you but I have my bicycle, unfortunately.'

'Oh, not to worry. I will pop it on the back.'

Lieutenant Uehara's use of informal idiomatic English is impressive, gleaned, he tells her, from reading vast amounts of popular English fiction. The lieutenant wanders the halls of the abandoned library and asks her for literary recommendations. She can't help offering up Wodehouse for his puzzlement.

Puzzlement turned to joy. Now he often throws Woosterisms into the conversation.

'Then thank you, Uehara-san. With pleasure.'

They share a smile. 'Tally-ho,' he says. 'Pip pip.'

Handsome Yoshio Uehara is a zoologist, an intellectual, and an aesthete. No contrast could be greater than that between Lieutenant Uehara and the strident martial image of the samurai. He is more like a silken-clad, elegant aristocrat out of the Pillow Book of Sei Shonagon than the twentieth century embodiment of the *Hagakure,* the samurai handbook handily translated into English, Malay, and Chinese for the enlightenment of the locals.

Guy, she perceives, harbours some small jealousy at her pleasantness with Lieutenant Uehara but there is little cause. Yoshio Uehara is besotted with a beautiful Malay boy, the son of one of the gardeners. The boy, fourteen-year-old Umar, helps both in the garden and the kitchen of the house that the lieutenant now shares with Hatter and Bertie. Uehara is their ostensible guard, keeping an eye on the possibility of subversive radio listening or even more ridiculous, clandestine plotting, neither of which he takes seriously.

He is lovestruck and, in the sensibility of his soul, affected apparently by the waxing and waning of the moon. When the moon is full in the soft velvet sky of Malaya, it is like a great golden lamp. Misty vapours mingle with moonlight. The perfume of cloves and cinnamon drifts like incense round the soaring tree trunks as if in the sacred precincts of a temple. Simone is not insensible to the pull of the Malayan moon in the Gardens. But Lieutenant Uehara is moon-haunted.

The lieutenant drinks to assuage his feelings and in his drink longs for companions. Simone, Hatter, and Bertie have become those companions on those full moon nights. Over time and close confinement she has come to know these two Englishmen very well.

John Hatter is awkward. The British civil service types he was occasionally obliged to meet before the war are all 'yoff-yoffs' for the snigger they give when amused by inanities. His instinct with women is to be either aloof and distant or condescending. She'd been surprised to learn from Bertie that Hatter had a wife and son whom he'd sent away at the first opportunity. He never mentions them. Before the war, his best friends were monkeys that he trained to run up trees and gather specimens. Yet even one of them had bitten him.

Now, with the Lieutenant safely put to bed upstairs, Hatter too retires. Simone is left with Bertie. They sit outside the house in the warm evening air and he pours her a glass of palm toddy. In the distance an owl sends a lonely hoot echoing into the jungle.

'Bertie, what are we to do?'

'About what?'

'The end of the war.'

'Not in our hands, is it?'

'No. But our survival might be. Have you thought about that? That we might simply be shot or beheaded. That the scientists themselves might commit suicide or be ordered to kill us.'

Bertie shrugs. Simone has never understood Hatter and Bertie's seeming dispassionate and scientific lack of interest in their own survival. Her own will for survival has been obsessive. 'You mustn't care so much,' Bertie had said to her long ago, 'or you merely exchange one form of death for another and become a shadow.' But she couldn't stop caring. If she didn't care who would?

'Can you see any of the scientists doing that? They're not fanatics.'

'No, but at the very end, can't they all become fanatics. Dr Ueno has a gun, I've seen it.'

'The Marquis isn't likely to allow that?'

'The Marquis is very unlikely to be here. I should imagine it is only a matter of time until he heads back to Japan or somewhere.'

'Yes, you're right. Of course he will.'

'If the British invade, the Japs will fight street by street and house by house. The gardens will be mined. We civilians will be hostages caught in the middle.'

'It's an interesting time,' Bertie says matter-of-factly. 'After the drudgery of the occupation, the long dark night of waiting, it is here. I can feel it. Can you, Simone? The trembling sense of a tide turning. People waiting for the moment when it will be safe to change loyalties once more. Not the British necessarily. We've let them down. Perhaps the commies. I dabbled a little in socialism in the twenties, you know. Lots of us young men did.'

But Simone is no longer listening. The turning of the tide? The blue feather. Old loyalties. What was the use of that? But she feels treachery in her gut. Surely that is too exaggerated a word? It was after all a mere refusal, a casual negation. But she can't shake the sense that her one tiny decision is a seed growing bigger and bigger. 'Betrayal,' Bertie had once said to her in a moment of reflection, 'requires neither size nor magnitude for its existence. All it needs is position. The moment, place, and circumstance.'

JOHOR

The Hill People

Java Force's camp is side by side with the native Jakun village and its plantation, and thus protected by their ancient and infinite knowledge of the land. Booby traps and pits ambush anyone who tries to navigate the densely wooded hillsides and the Japanese, though they know of these people, now rarely venture against them.

British airdrops are made along the ridges of the hills to prevent the Japanese getting hold of them. The British officers of Force 136, who camp with the Communist main forces of the Malayan People's Anti-Japanese Army, coordinate the drops. The Jakun, like many of the hill people have, since the beginning, cooperated with the Chinese and British forces as messengers, food suppliers, guides. In the first years, the hill people saved the British and Chinese guerrillas from starvation.

The camp settles for the night and the wireless set hums. Power is supplied by the bicycle rigged up to their generator. The antenna is only raised at night. Reception is often cut but when it comes through, it is clear. This marvel attracts some of the Jakun men, women, and children to sit in the light of the damar lamps—the kerosene of the jungle—and listen to the music and strange whispers that emanate. One of the men, young, curious, and vigorous, clad only in a loincloth, takes his turn on the bicycle, grinning, filled with the exuberance of discovering this newness; an unguessed at and revolutionary outside world.

They tune in to the British radio, which broadcasts out of Colombo. The news in English carries coded messages to the British officers. Submarine landings. Food drops. Times. Dates. She can't understand them but they can. Li Song was the deputy leader—now leader—of 1st Patrol of the 4th Regiment covering the area from Senai to Johor Bahru and their sole contact with the anti-Japanese forces. Yuan liaises with him. As far as Li Song knows, Yuan is working for a small independent group of Chinese Kuomintang guerrillas attached to the hill people.

Kay finishes writing up the report about Lao Wu and the attack on the police station for Yuan to relay to Li Song. This erratic cooperation ensures they keep receiving supplies from the airdrops and information about the Japanese movements.

Kay moves out of the circle of light to the small veranda of her plank and thatch cottage and the refuge of the mosquito net. She wants to open the tin of sardines and savour it, little by little, and watch the electric lightning flashing in the distant sky like semaphore. The voice on the radio changes to music. *There'll be bluebirds over the white cliffs of Dover.* Bugger Dover.

Nuns. She can't recall a nunnery at Kampong Laut but then she doesn't know the area well. She won't risk taking her squad down. She chews the sardines slowly. Eating juicy flakes of memory. The odour of wood smoke from the Jakun camp drifts through the trees. Down below, in the thick cover of the jungle, insects are eating the night guard.

News in Malay whispers over the airwaves. *Pigs slaughtered in mosques. Muslims forced to eat pork.* Black propaganda. She recognizes it. Might be true. *Women forced to unveil, wear trousers, and work in the fields. Japan and Germany, the enemies of Islam. Five Muslim countries have joined the allied cause. The King of Saudi Arabia met with Churchill. He condemns Japan for stopping Muslims going on the Haj.*

She's heard this stuff in Singapore from the Jap side. *Japan confident of victory. Thais and Indonesians sign up in their thousands to join the Japanese army.*

Singapore. The radio. 'Yuan', she calls, 'I need someone near Johor Bahru to scout out a nunnery in Kampong Laut.'

JOURNAL

New Year's Day, 1942

After weeks of unreal calm in Singapore, the raids began again last night. Without any true facts of what is happening up north, the people drift on rumour. Communiques are peppered with phrases like 'falling back to prepared positions' and 'strategic withdrawals', masking a multitude of disasters. Clever George follows the debacle by studying the Hong Kong & Shanghai Bank advertisements, which give a daily list of branches 'closed until further notice'.

At the General Hospital, there's evidence of terrible fighting. The place is packed with the wounded. The very young soldiers speak of a lack of leadership, no orders, getting cut off, surrounded by the Japanese even as they withdraw. They always seem to be one step ahead. It saps your courage. The Japanese have small light tanks which easily move through the rubber plantations. Confusion, chaos, exhaustion. And the growing impression on the soldiers' minds is that they are fighting a swift, silent, deadly, and unbeatable enemy. I suspect that they are. Desertion is seen as a perfectly sensible option.

JOHOR

A Murmuration

The Chinese couple who run the village shop supply the information.

The nunnery is Buddhist, attached to an old temple. Japs leave it alone because there are lepers inside. This horror they fear more than bullets. Three old nuns, the Chinese couple say. Might be a baby. The nuns have come begging for condensed milk. The Chinese wife has given it. She's devout. Merit in the next life. Offerings for good karma. She knows the nuns. Helps when she can. There's talk of burning the place down. And there's no food.

It's desperate. Even this sparse information tells her how desperate. If the Japs suspect the nuns of betrayal, they'll throw flames at them and walk away. Perhaps Teresa knew. There is no certainty that this child is there or alive. But they begged for condensed milk. The child, if it's even alive, cannot come here to the mountain camp. It is too far and too dangerous.

The sun is setting. Fire burns along the rim of the horizon and the sky blazes gold. The harsh, heat-baked rock of the day splinters. Russet streams seep into fissures. Silhouetted against the amber sky, a great flock of mountain starlings begins its evening gathering. The sound is like waves rushing the shore. Jean called it a murmuration. She blinks at the memory and the clear sound of Jean's voice. A murmuration of starlings—gathering, splitting, gathering again, forming shifting cloud patterns in the sky. Safety in their swiftly wheeling numbers, putting on a great show of confusion for the flinty-eyed hawks. She watches until the starlings gather like a dark shadow and swerve in perfect formation into the obscurity of the dissolving pleats of the hills.

JOURNAL

5 January 1942

Chinatown is bursting with refugees. Huge swathes of neighbourhoods obliterated by bombs. Hundreds of bodies never dug out. *Who are they?* No one knows. The ARP and the MAS do a wonderful job increasingly without equipment. Guides and Scouts cook food, bring water, make bandages, carry messages. Workers have gone the other way. Fled to villages with their families. At the mutilated docks nothing is unloaded.

Bombed out of my old digs. I've moved into the Tribune offices. George has prepared some rooms for the staff. Indoor plumbing is a boon, although actual water is erratic.

Raids are non-stop now. Bomber formations come in 21, 48, and 81 planes. They need no fighter escort. The RAF doesn't have any planes. They drop all their bombs at the same moment. A volcanic eruption. Devastating. Estimates of the dead are 200 a day. No one can count the wounded.

SYONAN

Radio Syonan

Samad will return tomorrow morning. Though there is food in this house, Zahra eats little. Her periods stopped long before the marriage but she doesn't want them to start. He doesn't even notice. Does he even know women have a menstrual cycle, the actual continuation of life, the filthy, ignorant idiot? She never wants to have children. She can hardly control how much she hates him. She wants to take an axe to him but she has no axe and fears for Noor. Yet sometimes she shakes with the desire to do this. He knows nothing of women except as they fulfil his wishes. When he does force himself on her, he uses her like a toilet. Used to be worse. Used to be every night.

Samad's started to look at Noor. Soon she will be old enough to marry as a second wife. She will have to kill him. Does that mean kill the entire household? It must be subtle and believable. She feels the desperation of such an act like a knife in her guts. She tries as much as possible not to think about it.

She picks up the folded paper that's been prepared by the Ministry of Propaganda and glances through the main headings.

The time has arrived for non-essential workers to evacuate Syonan
No cause for alarm... the final blow in the Pacific ... peace in the Great East
Asian Prosperity Sphere

The Heiho families relief committee will meet …
Four destroyers sunk off Okinawa

The housewife's recipe of the week is Savoury Papaya Soup.

The song this month is *Beiei Gekimatsu, Wipe out the British and Americans.*

> *Nami wa takeru, gekimetsu no toki wa ima da!*
> *Waves roar, the time to eliminate has come!*
> *Destroy hostile aircraft carriers and battleships entirely!*
> *These seas must be foes' graves and death places!*
> *These seas must be foes' graves and death places!*
>
> *Come now, the time to overcome is here!*
> *Achieve this sacred war to revive Asia, whatever may betide!*
> *We, the imperial subjects, are ready to die!*
> *Mitami warera no inochi ga mato da!*

She begins to translate all this into Malay.

Akiko-san, Yoshida's assistant, approaches. Akiko-san is there because she is the daughter of Dr Ando, the head of the Department of Health which is in reality the Department of Death. Yoshida is doing a colleague a favour. And Akiko-san, barely eighteen, is good-looking. In his unthreatening, avuncular way Yoshida likes to be surrounded by compliant young women. Dr Ando and his family were long-time residents of Singapore before the war. Akiko has never been to Japan. She was born, and has lived all her life, here.

'Zahra-san, sumimasen, telefon desu.'

'Arigato,' Zahra says. Who is calling her? 'Dare desu-ka?' Akiko merely shrugs and wanders away, checking her hair in a mirror.

Zahra heads to the office and picks up the telephone receiver. 'Hello?'

'A message from Java,' the woman says. 'Write this down.'

'What? Who is this?' Java? Can this be right? She looks around quickly. Takes up the daily newspaper and a pencil. The voice is Indian, speaking in English.

The woman gives a series of geographical coordinates. Zahra scribbles them down.

'Repeat,' the woman says. Zahra repeats them quickly. 'Yes,' she says. 'Go there. For Gray's child. I will call each day at this time. Tell me when it is arranged. Hurry.'

Click. She is gone. Zahra stares at the figures she has written on the paper. Gray's child? She is filled with confusion. Is this a test? Is someone here testing her? Is it Samad checking up on her? She looks around. Nothing is different. The usual crew on for the evening.

Yoshida approaches, gait uneven. He's been drinking most of the afternoon.

'Mondai ga arimaska, Zahra-chan?' he says, blearily looking at the telephone.

'Oh, Yoshida-san. No. No problem. Just checking on the recipe of the week. Wasn't sure if the papaya was green or ripe.'

He has no idea what she's talking about. He sways and proffers a tin of English biscuits. 'Ginger nut?'

JOURNAL

11 January 1942

Michael of the *London Times*, myself, George, and Norman of the AAP got permission to go to KL. By the time we got there, the British were abandoning it.

They've ordered everything destroyed. The tin mines flooded. The rubber estate factories wrecked. A Chinese man with tears in his eyes had to take a sledge-hammer to rods, valves, and pistons he had for more than twenty years oiled and greased. The British estate managers were ordered to leave all the labour force behind.

Looting is fantastic. White police officers gone south. Malay and Indian policemen returned to their homes. At the abandoned Governor's Residence, the Gurkha guards continue to defend the empty house. A half-finished whisky and soda stood on a small table by the sofa. Cases of silver ornaments, bejewelled daggers, gifts of Malay princes lay, untouched, in glass cases. The portraits of the King and Queen smiled down. The Indian medical officer in the hospital told us that all the European patients and staff had left for the south.

We went south too, weaving through milling crowds of looters heading north into the city to grab anything they can carry.

SYONAN

The Shokubutsuen

All botanical gardens are a paradise in miniature, a vision of the Garden of Eden. Before the war, this one had been a manicured place of neat borders, flowering bowers, carp-filled lakes, and elegant Victorian bandstands. For scientists and botanical lovers, it was a hive of taxonomy, experiments, and collections, the famous home of 'Mad Ridley', father of the Malayan rubber industry. Now, everyone within it lives off it.

Nothing here anymore is reserved purely for beauty or art. It is all for eating. The miles of neat borders and most of the lawns are for vegetables; the bowers for rattans and twining fruit. The lake is for edible fish, kankong, and ducks; the palm trees are tapped for sugar and toddy. Buffaloes and goats graze the meadows around the lake and the bandstands, and thousands of egg-laying hens peck the grass in the sprouting neglected paths under the coconut, mango and rambutan trees and the watchful eyes of their keepers. Even the Director's tennis court is thick with tapioca. Half-forgotten skills of village and forest, once found only in the displays in the ethnographic section of the Museum, were swiftly re-embraced. The Syonan Shokubutsuen is a farm-like country estate worthy of any eighteenth century nobleman. The nobleman here is the Marquis and this is his domain.

When she first came, it was a mess. Ancient trees, bombed and shelled, sprawled. Craters pockmarked the lawns. It had been the camping ground of regiments of Australian forces and at the surrender, they had abandoned everything. The first job Bertie had asked her to do was to arrange to record and stockpile into the storehouses and potting sheds the vast amount of tents, blankets, and tinned food left by the surrendered Australians. Whether the Japanese had given permission for this was now lost to her memory. What is certain is that it was forgotten in the fog of the first months of the occupation. This had never been discovered. So great had been the abandonment that they still managed to eke out those supplies today, over three years later.

She descends the steps to the Herbarium. Near the ancient ironwood tree, witness to numerous Japanese executions, is a black car. Two Japanese soldiers stand guard on either side of the vehicle. There are never any sentries at the Herbarium and few visitors. The soldiers both jerk their heads towards her. She has been summoned. What do they want? A niggle of concern. Her forbidden diaries of the occupation, three of them, nestle silently in amongst the folders of dried specimens in one of the glass cabinets lining the wall of one side of the room.

The Herbarium has always felt the most tranquil and peaceful of all the buildings in the Gardens: a haven that lives by the slow, rustling cycle of plants, not the hectic clamourings of man. When the bamboo blinds are lowered against the heat, the light thickens to sepia and the rooms with their rows of polished mahogany cabinets take on a monastic, ecclesiastical quality.

Every week one of her duties is to stroll the quiet rooms with her spray can and cudgel on the hunt for rat, termite, ant, beetle, fungus and mite which threaten to overtake the carefully organised folders and the library of books. On those occasions Simone and Carlos Pereira, the head of the Herbarium, play gin

rummy in the shadowy light under the whirling fan and drink
from his private stash of soda water hidden in the defunct drying
room zinged up with ginger or limes from the spice garden. This
concoction is accompanied by various worms, grubs and insects,
which Carlos dries and salts into crispy treats.

Should any sort of seed or specimen be required it is
Dr Pereira's job to seek it out and take it to the scientists. Other
than this and writing up the monthly Garden Bulletin—a balance
sheet of produce, distribution and occasional botanical discoveries
or advancements demanded by the Japanese authorities—he is
left entirely to his own devices, most of which concern the study
of rattans. It is a place of peaceful contemplation, so today this
Japanese incursion feels like an assault on a temple.

The man seated behind Dr Pereira's desk has a face of
impressive immobility. Under the red-banded kepi, dark glasses
hide his eyes. But there is no mistaking who he is. The large red
kempei characters on the white armband of his khaki jacket make
sure of that. At his waist are a cavalry sabre and a pistol.

The blinds are raised and the windows thrown open but the
kempei's dark presence sucks the light out of the room. The
officer looks up. She bows.

'Good morning,' he says, 'I am Captain Tsuji.' His English,
Simone notes with some surprise, is good. He has a pronounced
American accent. 'I understand one can study specimens here.'

She feels the rush of relief like cool rain. He has a hobby. The
Japanese do come from time to time. Orchids are a favourite.

'Yes,' she says with over-zealous eagerness. 'Dr Pereira will be
here shortly. Perhaps he can help you.'

'Yes, Dr Pereira,' the Captain says and from his pocket
produces a small notebook which he consults. She feels a flash
of envy. Where do they store their notebooks? Is there a godown
filled with notebooks somewhere? How can I find out?

'He is the head of this place. Is that correct?'

'Yes, sir, the head of the Herbarium.' She watches him, wary again now.

'The other scientists are English. But he is Eurasian.'

Warning signals fizz into her brain. The Japanese in Syonan have organized a strict hierarchy of racial suspiciousness. Chinese of all stripes, rich and poor, are on the top because of their loyalty to China and their support for Chiang Kai Shek and the KMT or, even worse, Mao Tse Tung and the communists. Next come Eurasians, like Simone, deemed tainted by miscegenation and fawning cronies of the British, their masters. Indians and Malays, as true Asians, are given most favoured subject status.

'Yes,' Simone says.

'And you, Miss Martel, have Swiss nationality?'

Simone feels her jaw clench and begins to count backwards. Ten, nine, eight, seven—it calms her down. He's looked into her life. She is on the radar of the Kempeitai.

'My father was Swiss.'

'And your mother was Chinese.'

'French-Indochinese from Saigon.'

Tsuji takes off his dark glasses and levels his gaze at her. Although his eyes betray nothing she feels, as she always does when confronted by a Japanese officer, that he's trying to examine the corpuscles of the filthy blood running in her veins.

From a pocket he takes a narrow jewelled box some six inches long. From the box he removes an object resembling by its handle a silver dagger. She can't take her eyes off it and grips her fingers together. However, beyond the handle in the shape of a gourd there is not a blade. It is, she sees, a toothpick, long and slender. He begins to pick his teeth, examining the contents on the stick before tasting them on his tongue. She has seen them chop off heads, hang people by their thumbs, slap and beat, punch and stab. But this she finds oddly more nauseating.

'Your father was once Swiss consul, is that right?'

She draws her eyes away from his face and the offensive sight. 'Yes.'

'Before Mr Muller who has recently deceased?'

Muller? Why does he want to talk about Muller? 'Yes. Long before. My parents both died of influenza when I was very young.'

Tsuji waves his hand towards the chair in front of the desk. Simone sits; glad of relief to the faint trembling in her legs but now forced to meet his eyes.

He delves once more into his mouth and tastes its contents. If I sit here long enough I shall see him regurgitate his entire lunch from his teeth.

'Have you noticed,' he says, clearing the apparently less tasty debris from the toothpick with his fingers 'that the life of human beings is like the flow of water.'

This sort of sudden philosophical meandering is not unexpected. It is apparently a Japanese trait. Uehara, in particular when drunk, is full of it and even the sensible scientific mind of Dr Ueno is not immune to sudden poetic non-sequiturs.

'Inga to kageboshi wa tsuite mawaru'. He intones this, filling each word with sententious portent as if he is an actor in an irritatingly slow Noh play.

Inga is their word for Fate. Kageboshi means shadows. She's almost grasped the meaning when he continues. 'Fate and shadows follow wherever we go. Death may come from anywhere in an unsuspected moment.'

There is no practical response. She does not respond. It is meant doubtless to intimidate her. However the molar probing reduces the effectiveness of the threat. She waits. At last his toothy inspection seems finished to his satisfaction so her lack of reaction apparently goes unnoticed. He replaces the silver toothpick inside the jewelled box and puts it in his pocket.

'Before his death Mr Muller was a good friend of Nippon. That is my understanding.'

'Yes. I believe so.'

'Are you a friend of Nippon, Miss Martel?'

His tone has become confidential, slightly ironic. Does he expect her to say no? Naturally she does not.

'Yes.'

Perhaps it would have been better to leave it at that, but the standard response comes easily to her lips. They'd all said it a thousand times to visiting Japanese military and civilian dignitaries.

'The Japanese scientists here are doing great work under the guidance of the Marquis and the enlightened vision and protection of His Majesty, the Emperor.'

Tsuji's face reveals nothing. He turns away and begins picking over the specimens in a tray of rattan flowers, seeds and leaves.

'My father is a dentist but his botanical interests are wide-ranging.' He engages Simone's eyes. 'He has asked me to obtain some books on Malayan trees or other such things which I can translate for him. Perhaps you can help?' He smiles. It is like the rictus on a corpse and disappears almost instantly.

'Of course.'

Tsuji consults his notebook.

'You came here with the British scientists after the victory. Is that so?'

'Yes. The British governor asked Dr Hatter and Professor Bradshaw to join the Japanese to take care of the Museum and the Gardens and preserve their collections. General Yamashita gave permission. They asked me to join them.'

The room is airless. Sweat trickles down her back. Her thoughts go to that day. She sees it in jerky snapshots like a faulty cinema reel jumping and crackling. The silence after such noise. No guns, no planes. Surrender. Cries and sobs somewhere, of relief or horror. The blood and guts on the ground floor where a thousand wounded men lay, limbs hanging off, wounds suppurating, dying. The suffocating heat and the sickly smell of disinfectant. She'd

escaped to the rooftop and fresh air and watched the smoke in
the sky. Below, exhausted soldiers lay sprawled about the pitted,
bombed-out quayside. Three were pushing the Governor's Rolls
Royce into the harbour. In the distance a massive Japanese flag
was flying on the Cathay Building.

It all led to this man sitting in front of her.

'I understand Mrs Muller works in the Gardens,' Tsuji says,
jerking her out of the reverie.

'She works in the gardens of Government House and for
Count Terauchi. She comes here when she needs extra gardeners.'

When Greta Muller came she treated the Malay men like her
slaves. Called them Muslim pigs and frequently and randomly
slapped their faces like the Japanese she so ardently admired.
The complaints were numerous and Mr Guan had appealed to
Dr Ueno. Nothing was done. She had the favour of the Supreme
Commander and the Marquis couldn't have cared less and,
even, Simone suspected, enjoyed the sight of squabbling aliens.
Dr Ueno had scuttled away.

Greta Muller has nothing but enemies in the Gardens. But her
special hatred is reserved for Hatter who treats her, as he treats
all women, with a haughty disdain. For Greta it is a red rag. She is
maniacally Catholic. How she reconciles the dead Catholic Bishop
of Singapore, the treatment of Catholics and the closure of all
but the Anglican church with her zeal for all things Japanese could
be found only inside her own warped brain.

'Mrs Muller is popular?'

'She is well liked.' Like a venomous spider. She tries to smile
at Tsuji without much success, instantly ashamed of her fawning
desire to get him on side. Her entire experience of the Japanese is
with civilians. The Stooges, quiet, unthreatening, unfailingly polite
and pleasant; the Marquis, goosy, wordy and supercilious but
patrician and polite, Mr and Mrs Sugiyama and the other Japanese
gardeners, efficient, calm and decent, a quiet bow and a shy smile.
She has no experience with a man like this.

'Mrs Muller was responsible for having the British scientists interned in January, isn't that so.'

'Yes.'

'Why?'

'I don't know. The Marquis had them released after six days.' Spite is the reason, sheer hatred of Hatter and even Bertie. Bitterness at the state of the war in Europe which, everyone had gleaned, was not going Germany's way. Her own bitter nature.

'I see. Miss Martel, do you know a woman called Teresa Wong?'

The question is so unexpected Simone has to force herself not to stare at him. What should she say? Why does he want to know about Teresa? The walls of the Herbarium seem to press in.

'No. I don't think so.' Such a dangerous question when they hate the communists. She touches her sweaty brow then drops her hand quickly.

'Ah.' Tsuji rises and walks slowly to the glass cabinet containing the folders of specimens. Atop one pile of folders sits the large female seed of the coco-de-mer, which resembles nothing less than a pair of buttocks. Beside it lies the male tree's phallic-looking catkin. They always draw attention. She bites her lip. Why on earth didn't she move those damn things to another cabinet? Cockiness. The confidence grown from the passage of time. The arrogance of her unthreatened existence. Amusement.

'What are these?' Tsuji asks.

She knew he would. The exhibit is too suggestive. She explains them and he laughs. It is a pleasant and genuine laugh. Unexpected, as if in another life he enjoyed a joke and pleasant company. He tries the door which is locked.

'Open the cabinet. I should like to take a closer look. I am most interested in plant specimens. I'm sure my father would like to have some. What else is interesting?'

'I'm sorry. I don't have a key. Dr Pereira keeps the keys.'

The smile evaporates. He touches the hilt of his sword and she wonders if he is going to take it and slash the glass. A distant growl of thunder. The barometer on the wall reads Change. Suddenly Tsuji turns away and yawns as if this whole business is a great bore. He moves along the bookshelf. Simone's eyes follow Tsuji and alight suddenly on *A Contribution to the Flora and Plant Formations of Mount Kinabalu* by Lilian Gibbs. She has never noticed it there before. She shakes her head. She doesn't believe in signs, yet somehow here is another. The blue feather flashes back into her mind.

Another growl of thunder and the wind picks up, rattling the bamboo chicks. Soon the rain will begin, as it does in the tropics, with a great whoosh of air and a torrent of water. The air freshens, filled with the tang of the sea, and she breathes deeply.

Tsuji's gaze stops on a large tome. He takes it from the shelf and lays it on the desk. She recognizes Hatter's magnum opus on Malayan mosses and lichens.

'Dr Hatter wrote this book?'

'Yes. I have heard that His Majesty, the Emperor, admires this book. He keeps it by his bedside.'

Tsuji's head shoots up and he stares at her. This might be utter nonsense, but the first Director of the Gardens, the ill-fated Tanaka, had insisted on this to them all. Flattery. Boastful. Untrue. It didn't matter.

'Really, the Emperor?' He lays his fingers on the book as if touching a holy relic. His hands are impeccable, manicured. He sits. From the pocket of his uniform he unfolds a paper with deliberate theatrics and lays it on the desk. She can see it is an old newspaper article from the *Tribune*.

'You say you do not know Teresa Wong, Miss Martel, but here you are with her in this photograph taken in 1939 alongside…' he peers at the photograph, 'Jean McKenna, the captain of

Halcyon Patrol'. He raises his eyes to hers but she lowers hers and leans forward.

The photograph shows Jean, Teresa and herself taken at the guide camp at Port Dickson. Memories of that time come flooding back. It was there that she had found out Teresa's secret and her shame.

Now she understands. She is certain that Greta has given him this photograph. Who else would know of the Guides? Of Port Dickson? Greta has combed through the newspaper archives. But why? And why now?

'Oh, yes. That Teresa Wong. It's a common name. I didn't … well we didn't call ourselves by those names. I know her by a different name.' She can see that she is digging a hole but she doesn't know how to stop.

'What name did you use for Teresa Wong?'

Oh God. I don't want to talk about Teresa. The sweat bursts down her back and she wants to get up. She doesn't dare. Tsuji's eyes haven't left her face. Does he know that Halcyon refers to birds? His eyes drill into her face. He does not blink.

'Just Tess,' she says. It's pathetic. Ridiculous.

He makes no noticeable reaction but puts his finger on Jean's face. 'This woman is a civilian prisoner. She was your group captain, is that right?'

'We were Girl Guides. That's all.'

'Girl Guides. Yes. A military youth organization. I see the uniforms. I have spoken to this woman.'

Jean's alive, that's all Simone registers for a moment, then realizes the import of his interpretation. A military organization. It would be ridiculous if they weren't all so paranoid. There is little point in answering this question. He will believe what he wants. She tries to change his focus.

'Jean McKenna, is she all right?'

Tsuji ignores the question. His voice takes on a soothing tone. 'I wish simply to ask some questions about this group. I'm sure you understand. It is my job. Do you know anyone named Java?'

She is fearful now. 'No. I've never heard of anyone called Java.'

Tsuji falls silent but it is an unquiet and menacing silence into which falls the soft trills of the mynah birds which nest on the roof.

'I want to know the names of all the members of this unit. Write them here.' Tsuji pushes his notebook towards her.

JOURNAL

15 January 1942

George Baker put his wife and children on a ship today. The official line is still to not encourage evacuation of the European women and children but some are getting out. The ships leave half empty. The utter abandonment of Penang by the Europeans is still a stinging scandal. The Tribune had made so much of it that now George feels he cannot go with any kind of honour. So he will stay with Daisy, the family spaniel.

The front line is now at Maur where the Indians and Australians are fighting. Michael says almost all the young recruits were totally unprepared for such an onslaught. The 45th Indian Brigade has been annihilated. In the space of a few days Percival has lost an entire Indian brigade and the best part of two of his Australian battalions as well as one brigadier, three Indian Army and one Australian battalion commander. Yet the press is still told that routs are tactical withdrawals. If the public knew what lies were being told, there would be a revolt.

SYONAN

The Banyan Tree

She watches the car move away and walks out into the rain, glad of its heavy, drumming power, getting away from the Herbarium, disappearing into the mist. He'd taken the notebook, scooped Hatter's opus into his arms, and left, hardly giving Simone time to rise and bow.

She takes shelter under the banyan tree and lights a cigarette. When she smokes, it reminds her of that fraternity of foreign correspondents. It is hard to remember that she'd been a journalist. That person. Before.

The smoke drifts up into the thick branches of the tree. The banyan symbolizes the sense of safety and peace she has found here. The mother tree and her babies, spreading out around her, all connected. A bird flutters on the ground. It appears injured, one wing at a strange angle. She approaches but it flies awkwardly into the tree, out of reach. Underneath the leaf mould and mud crawling things wriggle. The birds peck them, squashing them in their sharp beaks. High up, bats hang like black fruit from the top branches. She had not noticed them before.

Four names made up on the spot. How would that hold him? They have an efficient system of identity papers but she'd told him she had no idea if her companions had all survived the war. Now she's terrified that she's going to get someone entirely innocent into trouble.

She suddenly recalls what Kay had said about the banyan tree. It never allows a blade of grass to grow beneath it. It never allows for renewal of anything but itself. When it dies it leaves the ground barren and scorched. Like the devil's garden. Everything suddenly feels malevolent, tainted by death and uncertainty. Her languid avoidance of the outside world is shattered. She feels utterly alone.

As she reaches her compound she sees, tucked into the old rusty red Royal Mail letterbox on the gatepost, a brilliant blue feather.

JOURNAL

31 January 1942

The siege no journalist is allowed to call a siege has begun. Whatever else has been hidden from the civilian population during the shambles of the last month, the massive writhing plumes of black smoke boiling and coiling over the city from the oil fires at the Royal Navy base at Sembawang in the north cannot be concealed. The stuffy briefing room in the Cathay Building this morning was crowded with local newsmen and foreign correspondents. The only women in the room were Lorraine Hall, the tough, outspoken *Time Magazine* correspondent, and I. By now I'm toughened up too.

There was utter silence in the room and the sense of some momentous announcement. And so it was. The British, not the Japanese, had set fire to the oil dumps and the Royal Navy had evacuated the entire base. A naval fortress that had taken seventeen years to build and cost sixty million dollars has been thrown away without a fight. Millions of gallons of fuel might be burning but all the rest—miles of machine shops, dry docks, towering cranes, 22 square miles of deep sea anchorage, an entire town with cinemas and seventeen football fields, the great symbol of Britain's naval dominance in the East—has been left intact for the Japanese.

It was built for one reason and one reason only. This moment of destiny. Yet it has been abandoned, the briefing officer stuttered, before the troops had crossed the Causeway. The troops that, as one journalist pointed out, had been withdrawn to defend it.

Lorraine, George, Michael and I drove out there this afternoon. The deserted barracks housed a labour force of 12,000. Over an acre of ground was littered with abandoned equipment. Cranes and ships' boilers, spare parts for seaplanes, shelves of radios, boxes of valves, warehouses filled with wire, cord and rope awaited the Japanese navy. In the Mess Hall plates of food and piles of dirty dishes spoke of a panicked departure. It was like a scene from the *Marie Celeste*.

We got to the top of an embankment and looked down on the Straits. The Causeway had been blown up but it was obvious it would only take the Japanese the best part of an afternoon to repair it. We could see them on the other side moving around the lofty tower of the Sultan's palace from which all of Singapore could be viewed.

'Bet that bastard Yamashita's already up there,' Lorraine had said in her cool American drawl, 'looking down at us.'

SYONAN

Buyong Road

It's raining when Simone leaves that evening. The blue feather means a rendezvous at the Guide Hut at 6 p.m. That is Singapore time, an hour and a half behind Tokyo time. Syonan lives on Japanese Imperial time. It dictates their sleeping and rising, their working and leisure. The sun has no natural dominion here, only the Emperor of the Sun.

Her wristwatch reads 7.30 p.m. because everyone keeps their wristwatch on Tokyo time. Singapore time is for the privacy of the home and the hidden clocks. How else can they keep hold on reality when midday is officially one-thirty and they must rise in the darkness of night and call it daytime? It made everyone crazy for a long time but now they are all used to it, the distortion of time merely one more thing in the long list of dystopian facts they live with every day.

By the time she reaches Orchard Road, the rain has turned into a deluge. The deep storm drains are spilling their edges. She keeps to the covered walkway, skirting piles of skeletal Javanese romusha labourers whose bodies pile up like dying locusts all over the town.

Tens of thousands of these men have been transported by the Japanese to work in Malaya, on the Siamese Railway and throughout the far-flung Japanese empire as slave labour. When they become too sick through starvation and illness, they are abandoned and left to fend for themselves. It is impossible to feel anything but a fleeting compassion, for their appalling plight is distorted through the prism of familiarity. Their starvation, bloated misery, and death have become unremarkable. They are the daily visible evidence of the bestiality of the occupation and it has become simply commonplace. Ordinary is simply what you get used to. Evil has become banal.

Every other day a truck of British POWs makes the rounds, prodding bundles of bones ten degrees more emaciated than them. If the bones exhibit the merest sign of life, they move on; otherwise the bones are chucked into the back of the truck. She's heard they're shovelled into the sea somewhere off Changi Beach. The sharks won't get fat, she thinks in a moment of blackness, and she might never eat seafood again.

The romusha are without family and far from home. No one can survive in Syonan without a family or a tribe you can trust, a tribe that cares and a structure to protect you. The romusha have no one. The temple charities do their best but the numbers are crushing.

The romusha locusts are one of the reasons why Mrs Sugiyama writes haiku, makes art and rarely ventures out of the grounds of the Botanical Gardens or the Museum. Simone doesn't blame her. If she doesn't see she doesn't have to wonder why her sons died for this kind of world.

The rain means the Malay sentries take shelter to smoke and chat and pay no attention to the street. There are no Japanese sentries any more on civilian buildings because they need the Japanese soldiers out there, fighting, not here guarding non-military sites. For the most part the young press-ganged heiho don't check passes and don't care about bowing. They've had every bit enough of this relentlessly grim and bloody occupation as everyone else.

The Guide Hut is in Buyong Road and as she reaches it, she's forced out of the covered way and into the open. The rain is sheeting down, hard as bullets.

As she approaches the compound gates, the memory of that first encounter surges. Zahra was the first girl she met and she'd had ventured a wry smile as they'd sat by the flag which Miss McKenna had planted firmly in the shade of the big tembusu tree. How quickly any discomfort had faded and they had become filled with the excitement of that moment and thrilled with anticipation of the freedoms that lay ahead. Guides were girls who were free. Free to climb and swim and make fire and get dirty. Free to chatter and sing and dance like sprites. How quickly they'd felt sorry for any girl who was not a Guide.

'Welcome girls,' Miss McKenna had said, taking their hands in hers and planting a kiss on each girl's cheek. Ever cheerful, ever loving Miss McKenna. She suddenly and clearly remembers Miss McKenna reading a poem to them that first night when they sat together, not yet the friends they would become. They'd written it out and repeated it a thousand times.

> There is no friend like a sister
> In calm and stormy weather
> To cheer one on the tedious way
> To fetch one if one goes astray
> To lift one if one totters down
> To strengthen whilst one stands

The last time Simone saw Jean McKenna was the day she had walked into captivity on the long march towards imprisonment alongside her fellow teachers whistling *A Long Way to Tipperary*.

Almost every day of the occupation Simone has walked or cycled past the Guide Hut on her way to and from the Museum. It has come to represent a tableau of the shifting fortunes of the city, its people and herself. An elegant, well-proportioned bungalow on pillars, it was the epitome of empire in the thirties when it had played host to governor's wives, sultan's ladies and no other than Lady Baden-Powell. It witnessed the passage of European soldiers and civilians as they marched into imprisonment and then turned into a billet and guard post filled with Japanese soldiers. A month or so later it had been transformed into a clubhouse for naval officers who practised kendo on the lawn.

As things grew dire and the Grow More Food campaign started, a Malay gardener and his extended family had moved in to grow and supply vegetables to the various military clubs and hotels in the area. At least then, Simone had thought as she passed, there was the laughter of children. But a stray allied incendiary bomb had landed nearby in March taking out an electrical sub-station and surrounding buildings and the area had been officially abandoned.

After almost four years, it is eerie to be here on this silent, dripping veranda. The tembusu tree still looms in the darkness, sheltering the house from the tropical sun in the day and filled with whirling, raucous sparrows at night. They're sleeping now or sheltering, a dark shadow of birds, darker than the tree itself. They've survived because they're swift and not good eating.

In the blackness she sees the seven of them as they were, ruddy-faced girls in the glow of lanterns, listening to Java tell thrilling stories of evil and magic, Kadazan head-hunters and Christian angels. She recalls with a stomach-crimping memory the aroma of sausages.

Thunder. A shiver of cold. Time stretches. A convoy of trucks passes by sending spray into the night. She's made a mistake in coming. She gathers herself to depart when a familiar voice whispers at her shoulder.

'Red, you got your cooking badge yet?'

JOURNAL

5 February 1942

I ran into Kay today. George sent me to visit the KMT training school. A week ago, a call had gone out for volunteers from the Chinese population to take up arms. The response was enormous: students, middle-aged clerks and housewives, labourers, sing-song girls, cabaret dancers, veterans of China's wars, young women communists, teenage boys. Communists are trained in one camp. The Kuomintang in another. The officers are British from the Forestry Service, the Police and the Civil Service. The Commanding Officer of the communist-trained camp is Lt. Col. John Dalley, a starched soldier type. They call themselves the Singapore Overseas Chinese Anti-Japanese Volunteer Army, which isn't catchy. The Brits call it Dalforce, which is. The KMT trainees are headed by Major Hu Tie Jin and call themselves the Overseas Chinese Guard Force. It took me a while to get all this straight. The training seems totally inadequate. Even Frank Brewer, one of the trainers, admitted that they got a bit of parade ground drill and a lot of shouting so they get used to taking orders. Then they're shown how not to shoot themselves or blow themselves up with their weapons. The weapons are a shotgun, seven rounds of ammunition and two grenades each.

Kay was thoroughly disillusioned. The women were relegated to cooking and nursing. We watched together as the first volunteers went to the front. Truck loads of them, all cheering and singing and waving flags. Four days of training. Shotguns? What was the use? But I didn't say anything.

That should all have happened months if not years ago. When the Japanese invaded China. The Chinese have the greatest reason to hate the Japanese. They, not the British or Australians, are the natural defenders of Singapore. But this seems like suicide.

I had tea with Kay. She's not sticking around. I asked what she would do, but she just waved and left.

SYONAN

The Guide Law

Zahra's voice has a way of silencing the rain. The two women hug. No strain or awkwardness, just a quiet recognition of shared struggle and wasted time which fits like a garment over their natural affection for each other.

'The blue feather at the Museum. It was you.'

'Yes.'

'I didn't come.'

'No. This time you did. I'm glad. It is hard for me to get away.'

They move into the house. Rain pours through the fissured roof and seeps down walls now covered in meandering vines and patches of lichen. Zahra takes Simone's left hand in hers and leads her to the sitting room. The window is intact, the bamboo chicks are lowered and the verandah here softens the battery and noise of the windward side. It is dry but with an undernote of mould. There is no furniture. Doubtless looted for cooking fires long ago. In the middle of the floor stands a small kerosene lamp. Beneath the floorboards frogs create a raspy racket. She's surprised they haven't all been eaten. Jumairah catches them and fries them in palm oil and chilli. They're quite tasty.

Simone throws off her wet shoes and sits cross-legged.

'The left hand. The light. Is this a guide meeting?'

Zahra taps the brass trefoil badge pinned to her dress.

'The first meeting of Halcyon Patrol since November 1941. We were knitting for England. Do you remember?'

The thought is pleasurable. All together with Jean in the hot afternoon knitting woollen socks. Jean assured them that England was always freezing. As far as they knew she had never been, but neither had they. It didn't matter. They'd seen Santa on Robinson's Department Store. There was snow. Snow was apparently cold.

Zahra puts her fingers to her temple in the guide salute. 'The promise.'

'Blue, really?'

'Salute sister and make the promise.'

Simone feels faintly silly but Zahra's voice is serious so she curls her fingers into the familiar salute.

On my honour, I promise that I will do my best:
To do my duty to God and the King;
To help other people at all times;
To obey the Guide Law.

'See. It's an affirmation. Nothing has changed.'

'Everything's changed. I'm not sure I feel any duty for God or the King, if I ever did.'

'No. Well. God, as Jean always said, can be anything to anyone, even Kay's jungle sprites. As for the King, for now he will stand for Malaya.'

Simone grins. 'You know, for a Muslim you've always had a Jesuitical streak.'

'Well, as you know, I'm not much of a Muslim. Anyway the Muslims have had to play a very careful game with the Japs. Imagine how much the Imams and Sultans like facing East and bowing to the Emperor of Japan when they should be facing West, praising Allah and bowing to Mecca. Quite a dilemma. Requiring all sorts of Jesuitical justifications.' Zahra barks a laugh devoid of any mirth. 'Lucky for me I don't have to think about any of that. Old men's business. If the wrath of God is to fall, it will fall on them and their evil deeds.'

'What evil deeds, Blue?'

Zahra shakes her head. From her bag, she produces a tin of Huntley & Palmer's Ginger Biscuits.

'My Japanese boss loves these things. Always has a stash in his office. By two in the afternoon he's usually drunk so he has no idea we pilfer or maybe doesn't care. It's pretty lax at Broadcasting House. Cigarettes, vitamin pills and biscuits. If you ever need vitamin pills, tell me. Ciggies are fetching $70 on the black you know.'

'I don't know. No idea about the black market. Yes to the vitamin pills. The people in the house where I live could do with them. Haven't seen a biscuit for years.'

'Jap warehouses are full of them. Full of food, actually. They're hoarding it for the Apocalypse.'

Zahra opens the tin. It gives a small sigh as if longing for its cool English home. A fanciful thought. Simone takes one. It's fresh and crisp. She lets herself savour it and remember afternoons and tea at the Seaview Hotel. What had become of that good-looking Australian Flight Lieutenant who'd rather liked her? She hopes he survived. Those pilots were courageous, unhappy to desert, as they saw it, the island at its hour of direst need, but they had no choice. Their lumbering Brewster Buffaloes were useless against the fast sleek Japanese Zeroes, yet the delusion was that they could do service further south.

'There are things I have to tell you,' Simone says.

Zahra puts up her hand. 'Me first. I got a message. From Java. And I don't know what to do with it.'

Simone stares. 'Where is she?'

'I don't know. I don't know whom to trust. I don't know if the message is real or a trap. You see?'

'Yes.'

'So I knew I had to try to summon you again. We can trust each other and two heads are better than one. Actually I followed you one day. Did you know?'

Simone smiles. 'I didn't. You were always good at that.'

Zahra grins.

'All right, smarty-pants. What's the message.'

Zahra looks away into the darkness and frowns. 'I'm ashamed. I was scared of it. Even now I'm scared of it.'

There's stuff here, trembling below the surface of Zahra's words which Simone can't fathom.

'Was it in Kadazan?' Simone asks.

'It wasn't in anything. It was a telephone message. A bunch of coordinates on a map. From Java. Get Gray's child.'

Simone shakes her head. 'Get Gray's child? I just had a visit from a Jap kempei named Tsuji asking me about Teresa and a person with the code name of Java.'

The two women stare at each other.

'I tried to find a map, but no such thing is available to employees of Radio Syonan. Is this a trap?'

The two women chew. 'If it was a Japanese trap,' Simone says, 'why come to me then and ask about Java? Doesn't make sense. Where are the others? Are they alive?'

'I know Anita is.'

Simone finishes her biscuit. She feels slightly nauseous. The wind and rain pick at the walls, sending fingers of damp air swirling. Now and then the geckos stutter and run in the rafters.

'Did you never hear me on the radio?'

'No. No one connected to the Gardens or the British scientists is allowed a radio. They do spot checks all the time. The Jap scientists listen of course, but to the Jap programmes.' Simone suddenly remembers Tsuji's words. 'Jean is alive I think. Tsuji said he talked to her. I think that means she was interrogated.'

'Oh,' Zahra says. 'Poor Jean.'

'I'm pretty sure,' Simone says, 'he thinks Java is a man. All I know is that Tsuji has connected me to Teresa, Jean and Halcyon Patrol. A picture in the newspaper. Why Teresa now I don't know. But she is a communist so I have to guess it's to do with the guerrillas on the mainland. I had to give him some random names but we need to warn the others.'

'Do you know that Jean must be in a camp in Sime Road?' Zahra says suddenly. 'I know the civilians were moved from Changi in late 1944. Did you know that?'

'No.'

'Sime Road. Practically the very place where we met her on the day of the great crocodile escapade. Why the King George Curry Café must be right there for heaven's sake.'

A noise—the wind—slams against the hut and both look back into the darkness. Simone half rises then sits again. That lonely wet camp of starving prisoners fills her mind. 'The Nips won't surrender,' she says. They're digging in. I've seen the bunkers on the edge of the Gardens. Heard the Padang is mined. They're storing ammo. Dugouts under Bukit Timah Hill, tunnels, dynamite. Slit trenches.'

'We monitor the BBC, Voice of America and Radio Chungking. It's got to be just a matter of time.'

'Tell me.'

'The Americans are on Okinawa and have captured all but the tip of the Northern Philippines. The B-29s are dropping incendiary bombs all over Japan. There's talk of the Soviets entering the Pacific War and invading Manchuria.'

'Will any of that matter here? To us.'

Zahra shrugs. 'I don't know. I can't do this alone. My situation … is difficult. I was forced into a, well, they call it a marriage. It isn't. Anyway, I can't always get away. You understand.'

Simone clutches Zahra's hand.

'Nothing I can do about that now. But you know, meeting you, this thing Java wants. It gives me hope.'

'But do you believe this message, Blue? Why didn't Java give a more obvious sign it was from her? Anything. The guide motto? Anything. Are we just being stupid and putting ourselves into danger. And the Japs will kill us. Or worse, torture us. Is it a trap? And who can we trust?'

'I know. But it's all danger now, isn't it? Maybe we're better together than apart? I keep reminding myself of Ponompuan and Miss Lilian Gibbs.'

Simone grimaces. 'All right, Blue. No need to drag up poor Miss Gibbs. But can we proceed with caution. Where the hell do we start anyway?'

'With White. I know where Anita Shah is.'

'Where is she?'

'She's a soldier in the Rani of Jhansi Regiment. Her cousin works at Radio Syonan.'

'A soldier? Anita? In that women's Indian army outfit?'

'Yes. She's a captain.'

'A captain! Good grief. I've seen them parading. Unbelievable.'

'Well, there it is.'

'She's working for the Japs.'

'Not according to her cousin. He thinks the whole outfit is rubbish. But we need to see for ourselves. A woman with inside information, a map and a rifle might come in handy, don't you think?

'Okay. But what do you need me for?'

Even as she says these words Simone knows that she is glad she is here. These women of her youth are her family. She knows they've always given meaning and taste to her life. Without them there is only bitterness, solitude and an invisible death.

'I need you. When I go out anywhere other than my job I need to have a woman with me. A chaperone. I'm watched, you understand.' Zahra's voice has risen. Simone hears the note of panic. 'I'm scared of him. More than doing this. I'm ashamed of that fear, ashamed of what I've become. A mouse. I want to do this. But I can't do it alone.'

Simone receives those words as a blow. Ashamed to be afraid. Ashamed of what she has become. She herself has lived a life of safety, hidden away in a garden protected by the whimsical power of the oppressor, as suffering and evil swirl around. She flushes and looks away.

'And you have the Gardens,' Zahra continues, 'The Marquis and those Japanese scientists. We might all need them before this is over.'

JOURNAL

8 February 1942

The barrage began today after days of relative silence. Yamashita getting his army ready for this final assault. The bombardment in the north is no longer intermittent but continuous, sustained, loud, like heavy wheels on a road. And shelling has begun, which means their artillery is close. In the day, black smoke. At night, a dull red glow. The stink of oil and sulphur. Rain is filled with soot. At the Tribune, George was breathless. The Japanese have crossed the Straits and landed in the north-west of the island. The official communiqué by Malaya Command says they are mopping up the enemy. No one sensible believes any of it anymore. The Chinese don't. They've refused credit. No more chits for the colonial masters. It's cash or nothing.

That chinless wonder Percival is moving out of Sime Road Camp and into Fort Canning. George talks of leaving for the first time. But agonizes over what to do with Daisy. He wishes he'd sent the dog with his wife and children. By now the docks are being strafed continuously and the ships in the harbour bombed. The government has finally ordered women and children to leave. Too late. There are massive queues to get tickets of passage on any ship leaving Singapore for anywhere. We can't go. Not permitted. Anyway, we 'natives' have nowhere to go. For the first time, I'm truly afraid.

SYONAN

Carlos

Carlos Pereira, head of the Herbarium and rummy aficionado, places his cards on the table with a flourish. 'Gin,' he says with a grin.

Simone smiles. 'All right. No need to gloat.'

He writes the score on a banana leaf in Japanese ink, gathers the cards together and begins to shuffle.

'Carlos, I have to ask a favour of you.'

'All right.'

'I need a friend to be invited here to translate some of your books into Malay.'

'Do you? Really? Why?'

'To get her away from her violent husband two or three times a week.'

'And will she actually be translating texts into Malay?'

'No.'

'Right. Don't tell me anything else.'

Carlos goes to his desk, unlocks it and takes out a sheet of letter paper. It carries the heading of the Marquis Fujimoto. 'I presume you need the highest authority.'

'Yes.'

'All right. Slip one of these into the typewriter. I'm going to the toilet.'

When he returns the letter is ready. He takes the chop of the Presidency of the Gardens, drops it onto the red inkpad and stamps the paper. Mr Guan has always had a stash of the Marquis's letter paper. And the chop is a copy. Both have come in handy on the occasions they've needed to use them.

'I shall have to tell Mr Guan.'

'Yes.'

'Another hand?' Carlos says. He proffers the tin of dried, crispy bugs. 'Beetle?'

* * *

Samad

Zahra's prison is a large terrace shophouse in the traditional Straits style. Ordinarily behind the double doors of such a house would be the tiled hall for receiving guests, furnished with a lavish display of blackwood and mother of pearl inlaid furniture. Except for the heavy central altar table set against the screen which separates the public from the private quarters, every stick of furniture is absent. In pride of place on the altar, ordinarily dedicated to Chinese gods and goddesses, is a portrait of the emperor next to a kamidama, a shrine to Shinto deities.

Simone is seated on the floor in the centre of this room. Samad is thin and hard, his head shaved to the scalp. Simone can see he lives and breathes Nippon seishin. Erect. Severe. Disciplined. As near to a manufactured Japanese as you could get. She bows to him and addresses him in Malay. English is out of the question.

He had been selected to go to Japan on the special Japanese education programme, only one of a dozen so honoured. He studied at the Miyazaki Higher School of Agriculture and Forestry for a year. Zahra has told her to mention that. As best as she can in her struggling Malay, she does.

A look of what might pass for pleasure flits across his face. It's hard to say. He looks dyspeptic. Unhappy. As if he has a broom up his backside. Zahra enters with a tray. She pours the Japanese tea—a concoction that no locals, used to lashings of milky, sugary teh tarik, can stomach—and takes her place by his side, head bowed, waiting. Simone's knees, tucked under her bottom, are already protesting at the achingly awful but only permissible seated posture of the Japanese female. But she is more hurt by the way Zahra is behaving. She finally understands what Zahra couldn't explain.

'Keseronokan untuk bertemu Zahra selepas semua tahun ini.' Her Malay is excruciating. Dragging out that phrase—the pleasure of meeting with Zahra after so long—is exhausting. Samad does not respond. Perhaps it's so bad he doesn't understand.

'Baiklah, saya ...' She gives up. 'Mungkin Zahra dapat memberitahu anda.' She has asked for Zahra to explain. Has she? Was that right? Why on earth hadn't she bothered to learn to speak proper Malay? It is terribly wrong to live in Malaya and not speak the language. Like some dreadful English memsahib. Maybe the Japs were right. Eurasians never bothered to consider the local people. Always sucking up to the English. Bertie and Hatter speak it fluently. So does the damn Marquis.

Silence. She waits. Obviously this is the default position. Making women wait. Simone feels the pulse at her temple throb. Finally he nods in Zahra's direction. She turns, facing Samad and puts her head to the floor. Simone is appalled. She sits, jaw clenched, as Zahra mumbles her request. Asking this petty lord his permission. She wants to scratch his face, claw his eyes, punch his supercilious nose into the back of his head. Instead she simply hands him the letter.

How can he refuse? He wouldn't dare call the Marquis. If he calls Mr Guan, then he will get confirmation. As Zahra mumbles, he stares at the letter. Is he honoured? Or wary? His face reveals nothing.

Finally the miserable business comes to an end. Zahra resumes an upright position. Samad puts the teacup to his lips and Zahra slides a glance at Simone and even dares offer a wink. Simone looks down. Samad puts down the teacup, puts the letter into his pocket, then, with a curt nod of his head, rises and without saying a single word, leaves the room.

Simone shakes her head in disbelief. Zahra grins.

JOURNAL

10 February 1942

The Japanese are at Bukit Timah, five miles from the city. Drove George down to Clifford Pier. He's given me the car and the keys to his house. He's in tears, floods of tears. He had to put Daisy down this morning. The poor Chinese vet can't keep up with the numbers of animals he has to deal with.

Clifford Pier is total confusion. European women and children look lost until a Zero passes over and strafes the quay. Their husbands seek out the latest information, desperate. Cars are abandoned the length of the docks. Strewn suitcases punctuate the quay. Some never heard the order. Only one suitcase per family. Teddy bears lie crushed underfoot.

Soldiers, angry, armed and dangerous search for launches to get away. George pushes aside the tearful Chinese amahs farewelling their wards. 'Poor Daisy,' he sobs, 'the children will be so upset.'

I see Michael. He's getting out too. The correspondents have been told to leave. He tells George, a fellow journalist, a fellow white man, to tag along with him. He's found a Dutch launch. I say goodbye to them both. I'm not sure they heard me.

The Governor read a statement on the radio that in its sheer fatuity exceeded any of the numerous speeches, orders and pronouncements he'd ever made on the subject of Singapore.

'We are all in the hands of God,' he declared, 'from whom we can get comfort in all our anxieties.' Sir Shenton and Lady Thomas have quit Government House and moved into the third floor of the Fullerton Building. He has placed himself not into the hands of God but of the stewards of the Singapore Club.

SYONAN

Anita

The flint-eyed female sentry gives Zahra and Simone the once-over. The Rani of Jhansi Training Camp sprawls over the ground between the Museum and Waterloo Street. The women Simone has seen parading here and up and down Bras Basah had apparently included Anita, who had been, without doubt, the least disciplined, most lax member of Halcyon Patrol.

They are shown into an ante-room, spartan and bare except for a huge picture of the bespectacled, deceptively mild-looking leader of Azad Hind, the provisional Indian government in exile, and head of the Indian National Army, 'Netaji' Subhas Chandra Bose.

Alongside him is a poster of the warrior princess herself, Lakshmibai, Queen of Jhansi in northern India. These are standard fare. Simone has them herself for the Indian Exhibition together with Bose's photo alongside Tojo and the other Keystone Kops at a conference in 1943, and a banner declaring *Dilli Chalo!*—Onward to Delhi—and *Jai Hind!*—Victory India.

What is remarkable is the extent to which Japan has been excluded from this room. No portrait of the Emperor hangs here, as it does in every other military and civil building in Syonan. No Japanese soldiers or heiho guard the establishment. The women do that themselves.

The Rani on her horse, sword raised against British oppression a hundred years ago, will almost certainly make it to the walls of the Museum alongside the Massacre at Amritsar, the Indian Mutiny, Gandhi, the Quit India Movement, the Famine in Bengal, and the Klang estate workers' strike. But she's certain that there will be no photos of the women's regiment. The Japanese utterly disapprove of it and only allowed its establishment, from what Simone has gleaned, because of the powerful hand of Bose whose sway over 20,000 soldiers is needed to hold the British at bay in Burma. Instead there will be a variety of smiling willowy women in saris, all gratefully embracing, in their shy and obedient femininity, the bounty of the Empire of Japan in its support of a British-free India.

'We must be careful,' Simone says quietly to Zahra. 'The INA is funded by and supports the Japs.'

'Yes. This is reconnaissance.'

'Dyb, dyb, dyb,' a voice drawls behind them and they turn.

Zahra and Simone share a smile. 'Dob, dob, dob,' they say in unison.

Anita puts out her hands. Simone had expected tension and in an instant it is erased.

Anita radiates health. Not for her the skinny-armed and pasty-faced picture of semi-starvation. She is muscled, clear-eyed, clear-skinned and well fed, oddly elegant in her khaki shirt and jodhpurs, the soft cap hugging her short-cropped hair. Simone knows little about the women of this regiment except what she sees: the masculine and practical clothing and hair, the disciplined parades, the rifles. Anita had loved her long dark oiled plait of thick hair. What had induced her to chop it off?

'Come on. We'll have tea.'

A corridor leads to an office. Anita speaks to a young female soldier in Hindi. It's all very swift and military and the woman salutes sharply.

'Well, Anita,' says Zahra as they sit. 'This is all a bit incredible.'

Simone eyes the Arisaka 99 26-inch short Japanese rifle lying across Anita's desk. She is familiar with all the Japanese weapons. A reporter's never-quite-lost instinct for detail.

'What on earth made you join up,' Simone says. 'You have to tell us everything.'

'Well, the war came in the nick of time,' she says. Her voice and attitude seemed hardly to have changed. The languorous drawl, the disdainful tone. 'The man mother wanted me to marry got blown up, thank heavens. Couple of uncles and their families packed up and got off to India just after the first bombing raids. Father wanted mother and me to go as well, but Mummy refused. Really put her foot down actually, which was unusual and Daddy wanted to stay and look after the business and his warehouse, thinking they'd all be looted and destroyed. Really he didn't think for a minute the British would lose so of course we all stayed. Well imagine our shock at the surrender.'

Anita pulls her mouth into a mou of disapproval. 'Such a bunch of lies. Anyway, all the Indians were running around and terrified of rape and so on. So Daddy said I should get married. Again. But that bloody roti was already cooked.'

Anita laughs. It's loud and lusty and Simone can't help smiling. She'd forgotten how much, on occasion, she'd actually liked Anita's disobliging spirit.

'Said the Japs wouldn't rape a married woman. Can you imagine? Wanted me to hitch up to some old friend of his. Sixty if he was a day and ate raw garlic. Of course I refused, and there was a terrible fuss but I didn't care. And it blew over because Daddy was friendly with Pritam Singh who was involved in the Indian Independence League so of course he joined and the Japanese left us alone. And really that was when Daddy and Mummy got involved in all this Free India stuff. Before that, they couldn't have cared less.'

'Don't you want to free India?' Zahra says. 'I think I'd like to free Malaya.'

'Well, I don't want India or Malaya to be free if that means free just for men. If it means that women are still slaves. I don't want that. I'd rather have the British back. I'd rather have Jean McKenna and the Girl Guides and the freedom that gave us than purdah, caste, miserable arranged marriages and men telling us what to do.'

Anita's voice has taken on a hard and determined edge. Simone stares at her. Never in all her born days had she expected Anita to express such sentiments. Of them all in the Patrol, she had seemed the least interested in almost everything they did, the last one to react to Jean McKenna's sporadic and eclectic lectures on female emancipation, the writings of her idols, Eleanor Roosevelt and Marie Stopes, and the life and work of her aunt, Lilian Gibbs.

These words, here and now, are treacherous. Certainly the Japanese would take them that way. Anita seems to have had the same thought.

'But never mind that. It is good to see you. How did you find me?'

'I discovered that Kamal at Radio Syonan is your cousin,' Zahra says.

'Oh, that idiot.'

The three women chat, filling in missed time. Their stories are routine. The terror and uncertainty of the surrender, the shock and realization of the new, the adjustment, a search for security, a job, a refuge and the daily grind. Tea arrives, proper Indian tea, and the young woman, after depositing the tray on the desk, offers a salute and Anita returns it smartly.

'Thank you Sita,' she says.

'White,' Simone says, 'tell me about this regiment. I would like to keep a record of it. I'm still a journalist, I suppose. We should know about what is happening here, especially this: an armed regiment of women joined together to fight for an ideal.'

'You haven't changed, Red,' Anita says. 'Always recording. Writing things down. Those damn newsletters. I once thought it stupid, but now I see it for what it is. The need to make the history of our times.'

She sips her tea and puts the cup carefully on the saucer.

'The truth is that very few women in this army are fighting for an ideal. Unless you consider escaping slavery, poverty, forced marriage and hunger an ideal. Freeing India is quite a way down on their list of motivations.'

'I don't fully understand.'

'No. Well, Netaji and our brilliant female commander, Captain Lakshmi, of course are passionate idealists. I'd say that most of the officer class with close ties to India are genuine revolutionaries. For middle-class girls from local homes, they joined up seeking a bit of excitement and inspired by the message and, for some, a desire to prove the naysayers wrong. What was considered unthinkable is now noble. *Dilli Chalo*! Half of them have no idea what or where Delhi is.'

'Most are poor Tamil girls from the rubber plantations. Like Sita. She'd been raped and then hurriedly married off. Miscarriage, beaten, shunned, forced to do the filthiest tasks and always in danger of attack. She came in here dirty, ragged sari, skinny and fearful. A good wash, a good meal, a new uniform, a new purpose and now pride.' Anita smiled. 'Anyway you get the picture.'

'But you,' Simone says, 'why did you join?'

'Oh, Mummy joined. I didn't want to know anything for a long time. But in the end I was so deathly bored, you know. And once I was shown how to shoot a rifle and lob a hand-grenade I was hooked. Really the Guides should teach that stuff. '

Zahra laughs. 'I'm for it.'

'So now I'm the Chief Rifle and Grenade Lobbing Instructor.' Anita purses her lips and turns her eyes to Zahra. 'But I think you haven't come here today to simply catch up with old times.'

Zahra meets Anita's gaze. 'We are here to find Halcyon Patrol. The rest of us, Woody, Gray, Blackie and Java.

Simone and Zahra had agreed not to mention Java's message until they'd tested Anita's current loyalties.

Anita takes this in. Simone can see Anita has, over time and perhaps because of this experience, become more thoughtful and considered. 'What if there is a conflict with the Japanese?' Anita says at length.

Zahra's voice takes on a tight, determined tone. 'I don't care. Do you? I think we need to know that before we go any further.'

Simone tenses. This is the question. The answer will decide whether they can trust Anita or not.

Anita steeples her fingers. 'The last I heard Jean was alive. The guards at Sime Road are INA so I know a bit of what's going on in there. It's always risky to ask. The ones they choose for guards are loyal to the Japanese and they change them often. So that was four months ago.'

Zahra and Simone exchange a glance.

'So?' Simone says.

'So, I've no part in what the Japs want. They killed my friend, you know. I cared greatly for him. He was a Captain in the Indian Army and refused to join the INA. So they beat him and sent him to some filthy place to die. I'll never forgive them.'

Anita's voice thickens. 'They didn't want this regiment. And when the end comes, they'll stick us on the firing line or shoot us. But we are well trained and well armed. I'm not prepared to die for India but I am for this regiment.' Anita turns her gaze to Simone. 'You see.'

Zahra glances at Simone and gives a small nod of her head. In for a banana note, thinks Simone.

'We've received a message from Kay, from Java.'

Anita raises her eyebrows. 'Where is she?'

'No idea. The Japs want to find her. Is that a problem for you, White?'

Into the silence fall distant voices—women's voices murmuring like the deep flow of a river.

'No. This war is coming to an end. There are Indians fighting in the jungles too. What do you need?'

Simone exhales and allows herself to trust Anita. Now they are three and of them all Anita is the most useful.

'Java sent a bunch of coordinates. She wants us to go there.'

'What's there?'

'A child. Gray's child.'

'Teresa? Really? Her child? Is she … dead?'

'No idea. But that is the message. Go there and find Gray's child.'

Anita tugs an ear lobe, a habit when she's cogitating on something messy. 'Show me these coordinates.'

Zara takes a slip of paper and hands it to Anita who plonks a map on the desk and picks up a pencil.

'Hmm.' Anita marks the map. 'Don't know exactly what is there. It's near a coastal village called Kampong Laut.'

'If it's a fishing village we could go by boat,' Simone says.

Anita chuckles. 'Clear to see you've been living in a garden. The Straits are mined, patrolled and bristling with craft. No. No messing about in boats. We shall go by car. I can get a car. But I need a very good reason to go. You'll have to supply the reason.'

'You have to know,' Simone says, 'that there is a Jap Captain sniffing around. He knows about Halcyon Patrol and he knows that Jean and I were in it with Teresa. What he clearly doesn't know is that Java is Kay, or even a woman. I gave him four false names but inevitably he will get back to me. I may need help too.'

This ominous thought sits in silence for a moment. Then Anita nods, face serious. 'All right. Understood. Anyway only two of us can go. That's me and you, Red.'

Zahra pulls a face but shrugs. The reality is she could never get away. 'I know,' she says. 'I'll try to find the others. Somehow.'

'I know where Woody used to be.'

Something in Anita's voice makes Simone throw a sharp look at her. 'Molly? Where?'

'She lived on Cairnhill.'

Zahra gasps. 'Do you think she is still there?'

'I don't know. I hope not.'

JOURNAL

14 February 1942

Three days ago, Yamashita dropped an invitation to surrender. 'I advise immediate surrender of the British forces at Singapore, from the standpoint of bushido, to the Japanese Army and Navy forces, which have already annihilated the British fleet in the Far East and acquired complete control of the China Sea, the Pacific, and Indian Oceans, as well as south-eastern Asia.' Percival declined.

The broadcasting station is blown up. The central water reservoirs are in enemy hands. The town is rubble. Black smoke blocks the sun. Strafing, shelling, massed bombers. Unceasing noise. Unceasing barrages. The river is on fire. The looting is terrific. Hordes of men and women with carts and rickshaws strip everything from stalls, shops, warehouses. Doors and windows are smashed in the frenzy for loot.

Thousands of filthy, dejected soldiers wander around aimlessly. A million people are crammed like sardines into a tin of 6 square miles. Our backs are literally to the sea. The scrabble for boats is chaotic. I've been told the entire stock of paper currency in Singapore is going up in smoke. A million coins have been chucked into the sea at Keppel Harbour.

I'm exhausted. Tribune offices were bombed. Sheltered in St. Andrew's Cathedral, which has become a hospital. At least there the bombs are muted and there's safety in the solidity of its walls. The congregation sang Praise, my soul, the King of Heaven. Be interested to see if the King of Heaven is listening. In the morning the Bishop said I should gather with the neutrals whom the Japs might respect. Seemed unlikely but I headed to the Dietholm Building on Collyer Quay where the Swiss contingent were installed. Refused entry. No point in arguing. Muller's orders. No Eurasians, whether they have a Swiss passport or not, are welcome into the sanctuary.

Dead on my feet, filthy and stinking, I wandered towards Raffles Place with the vague idea of getting to the safety of the concrete and brick civic buildings in Empress Place. A plane flying low strafed, shooting a mass of bullets, it seemed, aimed at me. I hid behind Robinson's Department Store and there, hiding too, was Mrs Hutchins, the wife of the general manager. I'd done a story on Robinson's for the women's page of the Tribune, which featured her photograph. She'd been thrilled.

'My dear Simone,' she said. 'You look done in. Come in.' We passed through a courtyard stinking of whisky and gin. Broken glass lay inches thick. Days ago, the Governor had ordered all the stocks of liquor on the island destroyed.

She unlocked the door of the private staff entrance. We entered the vast, deserted store. 'There's a few of us in here,' Mrs Hutchins said, 'although for obvious reasons, it's by invitation only.' She laughed. It was nice to hear but I felt uneasy at the thought of the thousands of locals outside who could have taken shelter here within its solid walls. The class system prevailed even on such a day as this. Selfishly I was grateful and kept my tongue. It would have served no purpose in any case and I was done in.

'Would you like a nice cup of tea?'

In the furniture department candles glowed and a dozen men and women lounged on sofas and chairs that no one would now ever buy. Whisky and gin, saved from destruction, was being drunk from crystal glasses. Tinned meat and pineapples were on the finest bone china. Someone said: 'It's Friday the 13th,' and everyone laughed.

In the plumbing department I had a bath—oh glorious day—and washed my clothes. Changed into a silk dressing gown, which Mrs Hutchins had saved from looters in Women's Clothing. When the water supply was threatened, she told me, every bath in the store—over two dozen—had been filled. I found a brush and comb and some lavender toilet water in Ladies' Hairdressing. The battle raged outside but we lucky few spent that night clean, perfumed and drinking whisky and soda before dropping into oblivion in the most comfortable and expensive beds Singapore had to offer.

SYONAN

The Devil's Garden

The voice outside her bedroom window is shrill. Simone knows exactly who it is and can't quite believe her ears. She peers through the shutters. Greta Muller stands issuing orders to the Chinese trishaw man as to the disposition of her cases into the empty third bungalow. Never—and she does not think this lightly considering the predicament Singapore has found itself in for three and a half years—has Simone seen a more unwelcome sight. She looks at her watch. It is barely 7.30 a.m., which is in effect 6 in the morning. The light is just appearing.

What on earth has impelled Greta Muller to leave the flat she occupied in a rather nice apartment building near St Andrew's Cathedral in order to decamp to what can only be considered as a ramshackle mouse-ridden old house? Greta lost her husband Hans to tuberculosis in 1944. The Mullers had sent their two daughters away on a boat to Java just after the first bombs fell. But they had decided to stay on because Hans, an engineer, was Swiss Consul, an honorary position but one which he took pompously and seriously to heart. Hans had kept the diplomatic trappings of the Japanese Consulate shut down when all Japanese citizens had been deported to India. On their return he had made a great fuss of handing them back. He was thus a favoured son of the Empire. Greta had, for reasons of fanatical loyalty to Japan, also become the darling of the high command.

Simone thought that she was an amateur naturalist or something like that. She used to give lectures at the German Club—appropriately, Jean had remarked—on crawling species. However, her loyalty, not her knowledge was what was important to the Japanese. She had become the head of the gardens which surround the old Government House occupied by the Supreme Commander, Count Terauchi. Terauchi, she knew from the newspapers, was no longer in Singapore. He had decamped first to the Philippines and then to Saigon. She'd overheard during a conversation between Dr Haneda and Uehara that he'd had a stroke upon hearing about the loss of Burma to the Allies. That had cheered them all up for a time. Perhaps Greta no longer has either a patron or a job.

To find herself in proximity to Greta Muller is disagreeable and dangerous. Simone dresses and goes to the kitchen. There she makes coffee, the one commodity that is still available and generously supplied gratis by the Marquis. She goes in search of Mr Guan.

Mrs Guan is dressing her girls. The children turn their dark eyes to Simone. Do the Guans know they're breeding monsters? Will all the children of Syonan be monsters? Have they seen too much? 'Guan is in the devil's garden,' Mrs Guan says.

She leaves the house through the back entrance and crosses the road. The devil's garden is a place at once repellent and fascinating. Forty years ago, a previous head of the gardens had introduced a number of duroia species from the Amazon rainforest. Along with one of the species, duroia hirsute, came, apparently to his surprise, a colony of ants, which made this tree their sole home.

He had written a paper on the subject. The species are allelopaths. They are capable of biochemical interactions inhibiting the growth of neighbouring plants. This chemical inhibitor is aided in its process by the lemon ant, a resident on and in the tree, which plays an active role in suppressing plant growth in the vicinity of their host by injecting and spraying formic acid and defending against herbivores. The area around the understorey of the trees is therefore devoid of all other plant types leading to the local name, devil's garden. So effective is the ant's poison that it takes over large areas of jungle.

In the beginning, when she first came to live and work here, when everything was strange and new and made no sense, Simone had often visited this devil's garden. She saw in it a visual metaphor for the malign spread of the Great East Asian Prosperity Sphere and the ant-like Japanese.

She finds Mr Guan seated on a large flat rock observing the tree and the comings and goings of the ants.

'I used to come here often,' she says, taking a seat by his side.

Mr Guan is a slight man with an angled and bony face and poor eyesight, but over the years of their acquaintance Simone has discovered his capacity for kindness and decency. He has an impeccable soul.

'I too like to sit and contemplate them. Are they not the most interesting creatures?'

He points to one side, 'Look, over there is a colony of Malayan giant carpenter ants. Do you know that one of their number will commit suicide in order to save the colony? I've seen it happen. It blows itself up.'

Simone watches the giant ants for a moment. Perhaps it was these ants and not the lemon ants that most resemble the Japanese.

'Mr Guan, why is Greta Muller moving into our compound?'

'She has been told to move out of her apartment. Apparently since the surrender of the Germans, the Japanese are no longer prepared to be very accommodating to the German community. The high command has apparently offered her the visitors' bungalow. Unlikely to get any visitors now in any case, eh?

I understand the only planes the Japanese now possess are used to throw themselves into ships.'

Mr Guan smiles. He was being darkly humorous. It is unusual and she laughs.

'Dr Hatter and Lieutenant Uehara both dislike Mrs Muller,' Simone says.

'It was not in my hands. I have been asked to find her some work to do. Mrs Muller is a myrmecologist. She studies ants. I should very much like to know why and how the giant carpenter ant explodes. Wouldn't you?'

Simone shrugs. 'I suppose so.'

'One of her forebears was August Forel, a Swiss scientist who studied the social life of ants.'

'I see.'

'Thus I suppose her own interest.'

'Yes.'

'The gardeners will build her a small bamboo house for her studies. Better to be here than bothering Dr Hatter or Dr Pereira at the Herbarium, wouldn't you say?'

Simone smiles. 'Yes.'

'The war is drawing to its close,' Mr Guan says unexpectedly. She cannot recall ever talking to him about the war. 'The British will come back. Do you think they will shoot us as collaborators?'

The thought had never occurred to Simone and it startles her.

'We hadn't much choice, had we? And I think long ago the scientists agreed on a kinder word. Cooperation.'

'But Dr Hatter and Professor Bradshaw, they had the choice not to cooperate. I am concerned for them.'

'Yes, I suppose they did. They chose science and the wider culture. They saved everything here for future generations. Surely the British will see that.'

'I'm not sure that the sorts of British officers we may meet will be any more far-sighted than the ones the Japanese locked up.'

'No. You're probably right.'

Mr Guan's eyes follow the tracks of the carpenter ants. 'We have found relief in these gardens. Bounty and beauty. Everyone needs beauty. Perhaps there is even a strange beauty in the destruction the ants cause.'

She has never seen Mr Guan in this philosophical frame of mind. 'Now we shall have to discover who we once were. Who we deserted and betrayed and how we are going to make amends.'

She contemplates this. What did Mr Guan used to be? What did she? What amends did he have to make? Is what she and Zahra and Anita are doing an attempt at atonement? What on earth is atonement anyway? Reparation for sin. But who has sinned here? What even is sin if it isn't war?

'Perhaps,' he says, 'it is the things inside this Garden that are truly worth fighting for. Progress, science, our own cultures, the natural world of this region. Things we hold dear. Loyalty and friendship.'

Their eyes meet. She realizes that she doesn't know him at all, and his complacent, polite placidity harbours an unguessed-at fierceness. Things we hold dear?

'Mr Guan, I have to ask you to do something for me. It means deception.'

'Ah. Is it important?'

'Yes.'

He slides from the rock and holds out his hand for Simone, like a gentleman for his lady. He signals to the Malay gardeners. She hadn't noticed them crouching in the shadows. They begin to sprinkle paraffin on the duroia trees on the edge of the devil's garden.

'If we are to build a hut for Mrs Muller, the duroia stand must be destroyed. It has grown too big. It shouldn't really be here at all. It is a pity about the lemon ants but they are an invasive species after all.'

With a faint whoosh the trees begin to burn. The gardeners walk around tending the fire, setting new ones. Smoke coils into the sky and the faint acidic odour of burning ants fills the air.

Simone watches. 'Does Dr Ueno approve?' she asks.

'I don't know. I didn't ask him. He will not care. Not anymore.' They walk down the path to the Tanglin Gate. 'Tell me what it is you wish me to do.'

JOURNAL

15 February 1942

I awoke to the sounds of children's laughter. Mrs Hitchins brought me a cup of strong tea. With milk and sugar.

I went to the window. Children were dancing in little summer dresses, new shoes and hats. Little boys wore white shorts and shirts. It was like a party. The music was the waltz of artillery shells and the tango rat-a-tat of machine guns.

'Children's Clothing,' says Mrs Hitchins. 'Let those poor dears from up-country take first dibs for the children. They've not a stitch. They'll need something for prison.'

It is stark. But the fact is here.

'We've thrown the store open to all comers. Anyone can have anything they like. Help yourself dear. I'm off to the Cathedral for the service.'

I didn't take anything. As a neutral it was surely unlikely that I would be interned. I went instead in search of Jean in the Fullerton Building. The ground floor was a hospital stinking of blood, decay and idioform. The corridors were stacked with corpses, slowly and gaggingly melting in the heat but sights, sounds, and smells have lost all power to shock.

The Singapore Club billiard room was the operating theatre. I saw Jean lugging water from the basement alongside her fellow teachers. We embraced. But she was strangely aloof. As if she had already, like the cicada, shucked off this life and moved on. Perhaps they were all going to leave their shells behind and retreat into invisibility.

I offered to nurse but they had more nurses than they knew what to do with. Jean made sure I had a place to sleep in the fifth floor storage offices with the Eurasian staff. Went to the roof at 7 p.m. and sat with Mr Kiching, the Chief Surveyor of Singapore. He didn't seem to mind. Four shells fell on houses in River Valley Road. Some plopped into the river sending up fountains. Fires everywhere.

Lines of abandoned cars scattered willy-nilly. Three squaddies were pushing the Governor's car into the harbour.

Mr Kitching offered me a lunch of tea and sausages with the field officers, cooked on his stove in the Survey Department. It was nice.

Professor Bradshaw from Fisheries joined us. I knew him vaguely. A lovely man. Gentle. Call me Bertie, he said. He told me that we are surrendering. Percival will meet the Japanese at 3.30 p.m. Hearing it like that. No matter what, it was a shock.

Surrender. The end of the British Empire in the East. It took just seventy days.

I am staring at the words and can't quite believe what I have just written.

SYONAN

Cairnhill

The hilly area north of Orchard Road known collectively as Cairnhill is a series of leafy, winding streets filled with hotels and pretty terraced houses which, before the war, belonged to wealthy European and Chinese businessmen. Now it is a vast brothel behind a high wooden stockade like the wall of some frontier fort.

From the interior of a coffee shop Zahra eyes the snaking line of hundreds of soldiers, smoking and chatting. Waiting for their turn.

There are hundreds of women inside. She knows that they are mostly Chinese but there are Koreans too. Yoshida talks of this often. Doubtless he frequents the civilian brothels. Military or civilian, the women inside are enslaved. Just one of the many aspects of this occupation that she chose to ignore. Now she is enslaved too. Prostituted too. She is them.

But, unlike those women, now she has some small freedoms. It is heady. To come and go as she likes, free from hateful eyes. Now she has Simone, she wants to find the others. Anita's health and endless confidence fills her with courage.

She sips the coffee, uncertain how to proceed. Is Molly one of the women inside? Getting inside there. It seems impossible. To ask about Molly is too dangerous.

A door opens in the fence of the fort and a tubby older Japanese woman and a couple of skinny Malay kids come out. The kids are holding a covered basket. The Japanese woman says something to the boys and goes back inside. The boys, each holding one side of the basket, set off down the street.

Zahra gets up. She trails the boys. They turn into a shophouse. There are no indications as to the business inside. The door stands ajar. Can't think of the consequences. She steps inside.

The front hall of the shophouse is shuttered and gloomy, but beyond, through the open doors she sees the bright sunny light of an inner courtyard and, as she advances, hears the sloshing sounds of water. A turn and she arrives at the yard, which is crisscrossed with laundry lines and the gently swaying bodies of pegged-out jellyfish drying in the sun. The smell in the courtyard is of old drying fish. Not jellyfish, Zahra thinks, but transparent shapes, like narrow gourds. Cuttlefish perhaps. Against the blinding sunlight she can't make them out.

In a far corner the boys with the basket are emptying it into a vat of water. A Malay woman appears. Zahra puts her hands together in greeting.

'Salaam Aleikum,' she says.

The woman nods, seemingly unsurprised at this invasion of her home. 'Aleikum Salaam,' she says and gestures with her hand for Zahra to enter.

'I recognize you,' the woman says. 'From the newspaper pictures. You do the programmes for the radio. We listen. I am Noor.'

Zahra smiles, her vanity pleased despite herself. Noor. Her sister's name. They sit on the raised floor of a small verandah. A young Malay girl brings tea with mint. Outside the two boys are moving the water of the vat with a paddle and the odour of fish is strong.

'Forgive me, I followed these boys to this house.'

'Why?'

'I had a friend who lived on Cairnhill. I want to find out about her.'

'You think she is inside there still? You think she is one of the women?'

'I don't know. I want to know.'

'You cannot help her. If she is in there, she is ruined or dead. I've seen them.'

Noor points to the lines in the courtyard. 'Those are condoms,' she says. We wash, dry and powder them. We handle more than a thousand a week. I am paid one cent for every condom. There are four houses in this neighbourhood in this business. A woman services one man every fifteen minutes. Eight hours each day. Do you think she could survive that?'

Zahra puts down her teacup and stares at the lines of transparent latex. Condoms. She's seen them in the shops. The Kokusai Rubber factory is on Alexander Road. They are named Attack Champion. She feels tears well and puts her hand to her mouth.

'Yes,' Noor says. 'You see.'

Zahra's throat constricts. She coughs and swallows the mint tea.

'You could not know.'

Zahra shakes her head. She didn't want to know. That's the truth. If you want to, you see.

'I do not like this business,' Noor says. 'But it is how we survive. My husband is dead. Tuberculosis. He was a teacher at the Malayan High School. I do it for my children.'

She looks at Zahra, willing her to understand. Zahra nods.

'My relatives will not speak to us anymore. However, they are not above taking money when they need it.'

The cloying odour of fish becomes overwhelming as the boys remove the condoms from the first vat, trailing stinking water.

'Yes,' Zahra says and meets the woman's eyes. Hers too contain tears.

For a time the women do not speak. They watch the boys with their paddles, adding soap to the water.

'I would like to know,' Zahra says. 'Can you ask the boys? Is that all right?'

'Yes. They are spared nothing. They're not children anymore.' The woman calls her elder son, perhaps twelve, to her side.

'Number 22 on Cairnhill Road', Zahra says. 'What is that? Is it a brothel?'

'No,' the boy says. 'It's a restaurant for officers run by a fat Formosan. There are Chinese waitresses who come and go but they are old women.'

The woman pats her son on the cheek. 'Thank you, my boy. Allah knows goodness.'

'Thank you,' Zahra says. She rises and bids the woman farewell, glad to quit the stench of that tiny courtyard.

Molly isn't inside Cairnhill. Her home is a restaurant. So where is she?

She walks onto Orchard Road. She bows to the sentries. As she rises from the bow she catches sight of the Pavilion Cinema.

Molly had a brother who worked in film before the war. Molly told them once that she'd met Charlie Chaplin. Did we believe her? Hardly matters now. But the Shaw Brothers, the kings of Asian cinema, work out of the Pavilion. They didn't get away before the surrender. The Japanese make them run the Eiga Kaisha, the Japanese propaganda film industry, the cinemas and the entertainment venues, the Worlds. Molly and her brother, Charlie, knew the Shaws.

In the distance, to her shock, she sees Fatima emerging from the cinema. Before she can move, Fatima sees her too.

SYONAN

Suncus Malayanu

In the gallery, Simone listens for footsteps or voices. Lieutenant Uehara, Dr Ueno, Bertie, and Mrs Sugiyama are in the former meeting room of the Royal Asiatic Society, the gathering point for the collection, preservation, and despatch of the shipment of skins, feathers, insects, and artefacts to the Emperor. Bertie reckons it will never get through but they have to do it anyway.

She walks quickly to the spiral staircase which leads to the roof space of the Museum. The package she holds contains a week of newspapers and some recent leaflets warning the population against looking up during the passage of the B-29s and exhorting everyone confusingly to both greater efforts to grow food whilst at the same time quitting Singapore for the outlying islands.

With a glance around, she goes quickly through the trapdoor. Here in the rafters of the Museum are secreted all the copies of the Syonan Shimbun from day one of the occupation, alongside the rescued letters of Stamford Raffles and other historical papers saved from the initial looting. She places the newspapers on the stack at the far end of the attic where a breeze circulates air. Neem leaves and oils are sprinkled and spread about. It has proved a good check on insect infestation and a general preservative. The conversation about this work had come very early on, only days into the occupation. Bertie and Hatter were in agreement. They must preserve every possible item about the occupation against a possible day of final conflagration.

She shuts the trapdoor silently and joins the others with an armful of the newspapers for packing purposes. As is always the case, the Japanese are seated on chairs a good six inches higher than those accorded to the British. She is not sure when it might have happened but somewhere along the line the British chairs must have had their legs shortened as they are quite unnaturally low. Hatter is short and slight, but Bertie looks like an overgrown child in a nursery.

Lieutenant Uehara greets her with a bow. She returns it and smiles then joins Bertie at the table where he is bottling seashells and sea sponges in alcohol.

'His Majesty has requested sea slimes for the next shipment, Professor,' Uehara says.

Bertie nods. The pretence that any of this will occur must be maintained. 'Yes. Certainly. I shall need to go out to the islands. Perhaps Dr Ueno would care to join me?'

Dr Ueno's mouth takes a downward turn. Simone smiles. Insects are his game. He doesn't like boats and Bertie knows it. But a British scientist can't go messing about by himself amongst the militarized offshore islands.

'Perhaps,' Ueno says, 'the Lieutenant would like to go?'

'No can do,' Uehara says and pulls his handsome face into a grimace. 'I'm supposed to pop over to the mainland. Guan-san has told me that the Governor of Johor has made a request to arrange transport for his son to visit him. The young man is a lieutenant in the navy and his ship is currently in port. The military aren't very much interested in the Governor's son apparently and won't supply a car.'

Uehara wrinkles his nose. 'And then His Majesty has most particularly requested a specimen of the Malayan pygmy shrew, *suncus malayanu,* so I thought, jolly good, I can do both at once. But the problem is a car. No one seems to have one.'

Simone looks up from the sponge she has been pushing into the bottle with some difficulty.

'What about Dr Ueno's car?' she says.

'Tyre trouble. No rubber available.' This strikes him as amusing and he chortles. 'No rubber in Malaya.'

Bertie laughs and Uehara grins at him. Dr Ueno nods his head in a manner that shows his resignation. Lieutenant Uehara, in a swift mood change, pouts and stares, with a melancholy gaze, at a dried cephalopod. 'What on earth he expects me to do about it all, I really don't know. I ask you.' Uehara spreads his hands.

'Uehara san,' Simone says. 'Perhaps I can help.'

He turns to Simone. 'How so?'

'I have a friend who is a Captain in the Indian National Army. She was talking about going to the mainland. Would that be useful?'

Bertie frowns and looks sharply at Simone. She ignores him.

'Yes,' Uehara says and claps his hands with glee. 'Yes.'

'I should like to come with you,' Simone says. 'After all as you say, Uehara-san, all work and no play makes Jack a dull boy.'

Uehara laughs. 'Quite right. Quite right. Come by all means. We shall have a jolly time. Oh what a relief.'

'Thank you. Mr Guan and I will arrange for a specimen of the pygmy shrew to be prepared for His Majesty. You will have to organize the travel permission.'

Uehara smiles widely. 'Yes. Yes. Oh the Marquis will be pleased. And the Governor. Oh, jolly, jolly good.'

Bertie, having glared at Simone during this interchange, now releases her from his inspection. He has finished bottling and sealing his specimens He picks up some old socks and begins to insert the bottle inside. Dr Ueno gasps. Lieutenant Uehara looks over and Mrs Sugiyama draws a sharp breath.

'Professor Bradshaw,' Ueno says in scandalized tones. 'What are you doing?'

Bertie, surprised, says, 'Wrapping the specimens.'

'But,' Ueno says, 'they are socks. You cannot use socks.'

'They are clean, thoroughly disinfected,' Bertie says. 'And will make an excellent buffer.'

'No. Throw them away. You cannot send socks to the Emperor,' Ueno says.

Bertie removes the specimen and hands the socks to Mrs Sugiyama, who takes them with the tips of her fingers and leaves the room. Bertie grins at Simone. He's done it on purpose. A silent 'up-yours' to the Emperor.

The bell rings downstairs signalling the opening of the Museum for the afternoon session.

'Excuse me,' Simone says. She unlocks the doors and turns on the ceiling fans, checks the galleries and then heads to the Library. Two hours of peace and quiet reading. Today she will read again the slim book by Virginia Woolf, *A Room of One's Own*, rescued from a private home. Simone had discovered this book in the long hot afternoons in the vastness of this abandoned library—this treasure house, which was almost hers alone—and it had set her mind dancing. *What a change of temper a fixed income can bring. Women have served as a looking glass for men possessing the magical and delicious power of reflecting him at twice his natural size.* Why had she never read this book before? Why on earth was it not required reading by the Girl Guides? She was almost grateful to the war for bringing her in contact with Miss Woolf. What else was this huge library but a room of her own? Might she not write here? Write it all down as George had suggested.

And thus she had begun her dangerous activity, the finding of exercise books and paper, the compiling of the story of her life, those of her companions and this stricken island under the dark cloak of the Occupation. An activity so compelling and satisfying that she rarely gave a thought to the fact that it could cost her head. Her old diaries are in the Herbarium but she hides her new writings in amongst the books of the abandoned library, all 45,000 tomes. Early on, she'd separated out those written by women. It was a short shelf but she tended it the most carefully.

She throws open the windows and walks between the rows and stacks, checking for death-watch beetle and signs of decay, signalled by little piles of sawdust, spraying neem oil. The Japanese have their own exclusive library in St. Andrew's school. They do not care about these despised books that Guan, Hatter and Bertie had, with Tanaka's authority and a large truck, gathered in from all across the island in the first days of the surrender.

She is filled with quiet optimism and the thrill of adventure. Once you understand that life is essentially a tragic farce you can start enjoying it.

JOURNAL

16 February 1942

The Sound of Silence

A Jap officer turned up this morning. Everyone rushed to catch a glimpse of him. Wrinkled his nose at the stench of the stacked corpses but very politely informed the Governor, in passable English, that the British civilians must all go to the cricket ground on the Padang at 11 a.m. tomorrow.

Dr Hatter spoke to the foresters and agriculturalists about the need to approach the Japanese to secure and protect the collections and records of the Botanical Gardens. Met with resolute refusal. 'We British must stand together in custody and humility, and in a fraternity that wealthy times had scorned' was the reply. I wrote it down because it was so typically pompous and off point. How long those noble sentiments of fraternity will last when they're all slung together cheek by jowl inside some prison remains to be seen.

Dr Hatter just met with the Governor. He has secured a note addressed to the Japanese authorities asking them to preserve the collections of the Museum, Library and Botanical Gardens. Hatter went again to his companions, showed them the note and asked if they would accompany him to the Japanese. They would not.

'I see,' Dr Hatter said to Bertie and me, 'that, at heart, they are not true scientists.'

Mr Kitching deposited his diaries and photographs in a suitcase in Hatter's room for preservation in the Library. 'Singapore is lost. Perhaps forever,' he said to me. 'Dr Hatter is right. He knows that there is little hope of the British returning in the foreseeable future. The looting and senseless destruction has to be stopped. Places of knowledge must be protected.' These sentiments are unique to him. All the rest, except Bertie, see Hatter as a traitor.

Shenton Thomas is to make a radio broadcast this afternoon. That will doubtless be inspiring. In the Fullerton there is a sense of disbelief coupled with relief and apprehension. Some cry, but on the whole everyone simply accepts.

Went to find Jean. She was in good spirits. 'It's over. At least we know. I should have liked to bid you all farewell though,' she said and hugged me. I couldn't stop tearing up. I can't bear it.

But she took my hand and we climbed to the fifth floor. The rooms of the up-country wives who had fled Singapore on the last ships were overflowing with discarded suitcases and trunks. Bounty. Jean and the other nurses and teachers were selecting items for their journey. 'Last shopping trip we're likely to get,' said one.

This time I didn't hesitate. After all, I had only the clothes I was standing up in. I opened the suitcase of one Isabel von Hoff. Judging by the stickers outside and the clothes within, Isabel had been well-heeled and well-travelled. It was her bad luck to find herself in Singapore at its final shambolic and frantic hour. All Isabel's clothes are in good taste. And a good fit. There was not a stitch of Mr von Hoff's apparel apart from two dozen brand new monogrammed, over-large soft cotton Y fronts made by a Chinese tailor in Kuala Lumpur. Who monograms underwear? I choose to see it as a private joke. I like Isabel von Hoff. Hope she got away. I stashed the suitcase in Hatter's room.

SYONAN

To the Mainland

Mr Guan puts down the phone and turns to Simone.

'Your friend Captain Shah has given me all the details for the trip to the mainland. She will be here at 7 a.m. tomorrow. I will ask Lieutenant Uehara to be ready.'

'Be ready for what,' a voice sounds behind Simone and she turns. It is Greta. Nosy cow. But then she is here to do just this.

'The Lieutenant is going to the mainland to pick up some items for the Emperor.'

'Oh,' Greta says and plops herself down on a chair. 'Can I come?'

'I fear that it will be difficult. The car belongs to a Captain in the Indian National Army. She has offered it to us for this journey. Naturally we are delighted to take up this kind offer.'

'But why can't I go?'

'Aren't you mourning the death of Herr Hitler,' Simone hears herself say. 'Don't you think it's a little too soon to be enjoying yourself.'

Greta jumps to her feet, takes two steps forward and raises her hand. She intends to slap Simone but she is not fast enough. Simone grabs her wrist and pushes her away.

'You are now an alien of a defeated nation, just like me, Mrs Muller.'

'Ladies, ladies,' Mr Guan calls. 'Please settle down.'

Simone's heart is thumping fit to burst. She has dared. Greta has to know she is not afraid of her. And she cannot come on this journey to the mainland. All the trickling years of disliking this woman have swelled into a river.

'How dare you speak to me like that?'

'Times have changed,' Simone says.

'Now, now.' Mr Guan places himself between the two women. 'Mrs Muller, I will speak to Dr Ueno. Perhaps something can be arranged.'

Simone stares at him. Greta smiles. 'Thank you, Mr Guan,' she says. 'I have still some influence.' She glares at Simone. 'Perhaps you know Captain Tsuji. I am helping him with some of his inquiries.'

Ah. Good to know. Out in the open.

'Mrs Muller,' Mr Guan says. 'If you wish to have a peaceful life for yourself, may I suggest that you do not threaten anyone here. The Japanese scientists have not forgotten your actions in having their British colleagues interned. It was very good of Dr Ueno to grant you the Cluny Road bungalow, since the Japanese in general take a dim view of the surrender of Germany.'

Something deflates in Greta. Perhaps, Simone muses, she has realized how little power she actually has now. Terauchi is bed-ridden and couldn't care less about her. Tsuji is using her but if she doesn't produce any goods her influence will be nil and if all she has to tempt him was that photograph, it may not be enough. Then there is her daily life here in the Gardens where she is so despised.

Still she raises her chin. 'I shall inform Captain Tsuji of this trip to the mainland. We shall see if he approves.'

'Miss Martel is required to pick up some specimens for the Emperor. Will Captain Tsuji wish to thwart plans expressly made on behalf of His Majesty?'

Greta pauses. How far is she prepared to go in this new uncertain world that suddenly surrounds her?

'We shall see,' she says, turns on her heel and stomps off.

'I will ask Dr Ueno to telephone Captain Tsuji,' Mr Guan says. 'Since he is making inquiries in the Gardens it is only wise to do so and, in any case, doubtless he should give permission. It is always wise to get an extra level of permit and the Kempeitai have the greatest influence.'

It occurs to Simone that she can call Anita and annul the whole journey. An irreplaceable flat tyre would be an adequate excuse. But Java has sent for them. This is the way. But if Greta comes, what are they to do?

'Do you think Mrs Muller will get permission to go?'

'Doubtless.'

Simone sighs and Mr Guan raises an eyebrow.

'Let us see what tomorrow shall bring.'

JOHOR

The Quiet Resistance

Under cover of the night, Kay slips into the courtyard of one of the shophouses which line the street of the small town. It is strange but not unpleasant to be in these clothes, the utterly feminine kebaya and sarong. This is the part to play today. On the forged ID papers she is Rose Lim, waitress. Ravi had been angry. Yuan anxious. But the message had come from Zahra via a cousin of Uma's, Java Force's Indian doctor. They are the quiet resistance. The cousin's husband is also a doctor and she a nurse. This is their house. They have offered her shelter for the night. Her presence here can get them and their three children tortured and killed. They know this. They don't know her, but they greet her with smiles because she and her fighters shelter Uma.

She takes a little of the food they offer. In return she gives them ten thousand of the fake notes. 'Be careful,' she says, 'how you use it.'

'It will buy food and medicine on the black market,' the husband says. 'No one there ever asks where it comes from.' They talk of Uma, of the situation in the town, the places where the Japanese are, the places to avoid. The Japanese officer in charge of the small garrison in their town is an opium addict, he says, which would get the officer executed. It is a secret that he knows because he supplies the opium. He shakes his head. 'I am a man of medicine,' he says, 'but I supply this drug because it means we are safe.'

'War makes us do things,' Kay says simply. Whatever it takes.

Anita and Simone will be at the map coordinates sometime tomorrow. She settles on the bed of the eldest daughter. On the wall is a childish drawing of this house and five stick people. They are not smiling and the house is grey.

SYONAN

The Stuffed Boar

Anita sits waiting in a saloon car with a charcoal converter bolted to the back. Simone wrinkles her nose. The journey will be noisy and stinky. The vehicle carries the flag of the INA. For today's purposes it also carries a Japanese flag. Greta joins them.

'Is this captain an old friend of yours, Miss Martel?' Greta asks. 'An old Guide friend, perhaps.'

Before Simone can answer Mr Guan intervenes. 'The specimens you are to pick up will include a stuffed wild boar,' he says.

'A stuffed boar,' Greta says with a frown.

'Yes, a stuffed boar. The Governor of Johor and the Marquis often hunt together. They shot this specimen and the Governor has had it mounted in order to offer it to the Emperor.'

Simone feels like she has stepped into a Marx Brothers movie.

'Mrs Muller, Miss Martel, you may be obliged to squeeze up and perhaps commune with the boar on your return. It can't be helped. With so little petrol, these journeys are rare and must serve many purposes. Also, I must warn you that it is a dangerous journey. You are entering the territory heavily patrolled by the Malayan Peoples' Anti-Japanese Army.'

Greta looks as if she's swallowed a stone. 'I did not know.'

'Yes, it is a dangerous journey but I'm sure you will enjoy it.' Mr Guan smiles and adjusts his glasses.

'Does Captain Tsuji know this?'

'Why yes of course. It is common knowledge. But for the Emperor of course nothing is too much. No danger too great. And the Marquis has ordered it. Captain Tsuji has nothing to say on the matter.'

'Yes, yes, of course,' Greta says.

'I merely warn you. As a German national and thus a mortal enemy of the guerrilla army, you may be in danger. Miss Martel, it is dangerous for you also. The vehicles of the Indian National Army are often attacked. I wish you a pleasant trip.'

Mr Guan turns away. Greta stares at his back. So does Simone.

'Mr Guan,' Greta calls, 'Perhaps it might be better if I did not go on this occasion.'

Mr Guan turns. 'Really, Mrs Muller. I have gone to the trouble of putting your name on the permit. It is very inconvenient. But if you do not wish to go, I will remove your name. In future, please try not to cause such trouble.'

A vein throbs in Greta's temple but she remains silent and departs without a backward glance.

'Is that true?' Simone asks.

'Yes of course it is. It is very dangerous to be on those roads flying a Japanese or INA flag. I think the whole journey foolish. Mrs Muller is wise not to go.'

Mr Guan examines the notes in his small book. 'However, as you are to go, then these are the arrangements. The Governor of Johor has invited Lieutenant Uehara to lunch to thank him for transporting his son. You will take them to the Governor's palace, then pick up the specimens at the Governor's hunting lodge before returning for both the men and coming back to Syonan.'

'I see. And will we get some lunch too?' Simone says. 'If we survive that is.'

Mr Guan smiles. 'You will have lunch at the hunting lodge.'

'This will be jolly,' Uehara calls as he approaches the car. 'Let's be off.'

Uehara settles in the back. Simone gets in next to Anita. Once again Mr Guan has saved the day. She opens the window and settles in for the drive. Anita glances at Simone, nods and sets off. Simone feels a thrill of achievement. They've done it. They've fooled the Japs and got rid of Greta. She turns her face to the wind.

The jungle offers no interest as they speed by. A sea of green and oppressive heat. Kampongs dot the landscape. Nothing looks prosperous. Everything grim. Skinny children and sentry posts. The smell of rotting earth.

They turn to the naval base. She recalls vividly the last time she was here. Seven days before the surrender. Simone smiles and bows to Lieutenant Itami but can barely believe her eyes. He is the most astoundingly ugly man she has ever seen, almost a caricature of the buck-toothed, short-sighted Japanese soldier portrayed in the British newspapers. He does not return the bow and looks at her with all the haughtiness that he can muster in the presence of a good-looking but vaguely disgusting Eurasian woman. There is a guidebook for attitudes by mystified Japanese to subjugated populations. The natives were riddled with disease and defecated in ponds was one common theme. It was clear that whatever Uehara might truly think of the motley crew surrounding him at this moment, Lieutenant Itami considers them pond polluters.

The men chat in the back of the car. Itami has a rather irritating falsetto voice. Anita is silent and Simone feels her eyes droop. It is hot and monotonous. She begins to doze.

When the car draws to a halt, Anita nudges her and she jumps out.

'Thank you, Captain Shah,' Lieutenant Uehara says, then turns to Simone. 'Please pick up the specimens and return in four hours. Enjoy your lunch.'

Lieutenant Itami ignores both the women and strides away.

Anita watches in the rear-view mirror as the Governor's palace recedes. 'How did you get rid of that Muller woman?'

'Mr Guan. For a moment I thought we'd have to take her.'

'Well,' Anita says, 'Greta Muller is one lucky woman. She might have met with a terrible accident.'

'Would you?'

'Why not? Who would care?'

'Tsuji might?'

'Well I gave it some thought. Easily done. A fall perhaps which broke her neck. Still just as well it isn't necessary, eh?'

Anita is serious. Whatever they taught them in the Regiment made them ruthless. Perhaps Anita has always been ruthless. She pulls off the road into an abandoned rubber plantation and takes a map from the compartment of the car. The two women lean over it.

'About twenty minutes from the hunting lodge to the village,' Anita says. 'We don't know what we're going to find. Time will be tight.'

Simone looks at her watch then at Anita, suddenly suffused with doubt. 'Can we do this?'

Anita smiles and folds the map. 'Yes.'

The hunting lodge is an old bungalow on the edge of a rubber plantation. The Malay manager, an elderly, quiet-spoken man greets them. He has arranged the stuffed pygmy shrew and several other small creatures on top of a rattan trunk. These animals are dwarfed by a bristle-mouthed boar at least four foot long which lies next to them.

Simone walks around the boar. It has been prepared reasonably well and mounted on what appears to be a solid bamboo frame.

The stitching along the length of its belly, however, is already coming undone and the cavity is filled with newspaper. The whole thing reeks of rush. Simone can't think what Uehara will make of it. It will have to be remounted if it is to be offered to the Emperor. It gives off a musty stench.

Lunch is a modest affair prepared and served by the manager's servant. The manager's lot is not a happy one. His second wife left him and took his two daughters. She didn't want them married off to his old friends, he says, and shakes his head at this feminine dereliction of duty. She's joined a Japanese army women's auxiliary and gone to work in a factory in the town. The Chinese guerrillas killed his brother, a policeman. The manager lives every day, he says, in fear. On the one hand, the Japanese demand fanatical loyalty and obedience. On the other, the Chinese guerrillas of the Malayan Peoples' Anti-Japanese Army call him a collaborator. He is caught, he tells them, like all the Malays, like a mouse deer between two elephants.

Afternoon prayer time has arrived and the manager disappears. Prayer time is a trial for the Muslims for whom solar and lunar precision is so central to ritual. Since the Japanese had decreed that time in the East Asian Co-Prosperity Sphere was always to be Tokyo time, it means that the natural movement of the spheres has no significance. It made everyone crazy for a while. But the Muslims had got their heads around it all. Prayers continued to be sun-driven even if they had to be quietly observed.

'Load the car,' Anita says, 'everything on the back seat for the moment. I'll be back in a minute.'

'What?' Where are you going?'

'Change of clothes. I'm a target in this uniform.'

Anita disappears. So damn bossy, Simone thinks, and with a sigh of exasperation places the smaller specimens in the rattan trunk and begins to load the car to the faint chant of voices raised to Allah. Cicadas thrum in the bushes and somewhere Simone can hear the sweet whistling song of the bulbul. The rubber plantation has been utterly abandoned and the jungle has returned with a vengeance, filling the neatly hoed and organized man-made rows, down which the conquering Japanese soldiers bicycled to victory, with exuberant wildness.

With the help of a young boy, they manage to get the boar on the back seat, stuck with its legs in heraldic rampant attitude.

'Poor thing,' she murmurs.

'It's all pretty disgusting,' Anita says, wrinkling her nose. Simone turns. Anita has changed into a plain cotton sari.

She throws a bag onto the back seat next to the boar and produces a rifle from somewhere. She removes all the INA and Japanese flags from the car, slides the rifle next to her leg and takes a handgun from the glove compartment.

'Take this. Let's go. We have two hours.'

* * *

Fatima

Zahra can think of nothing else to do but advance towards the cinema and Samad's sister, Fatima. What can she tell her? Why is she here when she should be at the Gardens busily translating some botanical oeuvre? Her eyes go everywhere at once.

Fatima, however, does not advance. She stares at Zahra, eyes wide, as stunned as a trembling uncomprehending mouse-deer in the headlights. Behind her a man appears. He puts his hand to her arm. Fatima squeals as if burned. Zahra comes to a halt. The man is young and handsome. Possibly Malay but also possibly Eurasian. Fatima swirls round and half trips down the street. The man, dumbfounded, watches. Zahra turns and walks in the opposite direction.

JOHOR

The Chinese Temple

The road to the village is narrow and slow, oppressively overshadowed by the hot, close press of the jungle. This is communist guerrilla territory. Simone can sense that Anita is nervous and to take her mind off her own terrors as she stares at the old Japanese-made Nambu 94 pistol. It does not reassure. This is a gun so unreliable that Lieutenant Uehara calls it the suicide pistol. Could she kill someone? Perhaps. But not with a gun that was just as likely to kill her.

Anita pulls the car off the track, which is now impassable except on foot.

'Come on. If Japs stop us I have the permission slip. We're visiting my cousin.'

Simone nods and hands Anita the gun. 'This is a piece of junk. Goes off willy-nilly, you know.'

'Oh I know. It's for show. Japs hate the thing. That's why they gave it to us. Anyway it doesn't matter, they don't give us any bullets. Useful to wave about in case of need.'

Seemingly unalarmed, Anita takes the gun and puts it inside her sari. Underneath the sari, Simone sees, she has an army belt. She hands Simone a knife. 'Got to have a weapon. Put it in your bag.' Anita hands a compass and the map to Simone. 'I will follow and watch for trouble. We are in the vicinity of the coordinates. You were always the best at this.'

Simone smiles. Yes she was. She takes their bearings and writes them on the edge of Anita's map. She can see the village on the map which she puts on the ground, orients the compass to magnetic north and adjusts the map.

'All right. It's oriented. This way.'

The village is on the sluggish waters of the Straits. At their approach a thin dog barks then scampers away. Chickens cluck from the darkness under kampong houses. The odour of a cesspit floats on the breeze. The waterfront appears with small fishing boats stuck in the tidal slurry. Houses perch on stilts. An old woman, blind and emaciated, sits before one of them.

Just beyond the kampong, they take up position in a stand of bamboo. Dark clouds are gathering. Simone consults the compass and reads the coordinates. 'Need to head north-east. It's not far.' They follow a footpath through the forest.

'Should be near here. Can you see anything?'

Anita goes forward. 'Are we exactly on the coordinates?'

'No. A little off. Go forward.'

As they emerge from the trees into a clearing, they see before them an old Chinese temple. A violent squall springs up, tossing the trees, and the rain begins, heavy and drenching.

'Damn,' Anita says. 'Stay here. I'm going to take a look.'

'Not bloody likely,' Simone says. 'I'm coming with you.'

'All right. Stay close.'

Rifle in hand Anita enters the temple. As far as she can see it is deserted. She signals to Simone and they take shelter under the eaves of the surrounding walls. Anita wipes the rifle then places it against the wall. She unwraps her sari. 'Damn thing,' she mutters. She begins to squeeze out the water.

Simone approaches the altar. Buddha and the Gods are gathered on the tattered but elaborate gold and red altar cloth. Incense has recently been burned. Perfumed smoke hovers.

She hears a loud grunt and turns. A Japanese soldier is standing under the protection of the temple gate, staring at her through the sheeting rain.

SYONAN

The Secret

What power resides in a dangerous secret. Fatima has a boyfriend. Neither she nor Zahra speak of the meeting. They both know that, perhaps, Zahra could explain being on Orchard Road but Fatima could never explain being alone, unchaperoned, in a dark cinema with a young man. Samad would certainly kill her.

That evening, when Zahra goes out, a silent pact is made. The guard snores. Noor is asleep. Fatima goes one way and Zahra goes the other.

JOHOR

Ringing the Temple Bell

The soldier doesn't move. Simone doesn't move. Off to the left she sees Anita still fussing with the sari. From there, by the wall, Anita can't see the soldier at the gate. If she moves just two steps the soldier will see her too.

'Konnichi-wa,' Simone calls loudly and drops into a bow.

Anita's head turns sharply to Simone.

'Konnichi-wa,' Simone calls again louder this time, rising from the bow. 'Heishi-san. O-tenki hidoi desu-ne? Honourable soldier, the weather's terrible isn't it?

Anita shrinks back against the wall and takes up her rifle.

The soldier takes out the pistol at his waist. Simone turns and drops to her knees before the altar. She knows that she is hidden from his view by the large metal censer in the middle of the courtyard. She clangs the bell to waken the Gods and tell the soldier she is there. Not dangerous. Praying. She begins to chant. Nam-myo-ho-renge-kyo. Nam-myo-ho-renge-kyo. The chant of the Lotus Sutra. Merely by saying it one is granted entry into the Mystical Law of which human lives are the expression. She can't remember who told her that or when. She raises her eyes to the serene face of the Buddha and chants feverishly.

The soldier appears reluctant to step into the rain. Simone chants louder. She hears voices. From beyond the altar. There are people back there. Does she dare get up? She rings the bell again. A face appears above the altar. It has no nose. Nor ears. The fingers which lie on the altar cloth are stubs. A leper.

She turns her head to look at Anita, and the soldier. Neither has moved. The rain still falls. Lighter now. Soon it will stop.

The soldier steps out into the courtyard. Simone crawls backwards under the altar cloth keeping her eyes on his legs. One more step and Anita will be able to see him. Shoot him. But what if there are others? Dozens of others. Use your knife, Anita, she says silently and then realizes that she herself has it. She takes it in her hand, trembling, stomach churning, sweat steaming off her body. If he comes round the censer, she will rush him and take her chances. To her surprise, the soldier's pistol drops with a clang on the flagstones. His body follows with a low thud. A flowery sarong takes its place.

Kay wipes her knife on the soldier's jacket. 'Ladies,' she says, 'always be prepared.'

* * *

The Lepers

The old leper shuffles around the altar and stares at the body of the Japanese soldier. He has no toes and leans on a stick. He takes the stick and cracks it down on the soldier's head before losing balance and rocking sideways.

Simone stops hugging Kay and catches him. Anita is looking at the scars on Kay's face.

'Stop staring, White,' Kay says. 'Let's get this Jap hidden. I checked the perimeter. He was alone. No idea what the hell he was doing alone. Maybe he was coming here to pray.' She laughs. 'Red, you wait with this old boy behind the altar while we dispose of the body.'

'Yes, Java,' they say in unison. Grins. Joy.

Three lepers, all women, huddle in a corner, their eyes filled with fear. They are middle-aged, perilously thin, afflicted. The old man sits with them. Simone drops to the floor, back to the wall. Cicadas rustle like paper. She watches them on the branch outside lined up like soldiers, all pissing. She has never understood why the cicadas piss so much. She gazes at the leper women gathered under a painting of the Buddha and his bodhisattvas and recalls a passage in some book she'd read about how the cicada was an emblem of the soul's ascension that Buddhism taught as a parable.

Man sheds his body only as the cicada sheds its skin. But each reincarnation obscures the memory of the previous one. We remember our former existence no more than the cicada remembers the shell from which it has emerged. The cast-off skin represents the hollow show of human greatness. These leper women believe it and what a message of hope it is. One day they will shuffle off this deformed body and be reborn into a better life. One day Malaya will emerge from this darkness into light. It is a message of cheer and she smiles, her soul soothed. All doubt about being here and what they are doing evaporates and she rises with renewed vigour as Kay enters.

'Right. It's done,' Kay says. 'They won't find him.' She turns to the huddle of women. 'A baby.' The women separate revealing a basket.

Simone, Kay and Anita look inside. The baby is perhaps four months old, thin, but not apparently sickly. She looks at the three women with dark almond eyes.

'Gray's child,' Kay says. 'Zejian.' The words catch in her throat and she coughs. 'Do you have milk?' she asks.

The old leper points to the basket. Under a cloth are two tins of Carnation milk and a bottle. Kay is guessing that this is all they have. In a day or two the baby would be dehydrated and very soon dead.

'Thank you,' Kay says and touches the face of each. They have tears in their eyes. Each one touches the basket fearing to touch the child.

From her cloth bag Kay takes a wad of banana notes. 'Give them to the nuns. Use them carefully.' She picks up the basket. 'When the war is over, I will come back.' She looks at Simone and Anita. 'Which way is your car?'

* * *

Zejian

The rain stops. It's a respite but the black clouds signal a new storm. At the car, Simone dilutes the milk with water, fills the bottle and begins to feed the baby. Anita attaches the flags. Kay keeps watch, the Lee Enfield tucked under her arm. When the flags are done Anita retrieves her uniform and goes into the forest to change.

Around them the jungle steams. The baby finishes feeding and falls asleep. Simone puts her into the basket.

'Teresa,' Simone says, 'she's dead, isn't she?'

'Yes. We found her and Harold. He's dead too. She was, well, she was too wounded to live. We had morphine. She died peacefully in my arms.' Kay keeps her voice steady and factual.

Simone feels the wellspring of tears. She remembers Teresa and herself, so young and vulnerable, sitting next to each on the school bench. They were the same. Shy. Thin. Crushed. Alone. They found each other. Now she is dead but her child lives. So she lives. She knows Kay thinks this too. This child must live. She pulls her emotions under control. There is no place for tears.

'What happened here,' Simone says, touching Kay's cheek. The scars are deep welts.

'Not just here,' Kay says. 'Broken fingers, busted ribs. I was
betrayed. Captured.'

'Can you tell me?' Simone says.

'Gonna write it down?'

'Yes. Probably.'

Kay shrugs. 'I fell in with a group of the Dalforce communists,
a stay-behind cell of the Town Committee. But they were raided
and four of us were the only ones to get out. We got to the
mainland and found a place to lie low. I worked as a waitress in a
small town. My wages helped the unit.'

She doesn't mention one of the men. Big, brash, bold, an
MCP leader. He spoke of equality between men and women. She
was La Passionara, he said, and his words and his touch lit the
fuse. She saw his arrogance but longed for the smell of him. She
hated this weakness but it did not pass. Where he was she had to
be. She carried messages for them. Made money for them. All
for one and one for all, he laughed, like the French Musketeers.
Except that before long she was the one for all. And still she did
not leave. Shame is the terrible iron in her soul.

'I went back to Singapore in '43. Carrying information to Lai
Tek, the head of the MCP. When I got back to the mainland, I
was arrested. Fellow called Tsuji did this to me.'

Simone turns sharply to Kay. 'Tsuji? A man named Tsuji came
to speak to me. Is it the same one, do you think?'

Kay knows Lai Tek gave her up to Tsuji. She's sure of it. No
one else knew she was there. She was followed back to Johor to
lead them to the others. Because Lai Tek wanted to eliminate any
of the old guard who might threaten his dominance of the MCP.
But the Japs had jumped the gun. Arrested her too soon. So she had
to be made to talk. And talk she had. In the agony of torture she
could not find loyalty enough when the man she loved had treated
her like property and used her as his companions' plaything. Now,
years later, she knows that it was not fear but furious shame that

had made her give them up. That betrayal is yet another shame. All shameful choices that she tries to wash away in the sufferings and righteousness of this cause. The rescue of Gray's child. The fight to the death for the freedom of Malaya. 'Vicious and sententious,' she says. 'Always drivelling on about fate and shadows. The future of a man is in the darkness of the water. That sort of thing.'

'Yes. Fate and shadows follow you everywhere.'

'Yes, he's the one. If he ever threatens you again look him in the eye and tell him anything he wants to hear. Make it up. Doesn't matter. I learned that about them. Implicate the locals that they trust. They don't really trust them anyway. They think everyone is just waiting to betray them. It's easy.'

Simone glances at Kay. 'How did you get away?'

'A Sikh soldier, two Chinese volunteers. They raided the jail to rescue an Indian doctor who was in there for treating and feeding them. A half-dead woman like me. They rescued me too. We all live in the hills. They are my life now.'

'And what about us?'

Kay meets Simone's eyes. 'You are my life forever.'

Anita appears. 'I must go,' Kay says, 'take care of the child.' Kay hands Simone her cloth bag. 'Money,' she says. 'We'll meet again.' She draws smartly to attention and gives the three-fingered Guide salute. Anita and Simone respond. It feels wonderful and they all acknowledge it with a smile. Then with a wave, Kay disappears.

The rain begins again, falling harder. It blots out all sound but itself, the jungle fades and a gloom descends on the day. The air inside the car is fetid and damp. Anita cracks open a window. Simone examines the baby. She has soiled herself. Simone rips an edge of Anita's sari and, wetting it out of the window, washes down the baby, then fashions a nappy from a dry strip.

'Teresa's child. I don't know anything about her life really,' Anita says. 'I never asked I suppose.'

'She never would have told you even if you'd asked.'

Anita frowns. 'Why?'

'She was ashamed.'

'Of what?'

'Poverty. Enslavement. The fact her parents sold her. She was a *mui tsai*.'

Anita knows what the word means. Little girls sold into domestic servitude by their desperate and starving parents in China.

'Daughters are useless mouths.' Simone thinks that, in her own way, she too had been a useless mouth, a creature as despised as the slave girls of Guangdong, a half-blood Eurasian child, thrown into the unwelcoming care of her father's sister by the death of her parents. The Swiss didn't sell unwanted children although they might have liked to. Instead they did the next best thing. They put her into the missionary school, which took in waifs and strays to be turned into good Christian children and tried to forget all about her. Their last act before departing Singapore was to get her a Swiss passport. She'd had no idea how grateful she would be for that. It had kept her out of internment.

'She never had any luck,' Anita says. 'Unluckiest girl I ever met.'

'No, that's not right. In a way she was a very lucky girl. She was allowed to live. She told me once that at least two of her younger sisters were drowned as soon as they were born. She saw it happen. Two babies taken to the river, tied to a stone.'

'It happens, doesn't it? To girls? Everywhere.' Anita sighs. 'If this damn war does anything, it has to change that. We have to make it change.' The rain has ceased pounding on the car and the mist is clearing.

Teresa had been saved by the disgust of European women who forced the Mui Tsai Ordinance of 1932, and placed in the care of the British government. Eventually, like Simone, she turned up in the missionary school and found the protective arms of compassionate teachers. And Jean McKenna.

The jungle steams and drips. It's time to go. The baby wakes and cries.

'How are we going to do this?' Anita asks. Suddenly the problem of concealing the baby has hit them.

'We have to put her in the basket, along with the stuffed animals. Only way. We can strap it to the top of the vehicle and cover it with your sari. Stick the boar next to it. And hope to hell she doesn't cry.'

'I have chlorodyne.'

'Oh. Good. How much do we give a baby?'

Anita fetches the bottle from her first aid kit. 'Not suitable for children under six.'

'Bugger.'

'Never mind. My mother gave it to us and we're all right.'

Anita peers at the back of the bottle. 'For sleep and fever relief. Children 6 to 8 dilute 10 drops in a tumbler of water. What about we try one drop diluted in water.'

'What choice do we have? She has to sleep through this whole journey. If they find her we're sunk and so is she.'

Simone gets into the back seat next to the boar and the baby's basket. She wets a strip of cloth from Anita's sari, adds a drop of chlorodyne, squeezes to dissolve it then rubs Zejian's gums. The baby sucks on the cloth and gives a gummy smile. Anita takes a deep breath and engages the gears.

SYONAN

The Pavilion Cinema

Outside the Guide meetings, the seven of them met most often to go to the cinema, especially the air-conditioned Cathay. They bought fan magazines and ogled the stars, the clothes, the hairstyles. Each had her favourite actress. Zahra's was Merle Oberon. Simone's was Katherine Hepburn. Kay's hadn't been a woman at all. It was Johnny Weissmuller in *Tarzan*. They'd all laughed but it made sense. Molly loved Katherine Grayson. Jenny, oddly, had favoured Marlene Dietrich. She'd plucked her eyebrows out and nearly given her father a heart attack. Teresa's was Anna May Wong in *Shanghai Express*. She couldn't recall Anita's favourite. Perhaps she didn't have one.

The Japs had captured huge stocks of British and American films. They continued to show them until the end of 1943. The last film Zahra had seen was with Noor and their father. A musical with Carmen Miranda called *That Night in Rio*. After that, foreign movies ceased to be shown. The cinema lost its appeal.

What on earth had Fatima been watching with her paramour? Zahra eyes the posters in the lobby. Something called *Neppu* was the feature—Hot Wind. *An engineer working in an iron foundry devotes himself to raising the spirits of the workers and increasing steel production.* Well, they certainly didn't come to see that. Or the accompanying documentary on Japanese military successes in Burma.

She smiles. If Fatima leaves her alone, her secret liaison is tickety-boo.

She is here ostensibly for a Radio Syonan interview about the new offerings of the Japanese film studio being made in Singapore. Yoshida had been keen and arranged everything. She is shown to the upstairs office. Here she is inspected by a sharp-eyed, elaborately coiffed Chinese woman in a cheongsam and too much make-up and asked to sit on one of the hard Chinese chairs. The air-conditioning is deliciously cool.

She glances at the posters on the walls. *The Fall of Singapore. Mud and Soldiers. Fire on that Flag! The Man from Chungking. China Nights.*

She'd asked colleagues in the office about the Shaws. Run Je, Run De, Run Run, and Run Me Shaw had been the richest and most famous men in Asia. Their cinemas, their movie studios were famous. Their lavish amusement parks were famous. The Shaw Brothers ran the world of Asian entertainment from Shanghai to the furthest towns of the Dutch East Indies. The Japanese knew it. After their capture, they were invited to continue to run their now requisitioned businesses as salaried officials of the Japanese state film distribution company and the Department of National Propaganda.

Naturally they'd agreed. Advertisements about the Great World and the offerings of various cinemas appeared under their banner in the newspaper.

In Singapore, Run Run Shaw had established a Malay language film-making company at Jalan Ampas. Molly's handsome brother Charlie had been one of it minor stars. She sits. The time extends. She starts to have regrets. This man must be watched by the Japanese. The Chinese receptionist looks like a spy.

These wobbly thoughts are interrupted by the door opening. A young Chinese man departs and Mr Run Run Shaw appears. He is thin and looks tired.

'Sorry,' she says, rising, 'to bother you, sir.'

'Not at all. Come in. Would you like some Chinese tea?'

'No thank you.'

The office is not large and contains two desks back to back which cramp it even more. The windows look down on the roof of the long cinema behind.

'How can I help you?'

'Perhaps you can tell me what kinds of films we may expect to see over the next month. The public is keen on the cinema and gets little information about what to look forward to.'

Run Run Shaw sits back in his chair and gazes at Zahra, obviously appraising her. A silence falls. Zahra waits.

'Well, I think I can safely say that you will possibly see a wholesome light comedy. You are unlikely to see a film about the petty bourgeoisie, films that portray individual happiness, anything about luxury or the life of the wealthy, anything with foreign words, frivolous behaviour or women smoking and drinking.'

She stares at him. Then laughs.

'Is that the sort of thing?' He smiles.

'No. I don't think that Yoshida-san would like it.'

'No. Are you really here to talk about Japanese propaganda films? No one has asked me this for the entire duration of the war.'

'Well I do need to have something for the entertainment segment.'

'Certainly, I will have my secretary send you a review of upcoming offerings. Likely to be slight given the present situation. I'm not certain that the Japanese are still producing films somewhere else. We stopped long ago. No film stocks and the English POWs got too thin to be actors any more. They only want plump POWs.'

'I see. Thank you. Also I would like to know if you remember a man called Charles Salgado. I think he worked for you at Jalan Ampas.'

JOHOR

The Governor's Mansion

Anita taps her foot against the side of the car. 'Come on you idiots. Hurry up,' she says under her breath. Simone paces on the edge of the garden.

A black car sweeps into the drive. Simone with alarm recognizes the car and puts her hand on Anita's arm.

'Tsuji,' she whispers.

He steps from the car and walks towards the two women.

'Good afternoon, Miss Martel,' he says sweeping his eyes over the car and its baggage, staring for a moment at the boar.

'Captain, how nice to see you again. May I introduce Captain Shah.'

Anita salutes sharply. Tsuji doesn't bother. His eyes remain on the boar and the basket. To Simone's relief Uehara and Itami take that moment to appear accompanied by the Governor. As the Governor and his son make their farewells Uehara approaches. He frowns at Tsuji. 'Captain, what is it that brings you here?'

Before Tsuji can answer Uehara's gaze rises to the boar's head hanging out from the edge of the car, legs skyward. 'What on earth is this?'

'A gift from the Governor,' Simone says. 'He thought His Majesty, the Emperor, would like it.'

'A common pig?' Uehara glances at Itami and his father. Simone knows he dare not say anything nor remove the pig from the car. It would insult the Governor. He's stuck with the pig.

The Governor, having noticed Tsuji, approaches. From a different direction another kempei, a colonel, heads towards the group. Anita and Simone wordlessly withdraw.

A strange little altercation takes place. In rapid Japanese the two kempei officers face off. Clearly this man is annoyed that Tsuji is here on his turf. Voices are raised. Uehara approaches Simone. 'Blimey, for heaven's sake. These ridiculous soldiers. Do you have the pygmy shrew, Simone?'

'All in order, Uehara-san,' Simone says, pointing to the basket. 'I should like to see.'

'It would mean unlashing the basket. 'We should be moving, sir. It's not safe to be travelling after dark.'

'That's right, Captain' Anita says, 'the guerrillas operate after dark.'

'Oh. I see. Oh, horrid.'

The spat resolves with bows. Tsuji approaches the Anita's car. Simone glances at Anita. Outwardly she looks calm.

'Lieutenant,' Tsuji addresses Uehara. 'I shall accompany you back to the mainland. But first I must search these belongings.'

The Governor comes to Uehara's side. He looks up at the boar and frowns. Another sharp conversation takes place. Tsuji has no choice but to wait impatiently on one side.

Uehara turns to Simone. 'The Governor objects to the boar being on the roof and displayed in such an undignified manner. He demands it be taken inside the car.'

'Oh. I see. But there is no room inside the car.' Her pulse is racing.

The Governor and the kempei colonel issue a series of orders. Tsuji looks sour. Uehara smiles.

'The Governor has asked Captain Tsuji to take Lieutenant Itami and me back to Syonan. He has ordered the boar to be put inside your car.'

The Governor issues the order to two Malay men who rush forward and unlash the boar and with some struggle re-arrange it on the back seat.

'I would like to see inside the basket, Lieutenant,' Tsuji says, turning to Uehara.

'What for?'

'Security.'

'Security? It's got stuffed creatures inside.'

'Nevertheless.'

The basket is untied and put on the ground. Uehara opens it. He removes the pygmy shrew and examines it. Tsuji looks at the other creatures and puts his hand inside, touching the bottom of the basket. He straightens and nods, annoyance etched on his face.

The basket is strapped back onto the car, this time with ropes. The Governor farewells his son. The two Japanese get in Tsuji's car and the convoy sets off with Tsuji leading the way.

Simone crawls onto the back seat and pulls apart the loose stitching on the boar's belly. The baby is sleeping inside, now face down from all the handling. She turns her face up, sprinkles her with water and fans her.

Only once during the drive does the baby wake. Simone feeds her and gives her a drop more chlorodyne. They fly through the checkpoints. The kempei car and its passengers ensure a smooth passage. The boar, covered in Anita's sari, attracts little attention.

Itami is dropped back at the naval base. Once back in the Gardens, Tsuji disappears and Uehara goes straight into his house. Mr Guan greets them and two of the gardeners remove the basket from the car and take it inside.

Uehara pokes his head from the window of his quarters above them.

'Bring me the pygmy shrew,' he says. 'And get rid of that damn pig.'

'We'll take the boar to the Herbarium, Mr Guan,' Simone says, 'then Captain Shah can get off.' Exhausted, she is anxious to end this expedition. But Mr Guan opens the back door of the car.

'Let me have a look at this thing.'

Before Simone or Anita can say a word, Mr Guan removes the sari. Anita moves forward placing herself next to him, her hand on her gun. Simone shakes her head. Mr Guan looks down at the baby then up at Anita. He recognizes her intent and steps away and shuts the door.

'Yes,' he says. 'Get the pig to the Herbarium.' He stares at Anita. 'It will be safe there.' He goes inside the house.

'Will he say anything?'

Simone gives a short nervous laugh. 'No.'

At the Herbarium, finally, Simone changes and feeds the baby and they settle her into a drawer lined with old military-issue blankets behind the bottles of soda water in the cool of the underground refrigeration room.

'I have to go now,' Anita says and the women hug.

Simone watches Anita pull into the growing darkness and goes back to the baby. She will stay here tonight and keep vigil. Tomorrow she must settle this business with Mr Guan and find Molly and Jenny.

The boar stands, finally on its feet, at the entrance to the Herbarium. She is about to latch the Herbarium doors when, from the darkness, the two Guan girls appear like ghouls. They stare at her silently. How long have they been there? What have they seen? She had thought them incurious because of their blankness of expression but that, she sees, is not true. They are nosy and watching. Perhaps they are taught to tell on adults who stray off the path of Japanese righteousness, even their parents.

And they have no boundaries. They never knock. When she's in her room, she always puts the latch across the door to prevent them wandering in anytime they like. She has to get rid of them and see they stay away, at least for a few days.

With a swift movement she shoves the boar forward and towards them. They squeal and the youngest darts away into the darkness. But the elder girl, after a momentary recoil, stands her ground. The younger child, emboldened by her sister, returns.

'Sore nani?' the older one says and points to the boar. The girls always speak to Simone in Japanese.

'Buta,' she says. 'Buta no hara, mitai?' She thrusts her hand inside the boar up to her elbow.

Both girls squeal and disappear into the darkness. Apparently they don't want to see pig's guts.

She locks the doors but knows they will return. The baby can't stay here. And she would like a doctor. She must find Jenny.

* * *

Li Song

Yuan brings tea and two messages. The first is that Anita and Simone arrived safely back in Syonan. The second is from Li Song, head of the 4th Regiment of the MPAJA. He asks the chief of Java Force to meet him and one of the British officers. The time has come, he says, to coordinate strategy for the liberation of Malaya.

Ravi agrees. But Kay has doubts. She doesn't trust the commies. They are blind to the treachery within their ranks.

'Yuan,' she calls. 'Tell Li Song that Java will meet only the British officer at a place of our choosing.'

SYONAN

The British Exhibit

The American exhibit is all about the now: the war in the Pacific, B-29s, the bombing of the homeland, the Japanese response, sacrifice, and invincibility.

The British exhibit, by contrast, is about the past. A reminder of why the Japanese are here and how it came about. It must be factual. The Marquis has been adamant on this point. No vulgar triumphalism is necessary. The facts themselves glorify the Japanese and condemn the British. There is no question that this exhibit will draw in the most visitors. Who would not want to see what in hell went wrong?

A film of the Fall of Singapore rapidly put together from Japanese military news cameras had appeared in the cinemas six months after the event. It is here again. She has seen it a dozen times. It doesn't pall. It offers no explanation. It is spliced together from Japanese newsreel images, a stark exposition of events as they unfolded. It is not sophisticated, predominantly silent, and all the more powerful for that. This, it says, is what happened as it happened.

The deceptive news briefings of the British Ministry of Information are confirmed. The endless retreats in the face of the Japanese assault are shown for what they were, a rout. In the general population there was a belief in British invincibility, which penetrated all but the press. Almost until the actual moment of surrender everyone had believed. It seemed, in hindsight, ridiculous.

The exhibit begins with Japanese propaganda posters, the call to arms for Asians to join together to expel the imperialist oppressors. No photos of the bombing of the city are shown. Too many Asians died. Blown-up aerial photos of the sinking of the *Repulse* and the *Prince of Wales*. The ships flounder. Streams of sailors jump into the burning oily water like a scene from Dante's purgatory.

The evacuation of Penang by the panicked Europeans was a propaganda coup for the Japanese, who detailed the manner in which the Asian subjects of the British Empire were left to deal with the aftermath alone. The Union Jack was forgotten in the rout and remained floating over Fort Cornwallis; so the bombing of the town continued until a Tamil newspaper editor, Mr Savaranamuttu, took it down and ran up the white flag of surrender.

A map of the final battle for Singapore. The encirclement of the town.

Then, in pride of place in the middle of the wall, Percival carries the white flag and the lowered Union Jack, all captured by the Japanese newsreel cameras and photographers for eager consumption by the anxious and waiting Japanese public back home.

The remainder of the exhibit is mostly the news of the surrender as reported in the British newspapers via Japanese correspondents in Lisbon. *Singapore Lost! The greatest disaster in military history! The London Illustrated News* gives a thorough account of the battles with diagrams, maps, and drawings.

Other newspapers carry eyewitness accounts of the refugees fleeing the island. The story of the Fall and the reaction of the outside world after the island had been turned into a prison. Simone devours this part, unknowable to them all as the curtain fell.

Stories of gallant British officers and Australian soldiers making daring yacht escapes. Stories of brave European refugees fighting all the odds to survive the strafing and bombing of their ships. Stories of jungle survival and gallant escape by white wives, forced to dress in sarongs with blackened faces. Stories about those lost and captured by the Japanese.

Nothing about the millions of others. The millions like her. The natives. Except one passage.

Most of the evacuees deplored the inadequate preparations made in Malaya and Singapore to stem the Japanese onrush. They said the natives panicked in air raids and were not to be trusted.

Not to be trusted, the thousands of civilian air raid wardens and MAS women volunteers. Not to be trusted, the local doctors and nurses toiling though the raids without medicines, bandages or even water. Not to be trusted, the drivers ferrying their terrified masters to the harbour through shells and bombs, battling the gangs of drunken, panicked Allied soldiers throwing down their arms, ripping off their uniforms, pushing women and children off the gangplanks of departing ships in their desperation to get away from the endlessly rolling Japanese juggernaut.

And no trust at all for the Chinese amahs hugging the white children to their shoulders and breasts as they were jostled and shoved through the crowds, crying as the children they'd raised held out their arms and howled at the parting from their nannies, the women they loved.

Not to be trusted, the Eurasian and Chinese men in the Volunteers, the Malay Regiment, decimated in battle, the twenty-five thousand Indians who would not swear allegiance to Japan and walked instead into imprisonment.

Simone turns away, barely glancing at the final images. British and Australian soldiers surrendering their arms and walking into captivity. They are somehow an afterthought.

And so it ends. A litany of British blunders and lies, a war not lost so much as never winnable. Ancient planes, a lack of ships, arrogance towards the enemy, and no plan at all. Men with their heads in the glory of a Victorian view of their Empire simply unable to see what lay before their eyes and ignoring what was amply explained to them. In the end, none of that really mattered. Because Churchill had one aim only: the preservation of England. To that end, no death or sacrifice in the colonies was too great, even their loss. What a pity he hadn't had the honesty to just say it.

The Marquis is right. There is no need for triumphalism. The stark and miserable facts are enough.

JOHOR

Richie

Kay watches as Ravi leads the blindfolded Englishman into the camp. Ravi had gone down to meet one of Li Song's soldiers and this man. The soldier will wait in the jungle overnight. The Englishman will stay in their camp. The climb up has been hard. They both move slowly.

'Take off the blindfold,' Ravi says and steps behind Kay. The Englishman blinks in the light then stares at her, then at Ravi and back to her. She enjoys the expression on his face. Why would he have expected a woman?

'I am Java,' she says.

'Richie,' he says quickly, despite his evident astonishment, and holds out his hand. 'How do you do?' They might be at a garden party. Except she would never have been invited. She shakes his hand.

'Is this necessary?' he says waving the blindfold. That drawl. The lazy superior upper-class English drawl. She'd forgotten how supercilious they sound. Even in defeat. He expects to be in charge of this meeting.

She sits on one of the logs. 'Please,' she says indicating the place next to her. Richie sits. He looks at her scarred cheek then away. 'The first thing to know is that you must not reveal who I am, or that I am a woman. For Li Song, the chief of Java Force is a man. Chinese. The second is to know that the head of the MCP, Lai Tek, is a double agent.'

'A double agent? Really? You know this.'

'Suspect. That is enough to take precautions.'

'Shall I share your concerns with Li Song?'

'Yes. He won't believe it. The commies are all blind.'

'Good men though.'

'Maybe. We all fight for the same thing for the present. But he is being betrayed. Reveal as little as possible about this meeting.'

'Everyone is curious about you and your band up here. You are a bit famous. News of the daring raid to save Lao Wu has reached our ears. They'd die of shock if they knew Java was a woman.'

She does not look at him. 'Don't mistake me for your idea of a woman. That is an image created in the male mind through a thousand years of oppressive wishful thinking. I am not that. I will kill you without hesitation if you betray me or mine. I have endured everything. I have no compassion and no loyalty to you or them. If you don't understand that you can go down right now.'

'I understand,' he says. 'Agreed.'

Ravi brings a plate of food. Bully beef from the drops, jungle greens, biscuits.

'Zipper,' Richie says. 'Operation Zipper. The recapture of Malaya. Will start at Port Swettenham or Port Dickson.'

He chews. Java waits. She has told him nothing of her past. He has met none of the other guerrillas. All he knows is that there are about ten. Ravi brings him a glass of whisky and disappears into the darkness.

'Cheers,' he says.

'When?'

'Undecided. But the Japanese believe it will be 650 miles north on the Kra Isthmus.'

'Why?'

'We have three Malay agents on the inside.'

'Explain. Who are they?'

He smiles. 'Do you want me to name names?'

'Why not? It will never leave this place.'

'I will tell you one name. Ismail. Malayan chap. Dehradun graduate. Joined the Indian Army after the fall of Malaya. Conscripted to Force 136. Parachuted into Terengganu in '44. Betrayed. Captured. Tortured. Agreed to become a double agent together with the other two. Managed to get this information to us. Effectively those men are triple agents.'

It has rolled easily off his tongue. Possibly true.

'What is it you want of me?'

'Join forces with Li Song and Force 136 when the invasion starts. Safety in numbers.'

'Not if the Japs know all about it through Lai Tek.'

'You're obsessed with him.'

'Certainly am. You should be too. He wasn't massacred with all the other commie leaders at the Batu Caves. Who told the Japs about that meeting? How did they know? He comes and goes as he pleases on the roads of southern Johor. How?'

'I don't know about this massacre. All right. Look. I'll tell you directly when the time comes. Me. Not Li Song. There won't be any advance warning for any spy to tell anyone. Will that do?'

'Yes. Provisionally. We'll see at the time. Communicate only with Yuan, our radio operator. Who do you have in Singapore?'

He gazes at Java. 'Why?'

'Never mind why. Tell me and I'll trust you.'

He sighs and stares into the whisky. 'You know I proposed a guerrilla force of Indians, Chinese and Malays to Shenton Thomas in August of '41. He refused, the ass. Defeatist he called it. Extravagant and defeatist. If we'd had a crack force of trained guerrillas it would have made the difference. Men the Japanese couldn't detect. Not white men in uniforms untrained for jungle fighting. Local men, light, able to move quickly. Indistinguishable from the local population. Blowing up their camps. Harassing. Forcing them to look backwards as well as forwards. That force would have delayed the Jap invasion long enough for British reinforcements to arrive in Singapore. Singapore might not have fallen.'

'When they decided to do that, it was all too late,' Kay says.

Richie looks up. 'So you know.'

She shrugs. Everyone with sense knew.

'Even so, even with minimal training, they all went willingly. We had over three hundred agents scattered all over Malaya. All of us got stuck at the surrender. One of them was a man named Ah Gun. Dalforce commando trainee. I went to ground. He went with me.'

Richie finishes his whisky. 'Good stuff.'

'Yes. What about this Ah Gun?'

'Utterly loyal. Utterly trustworthy. Slight, wiry chap. A Chinese circus man. Ran an all-female acrobatic troupe out at Telok Kurau. I'd seen them before the war, would you believe?'

Richie takes a cigarette and offers one to Kay. She refuses. He has turned on a certain quiet-spoken charm. She can see he is enjoying this walk down memory lane. She can see he likes being with a woman. Not her particularly. Even the supercilious drawl has faded. A fixed and docile admiring female audience is obviously ideal. Doubtless he thinks it's fine for a woman to think so long as she's thinking of a man. Preferably him. His exploits form the centre of his conversation. He has taken his time to get to her question.

She sighs and gets up. 'If you've nothing but these dull and meandering recollections to tell me, I shall say goodnight.'

Richie stares at her and crushes the cigarette underfoot. She moves away. He rises.

'Stop. Right. Well, after three months, when things settled down, Ah Gun decided to go back to his family in Singapore.

We agreed it would be better than dying of malaria or starvation. He would work to pass information to me from there if possible. I joined forces with the commies to survive. In '43 I met the head of the MCP. He wasn't named Lai Tek. Chap called himself Chen Heng. He was with Chin Peng, his golden boy. Up north. Perak.

'If it was the leader of the MCP then Chen Heng was Lai Tek.'

'All right. Force 136 got men in and linked up with the MCP. The KMT Chinese fighters knew they had to chuck in their differences with the communists. Chen Heng agreed to work with us. The wonder is, if he's a double agent, why didn't he tell the Japs about that meeting? Could have caught us all.'

Kay shakes her head. 'Getting rid of almost all the MCP leadership put him in an unassailable position. There is no one left to challenge him. He's their God. They sing songs about him in the commie camps. Maybe he plans to take over Malaya when this war is done. A communist insurrection. The Mao of Malaya. He'll need his men. And lots of weapons. He cooperates. You supply the weapons. I don't think he'll give them back.'

Richie lets out a bark of laughter. 'Well. How shrewd. Perhaps you should take over Malaya.'

'No thanks.'

'It's always a risk. But we can only play the hand we have right now.'

Kay shrugs. 'Are you in contact with Ah Gun now?'

'Yes.'

'I want you to tell him to call someone at Radio Syonan. Someone I trust. Someone I like. A sister. If anything happens to her I will find you first. I know where Li Song's camp is.'

'Charming.' Richie laughs. 'You won't have to find me. Ah Gun is a brother.'

SYONAN

Great World

It only takes one mistake. One tiny little suspicion can get you thrown into the hands of torturers.

It's Sunday. Simone walks to Uehara's house. Bertie is sprawled, snoring, in a planter's chair in the garden. She knows the others are away. On Sunday, Hatter always goes on a study tour of his mosses. Uehara, she knows from Carlos, is inspecting the Garden's herds of goats and buffaloes with the Veterinary Chief, Dr Koga. She needs to contact Zahra, and Uehara has the nearest working telephone.

Hatter and Bertie occupy the downstairs in Hatter's old black and white house allocated to him as Deputy Director of the Gardens. Uehara occupies the upper rooms: living room, bedroom and bathroom. Simone has absolutely no business being upstairs in his private quarters. She looks around carefully for any servants but the house is quiet. She climbs the narrow staircase. Uehara's desk stands at the far end of the living room looking down onto the back garden. It is tidily arranged. Some specimens of small rodents preserved in glass jars of alcohol occupy one end alongside a scruffy-looking stuffed hornbill. She lifts the phone and dials the number Zahra gave her for Radio Syonan.

The operator, a sleepy-sounding Malay woman, puts her through.

'She is safe. With us.'

'White called me. I'm on air in five minutes. Can't talk. Meet me tomorrow night at Great World.'

'Great World? The amusement park?'

'Yes. I found Woody. Evening, 7 p.m. Main gate. Great World.'

'Great World?' a voice sounds behind her. 'What are you doing up here, Simone-san?'

Simone turns to face Lieutenant Uehara. He's dressed in a loose pyjama, his hair tousled. She feels her throat thicken and pulse race. What the hell is he doing here? She replaces the phone on its cradle.

'Oh, I beg your pardon, I thought you were out.'

'I was out. I had a headache and came back for a nap.'

He puts his head on one side like a curious bird. 'But why are you here?'

'I'm sorry. I took the liberty of using your telephone to call a girlfriend.'

'It is private here.'

Simone feels a tightness in her chest. In a moment, she thinks she might cry. The Lieutenant is an amiable man but she has invaded his quarters with a poor excuse for doing so. And the Japanese take these matters very seriously. Hatter and Bertie come up here at Uehara's invitation sometimes but only at his invitation. The Japanese have dozens of expressions for various degrees of apology none of which ever means sorry. She runs a few through her head but rejects them and waits.

Uehara glances at his desk and takes two steps forward. It is, as if, papers lie there on which depend the future of the Empire when in fact there are merely dead rodents and a stuffed bird. What a fuss. She goes from fear to annoyance in a second. What business does he have being here when he should be inspecting buffaloes? What the hell business does he have being here at all? When will they all just go away? When the hell will this bloody war be over?

'I thought you wouldn't mind. You're such a jolly good chap, Lieutenant. Obviously had I known you were here I shouldn't have come. I'm most terribly sorry.'

Simone looks downcast and clutches her hands, head bowed.

Uehara's expression softens. 'Oh, not to worry. Really. But I might have been naked.' He laughs and bobs his head up and down. 'Don't want to scare the horses, do we?'

Simone looks up and gives him her best little girl smile.

'You're right. Thank you.'

'What did you want to speak to your girlfriend about. Is it awfully private and confidential?' He giggles.

'Oh. No. I called to confirm that we will meet at the Great World tomorrow evening, Lieutenant. The amusement park. Perhaps you would like to go with us. There are a great many Malay singers, young men. And dancers too.'

'Great World, you say. I know it. I've been there.' His eyes gleam, he gives a little movement of his head and licks his lips. 'Yes. I would like to go. It's been a long time. And I know there are lovely boys who do the Malay opera. What's it called?'

'Bangsawan.'

Uehara nods. 'Yes. Righto.'

He turns back into the bedroom and Simone walks as calmly as possible down the stairs. She doesn't wake Bertie. She walks as fast as she can out of the Gardens and then bursts into nervous laughter.

The episode flits in her mind as the car, driven by Uehara, pulls round the sprawling POW camp on marshy riverine ground bordered by River Valley and Zion Road. At the surrender the Great World had been a defunct amusement park with ramshackle buildings recently purchased by Run Run Shaw. It had instantly been turned into an Australian, Indian, and Chinese POW camp. But the Japanese had soon desired a fun palace, so the prisoners were decamped to the surrounding mud. Now the

camp lies around its walls. The bright lights shine down on the
dark sprawling squalour of the straw-covered huts.

Everywhere is contrast: the filth and misery of the POWs,
the Javanese slaves, the labouring and hungry people lie cheek by
jowl with bright lights and music, where the Japanese military and
the local collaborators gamble, eat and ogle the cabaret dancers. It
is all part of the grotesque theatricality of the city. And what an
exquisite torture the Japanese have wrought to let starving men
gaze on plenty.

She glances at Uehara. He does not see any of it. He would
never consider himself a cruel man. Never. But she has seen him
grow tearful at the death of a sparrow, yet remain indifferent to
heads on poles and starving children.

They leave the camp behind and draw up outside the main
gates of Great World glittering with electric lights and fizzing
with life. On the archway over the gates in red and green neon
lights three feet high is the chunky katakana script of the trifold
Japanese writing system. It declares: DAI SEKAI. The Great
World. The penetrating falsetto wails of Chinese opera bleed into
the flutes and gongs of a wayang performance; aromas of frying
food and spice waft over the walls, enticing you in. Roll up! Roll
up! Outside is death and darkness. Inside is light and life. Simone
feels it herself, the itch to be inside, to join the throng and bustle,
forget everything for a night of make-believe.

Zahra is standing with a slight Chinese man. Zahra sees
Simone and a Japanese military man standing at her side, for
Uehara is in the crisp white shirt and freshly pressed khaki of
his lieutenant's uniform. Zahra whispers to the Chinese man who
disappears into the crowds. 'Hello,' she says smiling. She bows
to Lieutenant Uehara, offering a formal greeting in Japanese.
The Lieutenant beams. A small conversation takes place in rapid
Japanese much of which Simone doesn't understand.

Uehara smiles at Simone. 'You didn't say your friend was on
the radio.'

'Yes. Sorry. She's famous.'

Zahra wrinkles her nose at Simone.

'So we shall be a jolly band. What a wonderful idea to come out.' Uehara's eyes glitter. He holds out his arms and Zahra with a swift glance at Simone takes one of them. Simone quickly takes the other and they plunge into the park of earthly vanities.

* * *

Molly

Surrounding a central thicket of bamboo and palms is a circular open-air beer hall, the tables thronged with noisy Japanese soldiers. Chinese and Eurasian girls in tight-fitting cheongsams carry laden trays of sloshing glasses above their heads, threading through the tables with athletic skill, avoiding, as best they may, the attentions of patrons. A winking sign flashes, showing the way to the dance floor deep inside. Drums thump and saxophones sigh from the hall beyond, where taxi dancers ply their trade. The atmosphere is one of frenzied gaiety.

They move further into the park and beyond the heavy buzz of the crowd come the bells and gongs of the gamelan troupe, leading patrons to the Malay theatre. Uehara stops in the little pool of space outside the theatre. Nearby a series of stalls with flimsy corrugated-iron roofs offers fish balls, curried eggs, and ikan bilis.

Once the food stalls were half a mile long and heaving with the smells of spice, hot fat and sandalwood. There were lines of glistening Peking duck; satay roasting on charcoal fires; soto soup and wanton mee; vats of curried chicken; pyramids of rice; cauldrons of nasi padang and giant prawns; piles of durian and mango; small mountains of shaved ice and battalions of cakes and sizzling banana fritters. Once families flocked here to the food stalls and cinemas, the shadow puppets, street acrobats, magicians, snake charmers and flame throwers, their children running between the feet of the passers-by or sitting on shoulders.

Now this is a place only for men. Simone glances at Zahra. Why are they here?

Uehara's attention is fixed on the posters outside the Malay theatre with images of swaying, slim-hipped men and women. The gamelan music is insistent and hypnotic.

'Lieutenant, perhaps you'd like to see the Bangsawan,' Simone says.

'Oh, I could not leave you ladies,' Uehara says, peering around the door of the theatre. A pretty girl and boy dressed in flowery sarongs and elaborate headgear have spied the Japanese soldier and come forward, smiling, enticing them to enter.

Inside electric fans rake the audience sending a stream of cool air into the turgid atmosphere. Zahra speaks to the little boy and he runs away only to return a moment later with an older but equally attractive young man, a sarong tied against his hips, a loose sonket open on his smooth hard chest, and an elaborate headdress over his long dark hair. He bows to Uehara.

Simone frowns at Zahra who shrugs. There is money in Uehara, whose head is already bent eagerly towards the young man.

'He'll be all right,' Zahra says as they leave. 'I've told Mat to just look after him.'

'He's a prostitute isn't he? Or a pimp.'

'Yes. So what? We're all pimps aren't we? Pimps and prostitutes, one way or another, serving the master.'

Simone stares at Zahra. 'Do you believe that?'

'It's an honest way of looking at it. I have a rapist called a husband. What do you do but run about catering to the desires of the Japanese scientists and that ridiculous Marquis. 'Get this, fetch that. Laugh and smile on cue.' She shrugs. 'It doesn't matter. We all know what we know. We all have to survive. So do all the Mats and their families. I know where Molly is. Come on.'

Zahra veers off the main street emerging into a large clear space before a building, the façade of which resembles the red windmill of the Moulin Rouge in Paris. This is confirmed in letters two feet high announcing in katakana, MU RAN RU JI. A figure emerges out of the darkness. Simone recognizes the slight Chinese man who was at Zahra's side at the entrance to the World.

'This is Li Jun. He works with Molly.'

Li Jun is sharp-eyed and pointy-chinned, with the scars, pinpricks and craters of ancient acne on his cheeks. Shifty, thinks Simone. They enter the building, follow him down a dim corridor until he stops and knocks on a door.

'Come in,' a voice says. Zahra enters and Simone follows. Seated behind a desk of neatly arranged papers is Molly. But only just. She is made up with kohl-dark eyes and scarlet lips. Her hair is twisted into an elaborate bun and she is wearing a silk red and gold Cheongsam. She looks over thirty rather than twenty, the image Simone has of a 1930s Shanghainese tart. Molly rises and comes around the desk, holding her hands to Zahra and Simone. The women take Molly's hands.

'Welcome,' Molly says, 'to Tokyo Rose's world of make-believe.'

* * *

Make Believe

Scantily clad girls have finished with their finale—a high-kicking, squealing can-can. The room is filled exclusively with Japanese officers thumping their feet against the floor in time to the strident rata-tat-tat of the music.

In the shadows of the back of the room, Zahra, Simone and Molly watch.

'Make-believe,' Molly says. 'One evening French, the next Marlene Dietrich singing Lily Marlene, although we're thinking of dropping that since the Germans surrendered. Problem is the

Axis has shrunk.' She grins. 'On Saturday nights Rose Chan does her striptease with a python. That's always sold out.'

'Tell us about you,' Zahra says. Molly has produced some Chinese samsu wine.

'After the surrender, my brother Charlie was arrested. Locked up in Outram Jail. My auntie's house was confiscated. It killed her. She had a heart attack.'

Nobody speaks. Simone recalls a delightfully dotty and charming woman. All this would have just been too much. She puts her hand to Molly's. A piano is being wheeled onto the stage. She sees Li Jun. He is now dressed like a clown. He begins to perform a juggling act. He's good. And funny, tripping over his big shoes. The Japanese laugh with delight.

'I hate them,' Molly says. 'I couldn't do anything for my aunt but I could help my brother. You remember that Charlie was an actor for Mr Shaw. I knew Mr Shaw so I went to him and he convinced the Japanese that he needed Charlie released to help manage the Dai Sekai when it was re-opened. By then Charlie was very ill. Mr Shaw knew he couldn't do the job until he got better so he got me involved as well. The Shaw brothers saved our lives, you understand, found us a place to live, got us wages and rations. Charlie is alive because of them.'

Li Jun finishes his act with a flourish. The audience cheers. In one movement he throws off his shoes and strips away the clown's outfit. A small boy emerges and clears them away. The audience cheers again. Underneath he is neatly dressed in tails, as dapper as Fred Astaire. He does a few taps and the band gives a flourish.

'Gentlemen, tonight we celebrate the birthday of Lieutenant-Colonel Mori.'

The band strikes up 'Happy Birthday'. Simone shakes her head. More Marx Brothers. Cheers resound and the spotlight swings around the room, finally landing on the birthday boy in full uniform. He gets to his feet and raises his glass. More cheers.

'Now by special request, please welcome to the piano for an evening of chanson, Mademoiselle Giselle.'

Mademoiselle Giselle enters. She's Eurasian but dressed in an electric blue silk gown, her hair artfully arranged, she looks every inch Parisienne. The patrons clap and cheer.

'You can't see him but Charlie's on the piano. He and Mademoiselle Giselle have a thing.'

Mademoiselle Giselle begins her recital with *Mademoiselle d'Armentieres.*

'You hungry?' Molly says.

'Starving,' Zahra says.

Molly leads them through a long corridor and opens the door into the kitchen. Two dozen cooks are cleaning up. In a moment three plates are produced and placed on a table.

'Sit,' Molly says. 'The banquet for Lieutenant-Colonel Mori was quite lavish.' In succession arrive a heaped plate of crabs and prawns, a dish of white rice and a spicy soup of tofu and vegetables. 'Nothing but the best for the Colonel. Eat up.'

They fall on the food. After ten minutes of chomping, Molly wipes her mouth.

'We employ one hundred people,' she says. 'From these kitchens, each one feeds fifty more. You see? We keep thousands alive on the Japanese dollar. There are no shortages in the Jap warehouses.'

Simone and Zahra nod, picking over the prawns.

'We can skim a lot off the top before it's even cooked. We supply the temples who shelter the sick and dying. This place is for high officer class. They expect the best and ask no questions. We cook the books and no one cares.'

She laughs and picks up a crab, ripping off a large claw.

'There's something else I have to tell you,' Molly says. 'I wasn't sure I could trust you but I see that Java does. Li Jun is part of a network connected to the guerrillas. If anyone can help us in the final instance, it's them. They're well-armed now. They're ready for anything.'

Simone rises abruptly, scraping her chair. 'You'll get us all tortured,' she says. 'Or shot. I need to go. Uehara will be getting suspicious.'

'Relax, Red,' Zahra says.

'The Japs,' Molly says, 'reckon they can repel any force which the British can throw at them here. They think they can make themselves a fortress like the British did. But they haven't calculated internal sabotage. Attacks on communication installations, electricity substations, port facilities. The MPAJA is backed by a British force with money, weapons, food, dynamite. In the end, everyone may be called on. Even us. Street to street.'

Simone feels sick. Sweat breaks out and nausea sweeps through her body. 'I have to go.'

Simone moves through the alleyway towards the light of the main street and makes for the Malay Theatre. Noise beats against her like slapping hands. She staggers, leaving the opera behind but now the gauntlet that lies before her is even worse. The beer hall and its hundreds of soldiers through which she must pass. She looks around desperately, seeking a way. She feels as if she's drowning when a hand touches her arm. She looks down at the dark-skinned, hairy knuckles and wants to scream, but her throat is swollen by dread.

'All right missy,' the voice says. She looks into the face of Li Jun. He leads her from the main street into a side alley. Then the lights are gone. All is dark and she realizes that by some miracle they are outside the walls of the World and Li Jun is leading her towards a group of parked cars.

Perhaps he says something, she doesn't know. She is close to fainting. He helps her into a car. She tips into blackness.

* * *

Noor

Before she even closes the door Zahra knows something is wrong. Noor, who is in a prison here and bored, always comes to greet her. Always.

She calls the guard but there is no answer. She looks around. Samad's shoes are in a basket by the door. He always takes them off like the Japanese do. Insists they all do. What is he doing home at this hour?

That is when she hears the high-pitched keening. She goes round the screen which separates the reception hall from the back of the house. Noor is standing pressed against the wall, crying softly. Samad is standing near her. Too near.

'Samad,' she says. 'What are you doing?'

He is shocked. She can see that. He turns, takes one step, raises his arm and slaps her. She reels to the floor. Noor bursts into tears.

Zahra scrabbles away from him. He has touched Noor. He has hit her because she has seen. She gets to her knees, struggles to rise.

'Where were you last night?' he screams. 'The guard said you went out. Did not come home until late. Where were you?'

He takes a step forward, grabs her neck. 'Answer me.'

'With a Japanese lieutenant from the Gardens,' she says, the words rushing out. Her cheek throbs. His fingers bite into her throat. She can hardly breathe. 'With Simone. The Japanese lieutenant invited us to go. I should have told you. I was wrong.'

She knows if there is a Japanese officer involved in anything it will give him pause. He releases her and paces. Jittery. Angry.

He has touched Noor. Her sister. Beloved child. She who lives in a world of silence. Zahra feels hate like a rush of fire. She gets to her feet, shaking with the hate of him. She wants to throw herself at him. Beat him to death. But she does not. The sight of Noor, sobbing, stills her. For the first time he has hit her face. He seems to recognize it. She sees him grow uneasy.

Fatima appears. 'Samad,' she says. Quiet. Beseeching. Afraid. It is brave.

He ignores Fatima and flings himself around the screen. She hears him scrabble in the hall and slam the door. Zahra goes to Noor and takes her into her arms. Letting her sister sob the horror and fright away. Fatima is crying. She and Noor are close. They spend hours together. 'I'm sorry,' Fatima says.

Zahra signs to Noor. 'It won't happen again.' She strokes Noor's hair. It won't happen again.

JOHOR

The British Agent

Kay watches him shave, a cigarette dangling from his mouth. 'Why do you fight, Richie? How does this country matter to you?'

He removes the cigarette and arranges it carefully on a nearby log. 'I fight because its in my blood, I suppose. I join in this fight because I believe the Japanese are cruel and evil. Worse than us. Not much worse than the Dutch though.' He laughs. 'And they've got a lot of my fellow countrymen and women in prison. I'd like them to be free. I feel a duty I suppose. And we are the good guys.'

'You are not the good guys. White men, Richie, are like a weight crushing us with goodness and duty. Can't you see that? Goodness and duty is the warped reasoning of the master and we are the slaves. It would be better if you were less good and filled with duty.'

Richie finishes scraping, splashes water on his face and dries it with a towel. He picks up his cigarette and takes a drag. He begins to pack up his shaving kit. He doesn't look at Kay.

'You fight because you are in love with war. For men like you it is the proper outlet for those wonderful manly qualities without which, you imagine, men will deteriorate. Uniforms, ribbons, medals, these are your worthless loves.' He drops the cigarette and stubs it underfoot. 'Are you listening?' She knows he is hearing, but her words are too difficult for him to comprehend. He just doesn't have the mind. He's stuck.

'Yes, I'm listening. I'm not sure you quite understand the situation. But I'm listening because I like you, Java. Respect you.'

His words confirm her conclusion. He has no clue what she means. She releases him and addresses only what he can, possibly, understand. He cannot fathom the change that this war has wrought. He is consumed by his ingrained prejudices and a desire to return seamlessly to the status quo. He has made it personal, as if, suddenly, he has decided they could speak as equals. Very well.

'Is it surprising to like and respect a Chinese woman?'

'Perhaps, if I'm honest.'

'Because you hadn't expected me to be wholly human? Not just me, but the Indians here too and the Malays and the hill people. All half-human subjects. Do you not see what a stone you are around our necks? Why don't you just get out?'

She takes a step closer to him. 'Anyway, when this is over, we shall push you out.'

He puts a finger gently against her scarred cheek. 'I think you might just do that. Perhaps one day you'll tell me how you got that.'

She pulls away. 'I shouldn't think so.'

He smiles. 'I want to send you three of our fighters. KMT Chinese. The best. Do you agree? They'll parachute in. You'll have to prepare a drop zone.'

Java nods. It's time to join them. Not be alone. 'All right. At least they won't be commies.'

'Dear oh dear.' He laughs. 'But good.' He looks down the slope of the mountain. 'There,' he says pointing to a level plateau covered in scrub. Java goes to his side. 'Clear that scrub away. Use it to make a fire on each corner. It will signal the zone to the plane.'

'What will you tell the pilots? You don't know where we are?'

'Yes I do. I'm good at this stuff. I took bearings at the road. Before your fellow turned up. We more or less came up in a straight line.'

He sees her face. 'Annoying isn't it?'

She laughs. 'Yes. And no. Reassuring I suppose. You're not as stupid as I thought.'

'Thank you, I think. Tomorrow night. Seventeen hundred hours. Can you do it?'

'Yes.'

Ravi approaches. 'Time to go down,' he says. His voice betrays his annoyance.

'Righto, old chap.'

'Not your old chap,' Ravi says.

'No. Sorry. Just being a silly arse.'

Richie smiles at Kay. 'Goodbye Java. We'll meet again.'

SYONAN

The Corialis Effect

The dappled light of the afternoon lies like scattered grains of golden rice on the blanket. Simone's throat is congealed. She reaches for the glass of water and gulps, unsticking her voice. Jumairah rises from the corner of the room. How long has she been there watching over her like a hen with her chick?

'Jumairah,' she croaks and the woman comes forward and takes her hand.

Mrs Guan joins them. 'You've had a bad bout of malaria,' she says. 'But you're all right now. If you can get up we will take you for a bath.'

Simone looks down. Her shift is stained with sweat and she smells like a buffalo.

'What about ...?'

'She's all right. Guan moved her to a place of safety in the abandoned plant house. I have milk from the goats for her. She is taking a little rice water and some strained sweet potato. Jumairah stays with her. I want to get her onto solids. She is too thin. Really she should see a doctor and ideally get out of here. Anyone could betray her.'

Mrs Guan smiles. 'Guan made a little toy to hang over her. For her to look at. I have stopped the chloradyne. It's not good. The plant house is far enough from here so that no one can hear her if she cries. Really she should be in a hospital or a children's home.'

'I know. I need to get up.'

'A bath first.'

'Yes,' she smiles. 'That would be nice.'

Leaning on the two women, she creaks along to the bath house in the garden, joints aching like a seventy-year-old. They help her down onto a stool and begin to wash her, flushing her from time to time with ladles of water from the shanghai jar. There is soap and even, from somewhere, she recognizes by its scent, Drene shampoo. Whatever else has disappeared Mrs Guan seems to have an endless stock of Drene shampoo. She inhales the perfume and wakes at last.

She takes the flannel. 'I can do it, thank you,' she says and smiles at the women who leave. The words are weak and flabby. Inadequate. She is as weak as the words, but the soft shadowy light of the bath house, the cool water and the silence are restorative. She washes the shift, slowly, deliberately, rubbing soap against the stains, over and over.

Shadows move along the concrete floor. Mynah birds call and dance a tattoo on the corrugated iron roof. She rinses the dress and washes the spots again. They won't come out. She rubs again until a hole rips in the cloth. She throws the shift to one side and pours ladle after ladle of water over her head. The suds and bubbles gurgle down the drain hole. The corialis effect. That's what it's called, isn't it? Is it clockwise in the northern hemisphere? Or the other way? But they are on the Equator. One degree above the equator. It is important to know and she concentrates, tipping water, over and over but it splashes then swirls in no seeming pattern. Outside, the buzz of the cicadas is like the engines of a stricken plane, plunging to earth. She tries and tries to make sense of the water until her eyes ache and tears slide down her cheeks.

Jumairah calls, her voice soft and gentle. Jumairah. There is courage. She has lost everything she loved but not her core, not her unflagging spirit and love for the dreadful and faltering humans around. Jumairah, Ponompuan and Miss Lilian Gibbs. She wipes her eyes, straightens her back and puts on her shift.

'Coming,' she says.

* * *

Kadayannallur Street

The old St. Andrew's Hospital is located in Kadayannallur Street in Chinatown and now named Shimin Byoin. A Eurasian nurse looks up from her desk. The waiting room is lined with patients, all women and children. The hospital looks clean and well run.

'Hello,' Simone says.

'Hello,' says the nurse. 'What is your name and your illness.'

'I'm not a patient. I am seeking a friend who used to work here. Is there anyone who can help me?'

'Please take a seat.'

Simone sits on the bench and watches the passage of the room, the working of this hospital. Every face in the hospital is Asian of one stripe or another—patients, dressers, nurses, dispensers and doctors. It is quiet, clean and efficient. Before the war no Asiatic doctor, as they were termed, would ever be in charge of a department much less a hospital. Yet this hospital is being run in the most terrible of circumstances and with a lack of everything, without fuss. Keep calm and carry on. She feels a strange pride in them all and a touch of guilt. She's buried herself away in the Gardens. Out here everyone else is doing an appalling job with dignity.

It's a story in itself and she feels the old urge to interview the doctors and nurses and find out how all this came about. After the war, she thinks, and suddenly realizes she can think about a future after the war and a small surge of optimism beats in her veins. A Girl Guide solves problems. Teresa's sacrifice has to mean something. She lost her life for her cause. Maybe the rest of them can get through.

The lift door opens and a Chinese woman approaches. To Simone's surprise she recognizes the woman.

'Irma,' she says and the doctor smiles.

'Heavens, Simone.' She holds out her hands and Simone grasps them. Dr Irma Tan is a formidable woman, the first Asian woman to become the Director of Maternity and Child Welfare Services for all of Singapore, an unheard-of position of power in the highest echelons of the all-male, all-British medical establishment.

'How are you?' Simons says.

'As you see,' Irma says. She was always succinct and direct. 'And you? You look well. What on earth can bring you here? Are you pregnant?'

Simone laughs. 'No. I'm looking for someone. But what happened to you after the surrender?'

'Japs forced me to move the whole clinic here. Told me I'd be working for a Dr Ho. Can you imagine? Pigs the lot of them. Couldn't bear the thought of a woman being in charge.'

'Poor Dr Ho.' Simone says and smiles.

'Yes. Poor man. He saw straight away it wouldn't work. Said my department and his would be separate units. Best we could do under the circumstances.'

She removes her spectacles and begins polishing them. 'The wife, Mary, is an excellent doctor. Without her, well ... Let's say he's a good fellow, a decent doctor but a bit like tofu, if you take my meaning.' She puts on her glasses and peers at Simone. 'But tell me about you.'

'I'm afraid I've spent the war in a garden. The Botanical Gardens. But now I'm very keen to find an old friend, Jenny Tan.

She worked here as a doctor's assistant in the dispensary I think. She was a medical student.'

'Did she? I don't recall the name.'

Simone gazes at Irma. Should she ask her to help? What if she can't find Jenny? What if she never finds Jenny? She wishes now that she had brought Zejian here.

'Look I've got rounds. But we have records. The Japanese oblige us to submit a monthly report with the names and illnesses of all patients and the details of their doctors. They are vastly more bureaucratic than even the British. I'll take you along to the records room.'

The box room contains files and a small table. It is well-organized, everything neatly arranged and labelled.

'Which year?'

'I think 1942 and 1943. I don't know for sure.'

Irma takes down two tin boxes.

'Thank you, Irma.'

'Good luck, Simone. I hope we shall meet again.'

'Yes.'

Simone searches the employee records. It is quickly done. Much like in the Gardens, the report is short and the names rarely change. Documents tell a vivid tale. Increasing demands for scarce medical supplies as the months went by. Curt refusals. A growing list of staff and patient deaths.

She finds Jenny's name and sighs with relief then looks more closely at the card. Next to her name are some of the women Jenny treated and dispensed to. One of them is a Mrs Kay Chan. What was Kay doing here? There is no further address for Jenny but Mrs Chan is marked as living at CHIJ, Bras Basah. This had been crossed out and replaced by Victoria Street Girls School, the Japanese name for the Convent. In 1943, it appears that Kay was married and living at the Convent of the Holy Infant Jesus. Something here isn't right.

* * *

Sambal

Noor grinds red chillies into shallots, ginger and garlic. She adds dried shrimps and belachan and grinds again. Zahra adds palm sugar and fish sauce. Noor grinds again. Zahra adds lime juice and a touch of rice vinegar. They have made this paste a thousand times.

All the time Noor is grinding, a long silent conversation takes place. Zahra's fingers move fast. They have pork and long green beans. This is Samad's favourite meal. He will be here tonight and for three days he alone will eat this dish.

The little castor beans in the porcelain pot are beautiful. Each of the designs on the beans is unique. Like faces and fingerprints. Some say they look like ticks engorged with blood. With chopsticks, Zahra takes up one of the beans and drops it into the sambal paste. She adds water and a second bean. Noor grinds until the sambal is absolutely smooth.

* * *

The Exhibition

On the day of the opening of the Great Yamato-Damashii Exhibition at the Museum, no one is permitted to be absent. It is the thirteenth day of August and the Marquis's birthday.

The day is a celebration of all things Japanese. Mr Guan has told them what will ensue. First the band will play Kimigayo twice. General Seishiro, Commander, Southern Army, will give a speech. Japanese ladies will do a dance dressed in kimono. Japanese and Chinese children will sing 'Aikoku Kyoshinkyoku'. The Marquis will open the exhibition. A party of Japanese and Syonan dignitaries will be shown round the Exhibition. Orange squash and cakes will be served. The exhibition will be opened to the public.

It is all carefully arranged and everything goes to plan. Everyone sings Kimigayo, twice. General Seishiro's speech is received enthusiastically. The Japanese ladies dance nicely. The children begin to march in perfect unison, singing loudly.

Miyo! Tokai no sora akete
Kyokujitsu takaku kagayakeba
Tenchi no seiki hatsuratsu to
Kibo wa odoru Oyamashima

They have reached the bit about Mount Fuji 'Yonder, where the clouds of morn shed a radiant glow' when the American Air Force rains on the Marquis's parade.

Two B-29s drone low overhead. The little paper birds came falling from the sky, twisting and falling, eddies and whirls of red, black and white, fast and thick. They flutter onto the heads of the gathered throng. The Marquis swipes several away from his shoulders like unwelcome dandruff. Soon the ground is covered in leaflets. The Marquis and the General do not move, but angry orders are issued. Soldiers rush about gathering up bundles. But there is nowhere to put them so they stand a moment, nonplussed. Nothing can stop those around from gathering up a handful despite the shouts of the Japanese. Simone reads one. The American flag is on one side. On the other in Chinese and English—*Allied forces are on their way. We are coming to liberate you. Don't panic and stay calm.*

A volley of shots rings out. Everyone drops the leaflets.

'Inside, inside,' screams the Marquis. It is the first time Simone has ever seen the Marquis flustered. General Seishiro and his aide get into their car and speed away. The children and the Japanese dancers disperse. The rest of them make their way into the Museum. More shots and the spectators left outside scarper. Bertie finds Simone. He has a handful of leaflets. He smiles and heads up to the attic. Hatter and the Stooges gather in the rotunda behind Raffles and stare at his shapely calves.

Simone finds Mr Guan. 'How long do you think?' she whispers.

Already the smell of burning paper fills the air. The soldiers are making a bonfire and blackened embers float like joss paper up to heaven.

'About half an hour, possibly. They usually clear this up quickly.'

'No, I mean ...' Simone shakes her head. 'Never mind.' Mr Guan, in his calm way, thinks only of the day. Get through the day and you will get through weeks, months, years.

A great billow of smoke puffs into the building. The soldiers have made the fire too close to the entrance. Embers fly in and attach themselves to the banner. It blackens and flames leap upwards. Smoke swirls.

Bertie races downstairs. 'Come on,' he says as Mr Guan gathers the others. 'Out the back.' They run down the central corridor. Simone looks back. The banner has burned out and falls in sooty scraps on to Raffles' head then slides to his feet. There is nothing else in the cupola to easily catch fire and Raffles emerges somewhat blackened but unscathed.

'What a bloody shambles,' Hatter says to no one in particular.

An hour later order is restored. Hatter and Bertie have been ordered to pack up specimens for the Emperor. The rejected stuffed boar has joined the rest of the slowly rotting exhibits in the back rooms. Mrs Sugiyama instructs the Malay museum workers in the proper way to put up a new banner for the exhibition. It is vastly inferior to the first. A general lack of materials has meant a smaller and less imposing image and she rushes back and force, geta clacking, in order to make sure that no part of Raffles' head appears above the banner. Unfortunately that means his legs are prominent underneath. Simone is sure that Mrs Sugiyama will

find some means—pot plants are the usual choice—to disguise
the offending limbs.

Senyu—Comrade in Arms—Japan's most famous military
march has begun to blare and when she regains the hall, Raffles
has been concealed behind a screen and the banner is in place.
The exhibition is open to the public and a large party of flag-
waving Japanese school children are filing past the fuselage of
the B-29, shepherded by three Japanese schoolteachers. The
children march in step, their little arms and legs moving in perfect
rhythm. Beyond this group are several parties of Chinese and
Malay schoolchildren. Their entry is more slovenly. She smiles.
Three and a half years of Japanese discipline has made not the
slightest difference to the children of the southern empire. How
disappointing for the Emperor.

The final exhibit is for Hakko-Ichiu—all the world under
one roof—and the glories of Pan-Asian cooperation. It begins
with the story of Emperor Jimmu in various languages hung in
an elaborate frame over a cohort of a hundred dolls in his image
made by the children of Syonan. It is not without a certain charm
and someone clearly sacrificed a silk kimono for the cloth.

The first Emperor, and founder of the Imperial House, she reads, *a
descendant of the sun goddess Amaterasu and the storm god Susanoo, captured
the islands of Yamato and established the country of Japan in 660 BC.*

Captured the islands of Yamato. From whom? In 660 BC?
Who were those true people of the land?

*Jimmu Tenno wrote: It is the duty of Japan to extend the line of
Imperial descendants and foster right mindedness. Thereafter, the Capital
may be extended so as to embrace all of the six cardinal points and the eight
cords may be covered so as to form a roof.*

Well, they have followed-through, she thinks, even if it
was a mite slow. They'd been planning world domination for
1,345 years.

Mrs Sugiyama had dug out photographs of Prince Chichibu, the Emperor's brother, meeting with Hitler. It is a pity that his name so resembles Titipu or Nanki-Poo from *The Mikado*, the Gilbert and Sullivan opera which incenses them, but few amongst the Emperor's Southeast Asian subjects would know it, so perhaps it doesn't matter.

However it was wasted work. Chichibu has been thrown out. Without actually saying it, the Marquis has clearly decided that, since they had surrendered and Hitler was now dead as the dodo, all that stuff in Germany was inconvenient and embarrassing.

The exhibition's main focus is now on Japan's role in liberating the crushed and enslaved peoples of Southeast Asia. Several putative banners had been prepared. Burma for Burmese! India for Indians! Malaya for Malayans! Mrs Sugiyama had begun to write the East Indies for … and then abandoned it. Clearly she had no idea who the East Indies might be for. And then there was the awful issue of the Chinese, who she now knew lived all over the place. In the end she'd opted to drop all of that complicated stuff and now a large banner on the wall declared simply Asia for Asians!

Miracle in Malai, she reads. *In Three Years Food Abundant.* Pictures of happy and smiling Malay workers in the fields. Palm oil is there, but tapioca and sweet potato are prominent. The prize crops of war, which would grow on a stone, are the great leap forward in farming.

She picks up the newspaper. This week *The Syonan Shinbun* urges civilian evacuations to the paradise of New Syonan, a malaria-infested, unworkable stretch of jungle in Malaya from whose bourn, everyone knows, no man returns. The Catholic Bishop of Singapore, amongst thousands of others, had died there and even the newspaper is muted in its enthusiasm.

Mr Guan finds her. The Marquis is to hold a party in the Gardens this evening for his birthday. Naturally, gifts will be expected.

A gift for the Marquis? What do you get, when you are up to your ears in shit, for the man who has everything? For the first time in a week she laughs.

* * *

A Birthday Gift

The series of mismatched stools, chairs and tables set out on the lawn in front of the Director of Garden's house is unified, more or less in lumpy fashion, by a long white lace cloth, which she suspects might once have covered the altar of some cathedral.

Palm oil lamps flicker and the light from the verandah throws long shadows across the lawn. It is almost romantic. From inside the house music floats on the air. It is an aria from *Madame Butterfly*. Puccini, by good fortune Italian and therefore not a foe, is the Marquis's favourite composer. Clearly the reversal of the war in Italy and Mussolini's undignified exit has not altered his opinion. But then it wouldn't. Whatever he may truly feel about the collapse of the Axis in Europe—and Simone suspects not very much—the Marquis is royal and secure in his position as the Emperor's relative.

The Marquis likes the theatrical surface of things. He wants to give his captive guests the impression of a cultivated, if slipshod, elegance, far from the unpleasant inconveniences of war. He is dressed to impress in an austere black and grey samurai kimono, shod in white tabi socks and geta. Mr and Mrs Sugiyama, similarly dressed in traditional Japanese garb, hover sweating in the background. Lieutenant Uehara is in his uniform but the other Stooges are dressed as they always are in the rumpled shirts and trousers of the insouciant scientist and stand, silent and uncomfortable, nearby.

Ten of the older Chinese and Malay gardeners are gathered at one corner of the verandah alongside three Indian patrol guards.

Simone is offered warm orange squash. From what crevice of the Japanese warehouses this has come she has no idea but it is certainly over three-unrefrigerated-years-old. She declines and joins Bertie and Hatter.

'This is jolly,' she says. Bertie shrugs. Hatter ignores her. She notices a pile of feathers on the ground and looks up. Katsu-san, paws nonchalantly draped over the edge of the roof, stares down at them all with cool, mismatched eyes. *Madame Butterfly* comes to a crescendo and silence falls. As if on cue, the verandah clears, everyone shuffling onto the lawn, leaving the Marquis standing above them like Jehovah. He strikes a pose, smiling benevolently, his left hand gripping the hilt of the sword tucked into his *obi*, the right raised in dramatic declamatory fashion.

'Dearest friends,' the Marquis says in English.

Uehara sniggers behind his hand. The Marquis's accent is particularly thick tonight. The surprising thing she discovered over time was, despite all the outer show of harmony, just how much the Japanese ruling class disliked each other, how quickly cliques and factions, with their own greedy interests and desires, formed and reformed.

The army hated the navy and the air force. The navy hated the army and the air force. The air force hated the army and the navy. The secret police hated everyone. They all had their separate clubs and separate worlds. The civilian administration divided on departmental lines, all fighting each other. Officers replaced each other with monotonous regularity as they moved out and on to battlefields. Each new one changed everything his predecessor had ordained.

It was an important source of strength for ordinary civilians who knew how to navigate this minefield and the clamorous and venal demands of each new arrival. Mr Guan had worked all this out within weeks of his new overlords arriving in the Gardens and Bertie, Simone and even Hatter knew it. He and Mrs Guan had long hands and deep fingers in the black market to fulfil the ever-clamorous needs of the Japanese.

'Dearest friends,' the Marquis says. 'let us turn our faces to the East and sing Kimigayo in honour of Tenno Heika.' The East has long been marked by a white painted arrow on the pillar of the verandah like the Qibla wall of a mosque. All turn. The Malay gardeners do a sneaky half-turn, an acrobatic move, which involves having one part of the foot vaguely pointing in the opposite direction. The Qibla for them is West. Also when they should be shouting Banzai! they are usually shouting Bangsat! which means filthy scum in Malay. Small acts of secret, soul-easing rebellion.

Kimigayo is sung every morning in the Gardens so everyone knows the words. It's about the Emperor's reign featuring, oddly, pebbles, rocks and moss. It is mercifully short.

Kimi gayo wa
Chiyo ni yachiyo ni

With the Marquis's back turned and all the Japanese intent on the shining Emperor in Tokyo, various shufflings take place. The gardeners, under the severe eye of Mr Sugiyama, don't have the option to drift.

Sazare ishi no
Iwao to nari te
Koke no musu made

The anthem over, Bertie and Hatter wander towards a banyan tree where a suitable seat amongst its roots can be found. Simone steps back and into the shadows on the lawn. The Marquis never holds any event at which he does not make a long rambling speech.

The Marquis turns, plops his bottom on the big rattan chair, which has been brought for him and begins to read from a prepared speech. It is, as it always is, about Japan being the light of Asia, co-prosperity and the brotherhood of man. From somewhere in the twilight, a cuckoo calls.

Katsu-san pads out from the darkness and jumps into Bertie's lap. He strokes her. Perhaps she too is feeling change is in the air. *Allied forces are on their way. We are coming to liberate you.*

The Marquis finishes his speech. Banzai is hurled into the night air. There is a general movement towards the table. The meal, made up entirely from Red Cross parcels, consists of tinned spam, tinned sardines, tinned processed cheese, reconstituted powdered eggs, pickles, margarine, digestive biscuits and tinned jam, all of which must be eaten with either chopsticks or fingers. It's like a children's picnic. The chocolate, sugar and cigarettes have been siphoned off into Japanese pockets. But beside each plate is, ironically, a bar of Imperial Leather soap. Bottles of palm toddy made by the gardeners are produced. It tastes musty like the mildewed bottom of a bucket but that hardly dampens the enthusiasm.

The food is consumed all at once and indiscriminately with a great deal of chomping and licking of fingers. The Marquis smiles benevolently at them, enjoying the uncouth mayhem. Hatter picks at spam and pickles with a pair of chopsticks. Mr and Mrs Sugiyama eat tinned sardines with delicacy, their use of chopsticks being superior. Bertie doesn't bother with anything but digestive biscuits. Simone manages some processed cheese.

The meal devoured, the Marquis smiles expectantly and Mr Guan, ever mindful of the changing shades of the Marquis's face, rises.

'Your Highness,' he says.

This cannot be the right form of address for a Japanese Marquis, Simone has always thought, but the Marquis has never objected.

'As you know, the sad fact is that due to the continuing and inconvenient aggression of Western powers, the war continues in spite of Japan's calls for peace.'

The Marquis nods.

'Because of this our deep wish to offer Your Highness precious gifts and honours on the occasion of your birthday has been thwarted by necessity.'

The Marquis frowns.

'However,' Mr Guan goes on quickly, 'it is our great honour to offer you, in our most humble way, the gift of immortality.'

An old gardener shuffles forward and places a potted orchid on the table. A white slipper orchid with the faintest tinge of lavender.

'Sir, this new orchid has been developed by the head of the orchid garden in your name. *Paphiopedilum Fujimotum.*

Hatter peers suspiciously.

Mr Sugiyama shuffles forward and picks up the orchid cautiously, as if it might contain an explosive device, before placing it before the Marquis. A rapid-fire conversation in Japanese takes place. Then the Marquis beams.

Simone has no time for orchids, the spoiled brats of the botanical world. In the wild, their mortality is enormous. Much like humans in the East Asia Co-prosperity Sphere. What a perfect gift for an over-indulged fool and one which could never leave this island without dying.

What Hatter isn't privy to—for he would not approve and what the Japanese don't know, not even the scientists, none of whom is expert in orchids—is that this rather commonplace *paphiopedilum niveum* was this morning part of a clump growing behind one of the nightsoil cesspits in the Gardens.

Bertie grins at Simone and raises his digestive biscuit in salute.

The next morning word flies round the Gardens. The Marquis has left. Rumour is that General Seishiro and the Marquis had a row and the Marquis stalked out, ordered his car and went straight to the airport to fly to Saigon.

A faint miaow emanates from the roof top. Katsu-san stares down at them.

'Oh dear,' Bertie says. 'What shall we do with the cat?'

'Leave her alone. She takes care of herself.'

'We should change her name though. She can hardly continue to be Miss Victory.'

Simone shrugs. 'Bertie, I have to go somewhere. It's important. They won't ask but if they do, will you tell the Stooges I'm sick. Women's troubles. That should shut them up.'

Bertie purses his lips. 'Be careful, my dear. You know it's almost over. Five minutes to midnight is not the time to get into hot water.'

Simone leans in and kisses Bertie on the cheek. 'I'll be just fine,' she says.

* * *

Call the Doctor

Samad approaches the bed. Zahra has been ordered to lie here and wait for him. He disrobes. She hates his body. Hairy and bony. His penis is a tiny pencil. His breath stinks of chilli and ginger.

He sits on the bed but suddenly groans and throws his hand to his stomach.

'Ulcers?' she says. 'Sambal. You know it doesn't agree with you.'

His eyes glaze over and he squirms on the bed like a demented worm. Doubled over, twisted by pain, a great groan escapes from the depth of his being. She leans in to him and whispers in his ear. 'You shouldn't have touched Noor, you filthy rapist.'

With a groan of agony and a long exhalation, he goes still.

Zahra goes to the door. 'Fatima,' she says, 'call the doctor.'

Fatima puts her head inside the door and rushes to the bedside She lets out a sob of fear and anguish. 'What happened?'

Zahra looks at her. 'Ulcers?'

* * *

The Convent of the Holy Infant Jesus

Simone cycles to Tanglin Gate. On Orchard Road labour gangs are digging anti-tank trenches.

Men are drilling disconsolately in front of shops. Everyone has been ordered to join the MAS, the newly crafted ARP, or the labour brigade. It's like an old film they've all seen before.

With little enthusiasm, Mr Guan has asked them all to form a MAS unit in the Gardens. It's a ludicrous idea. When the British invade it will be a bloodbath and the least useful thing will be a bunch of no-hopers trying to sew on arms and legs.

Whilst there is no bow required by the heiho sentries, every sentry point manned by Japanese soldiers requires the obligatory O-jigi. Dismount and bow, dismount and bow. Once there would have been thirty between Tanglin and Bras Basah, now there are six.

At CHIJ the double gates are open, there is no sentry and she rides through into one of the inner courtyards. The once beautiful grounds are turned, like the whole of Singapore, to crops. It seems deserted. She knows a lot of the sisters and children had followed the Catholic Bishop to the settlement on the mainland.

She rides down the cloister towards Caldwell House, puts her bike against the wall and knocks at the door.

It is opened by a woman she recognizes, an Irish nun, Sister Catherine. The diminutive woman hesitates a moment then holds out her hands. 'Simone Martel, goodness.'

'Hello Sister. May I come in.'

'Yes, yes.'

Sister Catherine is the music teacher and choir leader. Simone's work on the women's page of the *Tribune* has brought her here in the past. They move into the sitting room. Circular, comfortable with ancient sofas. The motto carved around the top of the room reads: *Marche en ma presence et sois parfait.* Walk in my presence and be perfect. An optimistic and surely fantastical credo.

'Sister, I'm looking for a woman called Jenny Lim. Or perhaps another woman, Mrs Kay Chan. She is marked as living at this address.'

Sister Catherine reacts as if struck. She rises. 'I do not know either of those women.'

Simone also rises. 'That's not true. You are lying.'

'You must go. I cannot help you.'

'No. No.' Simone places herself between Sister Catherine and the door. 'I'm not leaving until you tell me what's going on. I need to find Jenny Lim. And Kay Chan may know where she is.'

The blood drains from Sister Catherine's face and she walks unsteadily to the sofa and sits. 'You don't know what you are saying.'

Simone goes to her side. 'What on earth is going on?'

'My dear, it is very dangerous to ask me these questions.'

'Why? Who could know what I'm asking you?'

'We are watched. There are spies in our midst. The Japanese suspect us of dealing with anti-Japanese forces. Now more than ever they watch us because we have contacts with the mainland at the Catholic settlement. They imagine we deal with the communist guerrillas.'

Simone takes this in. Kay is Java. But do the sisters know that?

Sister Catherine's eyes move along the wall. *Marche en ma presence et sois parfait.* She stiffens.

'You will have to ask Jenny. I can't be involved in this anymore.' She makes the sign of the cross as if to shrive herself of guilt and responsibility.

Simone gasps and stares. 'You know where Jenny is?'

'Yes. She is here. But you must never speak of it. We protect her. Come with me.'

They move into the church and along the aisle. At the back, behind the altar, Sister Catherine stops by a small door.

'Behind that door is a corridor. It leads to the cloisters. She is there.'

'You're not coming?'

'No.'

Simone searches Sister Catherine's face. Is she to be trusted? The nuns rely utterly on the Japanese. Is this a trap? She hesitates. She's come around asking about a woman the Kempeitai arrested and who is now possibly fighting them in the jungles of Malaya. But she wants to find Jenny and it's no good second-guessing herself now. She goes through the door and into the penumbra of the corridor. Light ahead rims a door like a halo.

She pushes the door and emerges into a courtyard. It is planted with rows of tapioca. Across the courtyard a cloister. Double doors stand open and give onto a long room. It's a small hospital. Children's eyes turn to her and so does the figure in a nun's habit. With a rush of joy Simone recognizes Jenny.

'God. It is so good to find you.'

Jenny runs forward and throws her arms around Simone. Jenny is stick thin. Simone can feel her bones under the habit.

'Come' says Jenny finally, leading Simone to a small dispensary at the end of the ward.

'We need your help,' Simone blurts, unable to wait a moment longer. 'It is for Teresa's baby.'

'Teresa's baby? Where is Teresa?'

'She's dead. But she left a child and Anita and I rescued her. A little girl. We've hidden her in the Botanical Gardens.'

'Dead? Teresa is dead?'

'Sorry, yes. I shouldn't have said it that way. But there is simply no time. We need you. We have to get the baby and bring her here. She'll be safe here.'

'I'm hiding here myself. You don't know what you're asking.'

Simone touches Jenny's hand. She snatches it away.

'I was arrested in '43 and held for three months. They accused me of … oh it doesn't matter. When you get arrested by the

Kempeitai, even if you've done nothing, when you get out—if you get out—you are tainted with the stink of them. No one will hire you. No one wants to give you a place to live.'

'My family was ruined. My father and brother, two cousins and an uncle were caught up in the great cleansing. They knew that the men were involved with the China Fund. They never came back. Our house was taken. We were thrown out. My mother died of a stroke last year.'

Jenny indicates the small ward.

'The convent took me in. I pay back by helping the children and nuns when they are sick. But food is so little, even growing our own. Everything goes to the children. The Japanese Christians give milk.'

'So you see. You can help Teresa's child. You must bring her here.' Simone grabs Jenny by the arms and shakes her.

Jenny pulls away. 'I'm too afraid. To leave here terrifies me.'

'I am terrified too. In my little garden I could shut it all out.'

'You didn't lose anyone to them. You haven't been inside their prisons. You don't know.'

'I don't know, but Java sent for us and now we need you. All for one and one for all. The promise and the law.'

A child cries out and a Malay nun rises.

'She was your sister,' Simone says.

Jenny turns. 'I thought that Java was dead, you know. The last time I saw her was in Saint Andrew's Hospital.'

'You treated her.'

'Yes. She … I … I can't say why.'

Jenny twists her hands. 'When I came here, the nuns took me in.'

Simone, impatient, clicks her tongue. 'Just tell me. I saw Kay in Johor. She's … Well. She's not dead.'

'Oh. I'm ashamed to tell you. I shouldn't.'

'For goodness sake, Jenny, just tell me.'

'All right. Don't yell. She'd met a man. You see. Oh, I shouldn't tell you.' She clutches the wooden cross on her chest. 'She got pregnant. She wanted an abortion.' Jenny bursts into tears. 'It was awful. I had no idea. I had no experience. And she trusted me. Mary Ho and the nurses got her through I suppose. I don't know. I was arrested the next day.'

Simone slumps. Jenny wipes tears from her eyes. 'But she survived.'

'Yes. She got back to the mainland.'

Simone is about to tell Jenny that Kay was arrested but she stops herself. Jenny doesn't need to know that. She tries to think it through. Kay was working for a cell of 'stay behind' men. She came to Singapore carrying a message for the head of the MCP. But she also came to get an abortion from someone she thought she could trust. So Jenny was arrested because Kay had gone to her and the Japs were following her. Kay was permitted to recover and go back to Johor. They knew. They followed her.

'Look Jen, it doesn't matter now. What matters is Teresa's child. You have to get the child and bring her here.'

Jenny recoils. 'I can't. I'll be arrested again. I couldn't stand it. '

'No. That's not an answer. Anita will get you. You'll be under the protection of the INA.'

'What do you mean?'

'Anita—White—is in the Rani of Jhansi regiment. She's a captain.'

Jenny bursts into nervous laughter. The Malay nun looks up.

'Why am I not surprised?'

'Don't laugh. She's terrific. Brave. If Anita fetches you, will you come?'

'Yes,' she says after a long silence.

The child who was crying is calm. The Malay nun is crooning a song. Simone points to a telephone on the small table in the dispensary. 'Does that work?'

Jenny nods.

'I'll call Anita now.'

Before she can pick up the phone, Sister Catherine appears in the doorway, flustered and sweating, her face contorted with fear.

'Come away, quickly Simone. Come.'

'But …'

'No. Come. You'll put Jenny in danger. I've been told a Japanese Kempeitai car has drawn up at the gate. You must come now.'

Simone grips Jenny's hand. 'Call Anita at the regiment. Promise you'll do it. Promise.'

Sister Catherine catches Simone by the hand and drags her along the corridor before Jenny has time to reply. The Malay nurse shuts the hospital door with a clack. They rush down the church aisle into the open. 'Go down the corridor and out of the Gate of Hope. I told you how dangerous it is to come here. Get away.'

Simone turns into the corridor.

At the end, advancing slowly towards her is Captain Tsuji.

* * *

A Funeral

Samad's body is wrapped in a white cloth and loaded onto the back of the truck supplied by the Japanese for its final journey. Samad's Indian physician has pronounced death from a burst ulcer. He has, he tells Fatima and Zahra, warned Samad many times about chillies and spice.

Women are not permitted to attend the funeral. The uncle who had bullied her into this filthy situation is not there either. He'd died of heart complications from beri beri. Little good it did him to have Samad as an in-law. Samad had forgotten him as soon as he had his way. It was a sort of justice.

* * *

Waiting for the Crocodile

It was always going to come to this. Tsuji had asked her about Teresa. But she had put it away. Ignored it to keep her courage. She had been foolish to heed Zahra's call. It has led to this. But what else could I have done?

She is inside a prison building. Not the YMCA Kempeitai headquarters—the building she has so strenuously avoided the entire occupation. She had been thrown onto the floor of the car and driven here, to this prison. She has no idea where it is.

The heiho corporal writes her name in a book. How meticulous they are even now at the end. She is marched across the small concrete courtyard and down a corridor. Stench from the line of cells. She holds back. Foulness is there. A sharp dig in the back propels her forward. The cell is four or five yards square, a narrow air vent in one wall. What light filters in is from a naked bulb some way down the corridor. The floor is wooden planks, damp with something she tries not to contemplate.

There is a floor drain and a tap. This she can see is the source for drinking, washing and all other bodily functions. There are ten other prisoners, all men. They do not look up but sit in the same attitude in two lines of five. She is ordered into the back line to sit on her knees on the stinking, damp floor. Within a minute she feels the strain of sitting, unmoving. Her knees and back begin to ache. She wants to look at the others, seeking some companionship but any turn of the head is greeted with a yell and a stick on the bars. She feels tears well. She swallows them away. Tears are signs of cowardice and fear. The Japanese detest you even more if there are tears.

One man calls 'O-benjo ka?' The guard grunts. 'Benjo hei.' The man rises and goes to the toilet and she smells the stench and hears the streams of shit pouring out of him. Dysentery. She knows the sounds. He splashes water on himself, groans then resumes his position.

Hours pass and the pain of sitting becomes a matter of mind over suffering. Her lower body is numb. She needs to use the toilet, an act now of humiliation, in front of the guard and the men but she longs to move and puts that passing shame out of her mind. She is scared of the filth at the drain but desperate. She dares to speak. 'O-benjo ka' she says. 'Benjo-hei.' She goes to the drain slowly, walking like a cripple, her legs an agony of needles as the blood rushes back. The smell, bad from the other side of the room, is here intolerable. She holds her breath and takes down her pants under her skirt, desperate not to touch the filth around the drain. She can't recall whether dysentery is a transmittable disease by contact. But it is an impossible task. She can't fail to touch the fecal matter. She sees that the men have all turned their heads away from her, giving her some dignity and this small kindness causes tears to run silently on her cheeks.

As she goes back to her place, she feels the swift movement of a hand touching hers. 'Courage,' a voice whispers so low she hardly catches it. It is enough to stop her tears.

She is not alone and soon this first, terrible day is over. They are ordered to lie on the floor. The guard departs. In an instant one of the men shuffles to her.

'I am Hong Pei,' he says and hands reach out to her and some names are whispered. Names she can't absorb. 'In the night they do not watch. You can drink, wash and go to the toilet. Tomorrow some food will come. Not much but some.'

The men surround her and guide her to the tap. She runs water into the toilet cleaning it, then drinks, washes her face. As she removes her underwear and skirt to wash all the men turn away. Such gifts in this tiny place and again tears come to her eyes. The gift of movement, the gift of dignity. How quickly she has become grateful for simple things. How fortunate has been her experience of this occupation and its miseries. She has not truly discovered this until now. She lies down, stretching her limbs luxuriantly among the men, glad of them, glad of solidarity in their little tin can.

She recalls a saying she has heard from Dr Ueno. Jigoku de hotoke—meeting Buddha in hell.

'Sleep,' Hong Pei says. 'It is the anaesthetic to get through the night.'

'Why are you here?'

'Black market. Said I sold food to the enemy.'

'Did you?'

'Probably. Sold food to anyone who paid. To feed my family. I don't know what's happened to them.' His voice is as bleak as a sand dune.

'How long have you been here?' Simone hears the fear in her own voice, afraid of the answer.

'I don't know. Perhaps three months. What is the date?

'August, the fourteenth of August.'

'Oh, then only six weeks. It feels like forever.'

'I'm afraid.'

Hong Pei puts his hand to hers and she grasps it tight. Her stomach aches for food. Outside, somewhere in the distance she hears the 'tock tock … tock' of the itinerant noodle seller.

She lies, back to back with Hong Pei, finding comfort in his presence. She closes her eyes and tries not to think.

It is not day when the peace is shattered by a stick knocked against the bars. She sits up. A name is called. A Chinese name and a man crawls to the bars. She watches as he lies face down on the floor and crawls out of the cell by the only means possible, a space no bigger than the span of an arm. You must go to them in the most humiliating manner possible.

He disappears ahead of the guard and silence returns.

'What will they do?' she asks Hong Pei.

He gives her no answer. She should not have asked. It would just terrify her and he knows it. The men lie down. And then a cry in the night.

A Guide has courage, she repeats to herself. The vision of Java at the lagoon shoots into her head. Standing in the swirling waters, braced against the bank, waiting for the crocodile.

* * *

The Cell

Gradually the night passes. She drifts but does not sleep. Sunlight from the air slit penetrates little by little, a parsimonious few inches of the world outside. She watches it crawl over the legs and bodies sprawled around her. The man with dysentery wakes groaning. She covers her ears. He crawls to the corner. A stream of stinking shit pours out of him. The smell sticks to the fetid and humid air. He will die without treatment.

We will all die. We will all die in this grave. Unmarked. Unnoticed. We will all die. All die.

Hong Pei wakes and grimaces. He has broken teeth. His face and neck are black from bruises. He is stick thin, but must once have been fatter for his skin sits on him like a Roman toga. The Japanese guards have gone. Why and for how long she doesn't know.

'Where are we?' she asks Hong Pei.

'Valley Police Station,' he says as they crouch over the tap and drink. Her stomach protests. It wants food. She fills it with water.

The Japanese guards return and with them two Indian workers. Half a coconut shell is filled with insipid, flavourless sago congee. She wolfs it down.

A guard knocks his truncheon on the bars. 'Marteru' he says pointing to her. She recoils, heart pumping. The guard raises his rifle.

She crawls out of the cell. 'Hayaku,' screams the guard, yanks her to her feet and frogmarches her forward. As she passes down the corridor she turns her head to the courtyard, to a glimpse of daylight.

* * *

Interrogation

Tsuji sits behind the iron desk, picking his teeth with his silver toothpick. The guard thrusts Simone onto a chair and departs.

'Now I want you to tell me nothing but the truth,' Tsuji says. He continues to dig for a moment and test the takings before placing the pick back in its container.

Simone is aware that she is dishevelled and smelly. Leaving her in the cell overnight has served its purpose. She is less than human. Look them in the eyes. Tell them half-truths. Implicate people they trust.

'I don't know why you had to put me in that cell. What have I done to necessitate such drastic action?'

Tsuji raises a pointed eyebrow.

'The problem is that you have lied to me. You said you did not know who the person called Java is, but you do. Java is an anti-Japanese terrorist. But you know this. The keeper at the Governor of Johor's hunting lodge said the INA officer and you left hours before you had to pick up the Governor's son.'

The little courage she had gathered evaporates. She realizes they had gone to the convent to get her. She was followed. They may not know about Jenny. A small relief.

'Where did you go?'

He waits. She is silent.

'Where did you go?'

'The manager of the hunting lodge went for prayers. We decided to go to the coast where it might be cooler. We had some time to ourselves. It was pleasant.'

'You went for a drive with an INA officer in a place where terrorists operate.' He laughs. Simone does not answer.

'One of the women who lives with you. The Malay woman. She is not in your house at night. Why? It is forbidden to sleep out of the registered address.'

'Who has told you that?'

'Never mind. I have sent soldiers to look for her. The names you gave me were lies. I believe you used the trip to Johor to pass and receive messages from the terrorists.'

'No. I gave you the names of my fellow guides. If you cannot find them that is not my fault. Mrs Muller is a liar and troublemaker. Ask Dr Ueno. You cannot trust her.'

'Do you know who Java is? Is it a woman?'

'A woman?' she says. 'But that's impossible. A woman cannot lead a troop of guerrillas in the jungle. A woman cannot be a military leader. You, yourselves, say it is so, do you not?'

Tsuji stamps his foot on the floor.

'Stop lying. I hate liars.'

The rattan cane strikes Simone across the cheek so hard that she crashes to the floor. It feels as if her eye will explode and when she puts her hand to her face it is covered in blood.

'Sit on the chair,' Tsuji twitches the cane.

Simone gets to her feet. Her cheek is throbbing and blood drips into her blouse.

'Now. Tell me what is your connection to Java?'

'I don't know any Java. It's ridiculous to keep asking the same question.'

Instinctively she puts her hands in front of her face but Tsuji does not strike her head. This time he whips the cane across her ankles. They too burst into seams of blood. She can't stop herself crying out. She stifles it as quickly as she can. It pleases them and makes the other prisoners tremble.

Tsuji lays the cane on the desk.

'It is no good lying to me. Everyone talks in the end. Or they die. I'm sure you don't want to die, Simone. You western-educated bananas are all cowards.'

Tsuji takes a packet of cigarettes, puts one between his lips and lights it. Simone's blood throbs where he has struck her. Her heart however calms and a sense of deep serenity takes hold of her spirit. This caning, this pain has brought a revelation. She is glad she is hurting. She no longer fears him. Tsuji has done something nothing else could do. It has made her one with them all, it has given her back to herself, it has given her back the great, singular power of self-respect.

She knows what to expect. Denial will only result in endless beatings. Now she has to be smart. Half-truths. She has to implicate Greta. Who else is there?

Tsuji's mind seems to have wandered onto a different subject. One close to every Japanese heart. The appalling lack of seishin. 'You people are disgusting,' he says. 'Yurasia-jin. How can you bear the humiliation and disgrace of being puppets of the British? Do none of you have any shame? A Japanese woman would have killed herself. A Japanese woman would not be afraid to die. A Japanese woman has a code.'

Tsuji leans back in his chair. Smoke seeps from his mouth. It's as if they've all seen too many James Cagney movies.

'Disgrace.' Simone says. 'Well, we have a different view of what you call disgrace. Like danger we believe it must be bravely lived through. Not run away from by the pitiful and cowardly taking of one's life.'

This view is apparently so novel that Tsuji stiffens and stares at Simone, then crushes the cigarette into the ashtray. His hand is shaking. She is glad she has found something to shake him, even though it may be the death of her.

'No, no. Liar. You are the cowards. Cowards,' he screams. He grips the cane. Simone rises. If the end is to come she wants to be standing.

A guard enters. Tsuji whips round furious at the interruption. The guard flings himself into a low bow. A rapid exchange of Japanese. The only words she understands are Tenno Heika, His Majesty the Emperor. Tsuji stands very still, his grip on the cane tight. He stares at the guard who is still bowing. The face of the guard is a rictus of horror as he stares at Tsuji's boots.

Tsuji strides from the room. The guard follows. She is left alone. She goes to the window. Locked and barred. The door opens. An Indian guard ushers her to come.

He takes her back to the cell and she crawls inside. There are no Japanese guards in the corridor. She cleans her wounds at the tap and tears a piece of her skirt to bind her ankles and soothe her cheek.

Food is brought by the Malay guard. A tiny amount of rice. A tiny dried fish. She eats. Lies down.

'Something has happened,' Hong Pei whispers. 'All the Japanese guards suddenly disappeared.'

In the distance she can hear the crackly sounds of a voice on an ancient phonograph record. Then, abruptly, silence. They all sit facing the bars like dumbbells. Her stomach is eating itself. Outside a baby's crying. Who can she give Tsuji? Who do they trust?

Then, like a little flash, she remembers Samad. She will give them Samad. He lives and works in the north of the island. He is a double agent, liaising with guerrillas over the Straits. He appears to work for the Japanese but he has always worked for the British. She will give them Samad.

JOHOR

The Drop

The drone grows louder. Java signals to Yuan to light the pile of damar-torches at the corners of the drop zone. They catch instantly. The drone becomes a roar. The plane sweeps across the drop zone and turns a lazy circle.

It sheds height. The men jump at 800 feet. The B-24 skims the tree tops on the approach. The roar is tremendous. She ducks down. Parachutes billow. Yet the shapes don't seem to drift but plummet. She can't believe they can land safely. Leaping into the unknown. Flying into the trees. What steel does it take to do this?

The plane arcs back to sea. Ravi and the others head into the forest. Java returns to camp. The Jakun men are building a small hut for the new arrivals. Piles of bamboo and attap are neatly stacked.

An hour later they come in. Scratches and bruises. A triumph of luck over sense and the feeling in the camp is buoyant. Tea is brought to the men who jump into trees. Suddenly there are allies from the outside world. Suddenly there is hope.

Yuan sets up the radio. A message to Richie. Safe arrival of three packages.

Richie asks to speak to Java. 'News from Ceylon,' he says. 'The Japs have surrendered.' He sounds disappointed.

The thumping script for the liberation of Malaya by triumphant British heroes has not found an audience. The shame and disaster of the surrender cannot be transformed into their noble return.

SYONAN

Harikiri

The gloomy martial thud on the radio in the distance has gone on for half an hour. A gunshot. An explosion. They all turn their heads towards the sound.

Gunshots in quick succession. Crack. Crack. Crack. An explosion, closer. The light in the corridor trembles from the force of the blast and shadows move on the wall. The shadows are people, suddenly, with arms outstretched. The inmates see the shape of a machine gun and retreat to the back of the cell.

But the voice they hear is not Tsuji's. It's not Japanese. It is a woman's. It's Anita's. 'Open the cells,' she orders the three women with her. Simone crawls to the bars. 'Here, here,' she calls, frantic. 'It's over,' Anita says, 'Japan's surrendered.'

Dazed, the prisoners wander out into the daylight, which burns their eyes. Gradually they take in the chaotic and bloody scene in the courtyard. A dozen Japanese lie in great pools of blood, blown to bits by grenades. None of them wears the uniform of a Kempei captain. Tsuji is not among them. Two army officers slump next to a wall, swords sticking out of their stomachs. One is alive, groaning. Nobody goes to him.

Outside the prison Japanese sentries stand on guard as if stunned. Passers-by still bow to them as usual. Yet none of the sentries stops this rag-tag bunch of emaciated escapees. As if a spring in the clock has wound down, they stand stopped at midday. Simone supports Hong Pei to Anita's car. People walk the street. Glances. Eyes raised to each other. No one speaks. No one cheers. No one is jubilant. A truck loaded with Japanese soldiers speeds by.

'Is it really over?' Simone says. 'It doesn't feel like it.'

'The Emperor gave a speech on the radio. Unconditional surrender. The Regiment has been ordered to stay in barracks, but I had to come and get you.'

'You knew where I was?'

'I knew where Tsuji was. Jenny called me.' She passes a tin bowl. 'Cold rice. All I could get quickly.'

Simone and Hong Pei share it. Anita takes the first aid box and cleans up Simone's wounds. Bandages. Idioform. Some of the inmates, supporting each other, approach the car.

'Get in,' Anita says. 'I'll take you to a hospital.'

The inmates eye the INA flag on the car. Eye her uniform. Hong Pei gets up. 'We will be all right. I will take them to my shop.'

'I will take you,' Anita says.

But none move. Hong Pei shakes his head. 'It's all right. I will care for them. It is not far.' Two of the inmates spit on the ground at Anita's feet. She steps backwards.

Simone hands Hong Pei the first aid box. 'Use it, my friend. Care for yourselves. Anita, let's go.'

Anita does not move, staring down at the spit in the dry dust at her feet. Perhaps the import of that act of disdain enters her consciousness. This wasn't a game. Playing soldier. People she would never know had suffered and died. And they saw her as part of the system and the pain.

'Come on,' Simone says. She pulls at Anita's arm. These men are weak and sick. But there will be stronger ones. Filled with hate. It is there. The first inkling. The first pattering drops of revenge. Soon it will flood. 'Drop me at the Museum. And get yourself into your camp.'

Anita's car chugs along Havelock Road and over the river, soot flying, fumes of sulphur.

Japanese flags still flutter the length of the bridge, from balconies and flagpoles. Japanese sentries stand, heads bowed. None ask to see a pass or berate them. A hush on the city. A breath held. Waiting. Hoping to believe. Finally it has happened. Can it be true? The end of the Noh play not with a crescendo but with a sigh. A world changed. Yet the sun still shines. Trees still throw their shadows on the ground. Birds still fly.

She recalls her conversation with Mr Guan. A swift change of loyalties has begun. Who will I be loyal to? Perhaps no one. Just them. The women who have become my life. Teresa dead for nothing. Was it nothing?

A Japanese soldier puts his gun to his temple. His brains spatter the wall. Two old Chinese women nearby watch then simply turn away. A little boy laughs. 'Nippon Go!' he screams.

* * *

The Museum

Bertie stands in the courtyard. He has a suitcase in his hand and drops it when he sees Simone. His arms go around her.

'Thank God, Simone. We were frantic. Dr Ueno made a fearsome complaint. Never seen him so agitated. We've been trying to find you.'

He touches her cheek. 'Oh. Poor child. What did they do to you?'

'It's over,' she says. 'This doesn't matter.'

Uehara's head pops out of the window above them like a dyspeptic turtle. 'Simone-san. Oh. What has happened? Oh dear.'

You lot happened, she thinks. But she bows to him. Why? Will they never unlearn the O-jigi? She has no reason to bother with them anymore. Except they are still there and still armed and harmful. His head disappears.

'The Emperor himself spoke on the radio,' Bertie says. We heard it here. Uehara says they'd never heard his voice before. He flung himself to his knees and put his head on the floor. Listened to it in that posture the whole time. Said he barely understood a word, but Ueno knew.' Bertie shakes his head. 'What a strange lot. But apparently there's a bomb. Whole cities obliterated by one bomb. People turned to cinders. What a terrible thing that is.'

Simone can't think of anything except the pain of her cheek and this idea of freedom.

'Simone, listen. Dr Hatter and I have to go into internment. Dr Ueno has received orders. All British civilians outside must go to the Civilian Internment Camp at Sime Road. I think it's a condition of the surrender. Anyway a lorry from the camp will be here at 2:30 p.m. to pick me up, then swing by the Gardens for John. Uehara's here to get his things and Mr Guan will take him back in the car. You go with them. I'll stay and put up the notices Mr Guan's prepared and wedge all the doors shut from the inside. There will be Japanese sentries stationed around the Museum but it pays to be careful.'

Lieutenant Uehara steps out of the Museum with a suitcase. Tears in his eyes. 'This is a dreadful day,' he sniffles. She wants to slap him but he might slap her back. He has seemingly not noticed the marks of cruelty of his fellows on her face. 'A most dreadful day.'

Bertie grins. 'Not for everyone, of course,' he says. Uehara stares at him. She waits. All those evenings with this man, enduring his melancholy bullshit. She would smile but it hurts.

Mr Guan appears. He's surprised by the sight of Simone and momentarily nonplussed. She sees his relief and goes to his side.

'You are safe,' he says and frowns at the wound on her cheek, then turns to Bertie. 'Professor, I will see you in the Gardens with Dr Hatter. Lieutenant Uehara, Simone will come with us.' He has dropped the Japanese honorific on his name and hers. 'Shall we go?'

JOHOR

Changing Places

Java, Ravi and Yuan meet Richie's truck on the road to Sendai. The truck has Ichiban Soy Sauce Factory on the side in Japanese and Malay. Chinese characters in red paint half-smother the sign. Two Chinese communist guerrillas with sub-machine guns are in the back. Richie pats the seat next to him up front. Java ignores it and holds out her hand to Ravi who pulls her up.

As soon as the Japanese retreat the MPAJA guerrillas swagger in. They have come to liberate the town they cry on loudhailers. Marching. Shouting orders. Arresting. Kidnapping. Bullying. Executing. Settling scores. The innocent, the guilty—Malays, Eurasians, Indians, Chinese—policemen mainly but anyone they hate.

Tonight in this town there is a celebration. The Java Force is invited to Sendai. To the headquarters of Li Song in the former Hotel Nippon rapidly renamed Red Star Hotel. Towering bamboo triumphal arches stand over the road carrying slogans in Chinese. Yuan reads: 'The People's Autonomous Council Welcomes the MPAJA. All Heaven is Rejoicing.'

She does not say she is Java. Li Song is intrigued. He is small and wiry with sharp, clever eyes. There is no leader, Yuan says. A council. All equal. Whether he believes it or not, Li Song is forced to salute this central tenet of the communist party. Richie is silent.

The men get drunk on air-dropped rum and songs of red patriotism. She despises them all. There are few women. Those who are there are working in the kitchen.

'They should be occupying the radio stations and the newspaper offices,' she says to Richie. 'If they want a revolution, they should be moving men into the ports to repel the British and firing the Malays to fervent nationalism, not settling scores, creating division and drinking rum.'

'You're right. But I won't tell them. You wouldn't expect me to. Actually I've contacted the Japanese commander in Sendai. They know they have to surrender but they won't cease military operations while the commies are attacking them. The sooner we take control, the quicker this will end. But MacArthur won't allow troops to land anywhere until the formal surrender is signed in Tokyo.'

'When?'

'30 August is the date I've been given. I'm hard at work trying to convince Li Song to cooperate with us. Mountbatten wants Force 136 agents to be the liaison between the Japs and the Reds. He's very annoyed at this delay.'

British understatement. He's probably furious at being told what to do by an American general. But the tens of thousands of military and civilian POWs all over the Japanese Empire languishing in stinking camps will be more than annoyed. They'll be dead. Jean is there. Waiting for this all to end. Is she, even now, at the end of her tether?

'I'm going to Singapore tomorrow,' she says. 'I need your Soy Sauce truck.'

SYONAN

Going Home

Zahra looks down from the house onto the street. A Japanese man, sword raised, is slashing at the Japanese flag and shouting. It falls in ribbons at his feet. She watches, fascinated. The man flails and cries, agitated beyond all sense. After five minutes he collapses, foam on his lips.

She goes down. The man lies still. He has fainted completely away. She sees a neighbour. 'What's happened?'

'Nippon has surrendered.' His eyes grow wide as if he can't believe what he's just said.

She walks to the crossroads. The sentries hang their heads. She bows but they don't look at her. As she turns back she sees, a little to one side, the body of a man hanging from a window. It is the one-star man—the Tamil shopkeeper who'd been ordered against his will to be the Japanese neighbourhood spy. She can't recall him doing anything cruel. He'd been a decent soul stuck with an unpopular job. His body hangs straight, his tongue caught between his teeth.

The man's wife stands looking at her husband. Zahra approaches. 'Mrs Veeraswamy,' she says. 'Come into my house. Come away.'

The woman shudders. 'My brother is coming.' She turns to Zahra. 'They will come for you too. Look.' She points to the door of the Chinese house. Noor is there staring at the Japanese man on the pavement. There is a red painted sign on the door in Chinese. 'They mark the houses of those they will kill.'

Zahra rushes back into the house. She signs to Noor. Go upstairs and get your things.

'Fatima,' she says to the girl peeping around the screen, terrified. 'Get ready. We're going back to my father's house.'

* * *

The Lorry

Mr and Mrs Guan, Carlos, Simone and the Chinese and Malay gardeners wait outside Dr Ueno's house. The lorry from the internment camp sweeps up the drive with four sullen Japanese guards and Bertie in the back. The gardeners all cheer and Bertie raises a hand like Caesar in triumph. He jumps down and begins shaking everyone's hands. To Mrs Guan's astonishment, he gives her a hug, then puts his lips to Simone's undamaged cheek.

'Keep everything. Newspapers, leaflets, everything,' he whispers.

Dr Ueno accompanies Hatter to the lorry. After the exuberant farewell of Bertie, Hatter simply bows to Dr Ueno and gives a wave to the others. Nothing, Simone reflects, could more aptly describe the relationship of these two men to everyone in the Gardens. Bertie takes the two suitcases and slides them on the back and puts his hand out to Hatter.

Then they are gone.

* * *

The Atom Bomb

Mrs Guan prepares the milk. 'Powdered rice and some strained carrots,' she says in Malay. Jumairah pounds rice in the pestle.

The girls sit and watch these proceedings, gazing at the baby with interest. Milk is suddenly abundant. And Dr Ueno has ordered it to be distributed to all the employees of the Gardens. The Red Cross has begun liberating rice and provisions from the warehouses.

'Aka-chan,' the eldest girl says to Simone as she arrives, pointing at Zejian.

'Bao bao,' Mrs Guan says. 'Baby. It's a baby. English now.'

The girls gaze up with their slender eyes at their mother. They have no idea what she is talking about. How can Mrs Guan undo years of indoctrination? 'Baby,' she says. 'English. The word is baby. 'Say it,' she orders in Cantonese. The girls, used to the discipline of repetition and obeisance, say it. 'Bay bee.'

The Syonan Shinbun carries a report from Lisbon about what they call the atom bomb. The Archbishop of Canterbury in England declares that 'humanity has received a searing wound by the fact that half a million people were destroyed in a moment by a new diabolical weapon'. None of the scientists—actually no one—can grasp it. There are no pictures. Dr Ueno, Professor Haneda and Lieutenant Uehara go to the temple. Ring the bell. Light the incense. They make no complaint.

'I have to go to the POW camp at Sime Road,' Simone says.

'Guan is going,' Mrs Guan says. 'Dr Ueno gave him the key to the storehouse and the car. He wants to take food and medicine. He's at the Herbarium.'

JOHOR

Leaving

Kay holds out her hand to Richie. 'Goodbye,' she says. He takes it. Holds it. Ravi in the driver's seat toots the horn.

'See you in Singapore?' Richie says. 'I have to talk to Lai Tek.'

'See he doesn't bite off your hand of friendship. And watch your back.'

He laughs. 'I'd like to see you in Singapore.'

She swings into the passenger seat. Java Force has disbanded. Yuan and the other Chinese guerrillas have joined up with the MPAJA. Uma Nair has gone to find her cousin and taken the Malay sisters with her. The others have returned to their villages. The Gurkha soldier was delivered to a hospital. The farewell was intense. They've fought beside each other. Cared for each other. War makes life exciting but cruel too, monotonous, terrifying and hopeless. A time, an extraordinary experience they would never have again. Perhaps, she thinks, we will not really realize how it was until much later. Perhaps, one day, we will be able to dwell on it more fondly than we think.

She looks up to the mountain. To a grave where the Jakun children play. Love is a mortal thing. You hold it close, in your skin, for your own life is part of it. But you know when the time comes you have to let it go. She can't quite. Not yet.

'Java,' Richie says. 'Tell me where?'

She smiles. 'Raffles Hotel.' She clangs the door shut. 'Oh. I forgot. Sorry. No natives allowed.'

SYONAN

The Banyan Tree

The Herbarium has notices pasted everywhere in Chinese, Japanese, English and Malay warning trespassers and looters of death. Two Jap soldiers have been posted to protect it. A group of Malay gardeners is gathered to one side, clearing the paths. The life of the Gardens goes on. But now the Malays don't bother to bow.

Greta Muller emerges at the side of the building so abruptly Simone has no time to get out of her way. Greta flings herself on Simone knocking her to the ground. She screams in German, venting her fury with flailing arms and legs. Simone feels the wound on her cheek open and blood pour down her neck.

The Malay gardeners drop their rakes and come forward. The Japanese soldiers watch, indifferent. Greta gives a shriek of pain. Katsu-san is attached to her shoulders by her claws, and Greta, turning and whirling as she might, cannot detach her. The cat rakes Greta's cheek into lines of blood before leaping lightly to the ground. Greta screams and lunges but in an instant the cat is on the roof of the Herbarium licking her paws.

Simone gets up, goes to Greta and slaps her across the face as hard as she can. The Malays clap and cheer. Greta bursts into tears and runs, arms flailing, down the path. Mr Guan appears during all this pandemonium.

Simone holds her cheek. 'Damn,' she says.

'We have a first aid kit in the Herbarium,' Mr Guan says. 'Red Cross parcels the Japs had hoarded. Dettol and Elastoplast. Wonder of wonders.'

'I want to go with you up to Sime Road,' she says.

'Yes. But let's deal with your cheek first.'

A miaow. Simone looks up. 'We need to get Katsu-san inside,' she says. 'Until things settle down. Someone will eat her.'

'She's practically feral,' Mr Guan says. 'Not much chance.'

To her surprise—and his—Katsu-san leaps elegantly from the roof and curls her tail around Simone's bandaged ankles.

'She knows what side her bread is buttered on. I wonder how you say that in Japanese?' Mr Guan laughs. 'Of course, I don't have to care anymore.'

Dettol, gauze and Elastoplast are applied to her cheek. She looks in the mirror. 'It might be a good thing,' she says. 'Better dressing. Perhaps less of a scar.'

'I have to get the Red Cross parcels to take up there.'

'I need to settle the cat. Let's not call her Katsu-san anymore.'

Mr Guan smiles. 'No. Perhaps she will find another who will give her a new name.' He hands Simone the keys to the Herbarium. 'Lock the doors and meet me at Tanglin Gate.'

Simone makes a bed for the cat and prepares a bowl of water. There are plenty of rodents in the Herbarium to keep her going for a day or two. She sits, watching the cat lap up the water in the cool, quiet familiarity of this place. A few short days ago she thought she was going to die.

If no one turns up to love this cat Simone knows she will. Miss Victory has become a part of this story. Bertie and Hatter will head back to England as soon as the Brits arrive. They may never speak again. Will this cat remember Bertie? Does she remember the Governor and the fire in the grate. What do cats remember?

The cat looks at her. Glossy. Healthy on her abundant diet of small creatures. One eye blue, the other green. Glittering. Calm. She purrs, a rattle, deep and heavy, settles onto the bed and goes to sleep. Simone grins. Protected by her privileged position: by the Governor, by Tanaka, by the Marquis, by the vastness of the Gardens. Otherwise she would have been cat soup. Survival never depends on you alone. What did the Japanese say? *Jigoku de Hotoke.* 'Finding a Buddha in Hell'. Everyone needs to find a Buddha in Hell.

She locks the Herbarium. The Japanese guards do not look at her. She does not bow. It's as if they now live in parallel universes. Their realities are no longer the same.

She begins to climb the steps, up the rise to the banyan tree, weary now, her cheek throbbing, but ready for the drive to find Jean. As she puts her foot on the final step, she looks up. Mr and Mrs Sugiyama are hanging from the branches, faces purple, feet swaying. They are dressed in their finest kimonos and around their necks hang the white boxes of their sons' charred hands. Their wooden geta lie below them like the dots on an exclamation mark.

She knows they could never have lived with this surrender. It doesn't stop the rush of unutterable and inexpressible sorrow, which brings her to her knees.

* * *

The Red Corpses

Three bodies are lying alongside the railway tracks. Three men. Naked. Japanese. A blood-soaked Japanese flag draped over one of them. Their clothing strewn to one side. Kay approaches. They look as if they've been dried and shrunk. Reddish stripes run the whole length of their bodies. Were they skinned alive or after death? She takes a step back. One is halfway into a ditch, one arm slightly raised as if trying to grab hold of the sky.

Private vengeance? Ordinary people turned into slayers and flayers. It is possible that these men were civilians. Possible they had done nothing terrible. That they stand in for the anger and frustration of common people forced to be complicit in war. Expiation for all the other bastards who will get away with it. She feels that too. The deep quivering anger. The desire to kill. Tsuji's death will be balm for her soul. He will be her red corpse.

Ravi slides his hand into hers.

* * *

Kranji Camp

'I escaped from here,' Ravi says, 'with two others. Swam across the Straits.' He gazes at the camp. It's quiet. The men are thin. Starved. 'If I'd stayed, I'd be them. A skeleton.' She knows the other two died of disease and hunger in the jungle. He's thinking of that now. Uma Nair had saved him. Taken him into her home and nursed him to health. In return he had saved her.

Ravi has to join whatever remains of his regiment to wait for the British. He has to go back to India. Get the whole war mess sorted out. He has a wife. A son. A family who think he is dead. They both knew it would come. She can feel her hand in the long silky hair running like water down Ravi's back. The Sikhs never cut it. It is magnificent. Luxurious. She wrapped her body and her spirit in it and him. Ravinder Singh. It sounds like a breeze or a rilling stream. Like poetry. His body, his determination, hard as iron, but his mind wide and open. Their nights together never changed her authority in the day. They will never know again such a strange meeting of souls. Their bones will ache with missing each other and dwell silently on that time, in odd moments, forever.

He pulls her behind the truck. To kiss her for the last time. For the memory. For all the days and nights of heartache to come. She holds him as hard as she can. His eyes meet hers. Then he releases her and walks into the camp. She gets into the truck. The gears grind, harsh and hard, in her anxiety to get away.

* * *

Hurley Burley

MPAJA lorries, nose to tail, rumble down Bukit Timah Road.
Flags wave. The soldiers roar in song.

Zhe shi zuihou de douzheng
Tuanjie qulai, dao mingtian

Loudspeakers declaim. They have come to liberate the people.
The time has come to throw out the colonisers, the capitalists, the
oppressors.

So comrades, come rally,
And the last fight let us face.
The Internationale
Unites the human race.

The Japanese travel in the opposite direction. Armoured vehicles.
Tanks. Cars. Trucks. Motorcycles. They carry ammunition,
stores, furniture. Loot. What they do not take, they buy with
mountains of banana notes. They've printed millions over the
past three months.

The British will honour the money, some say. To those who
believe that, others offer banana notes for Straits Dollars. A
thousand. Two thousand to one.

In all the military and civilian offices a great conflagration
has begun. The destruction of every picture, paper, document, all
trace of what was done here. It is steady, thorough and efficient.
Fires crackle and smoke in courtyards, gardens and parks and
embers float like orange glowworms day and night.

At Adam Road, people meld from every direction to climb
up the long steep rise to the POW camp. Chinese and Eurasian.
Carrying bundles of clothes. Baskets of hard-found food.
Christians seek their fellows. Nurses, doctors, clerks, scientists
and teachers seek former bosses and colleagues. Amahs, cooks

and maids seek the mems and children they remember. In the Indian houses and Malay kampongs they stay quiet. Retribution is in the air. The only policemen visible are shot through the head or hang from trees. The rest have melted away.

The Red Cross truck—the Blue Angel—is at the gates of the camp. Throughout the occupation the Red Cross has tried to feed the prisoners, send in medicine. Banging against a wall. The Japanese allowed only one distribution of food in three years. On the Emperor's birthday in '44, a gracious gift of their own parcels. Even then it was one parcel between forty men. No medicine was ever given. Now they've released stores, parcels, rice, drugs. Abundance. To fatten the prisoners before the British return. Nothing terrible happened here.

The camp kitchen is bursting with activity, smells, heat. There are no guards. The Japanese have withdrawn. The INA soldiers have disappeared.

This valley was a golf course once. Then Percival's headquarters. Then a military POW camp. Now it is a farm. Rows of tapioca. Attap-covered huts. In the valley a fence runs the length of it. On one side men. On the other women and children.

On a knoll sits the house of the Japanese commander, Tominaga. He is there, to her surprise, seated on the veranda, looking down. Unmoving. He has decided not to rip open his guts. Why? There will be a judgement. There will be a trial. He must know it. The British will not care about the local people—their massacres, miseries and deaths. But these people—their own— those they will avenge. The graves and the starving witnesses to his actions are all around him. He will be hanged.

A voice calls Simone. She turns. She doesn't recognize him. Emaciated. Scabrous. Arm in a sling. Walks with a crudely fashioned crutch. His heavy-rimmed glasses are stuck all over with a variety of tapes.

'It's Leslie.' he says. 'Leslie Hawkins. *Straits Times* editor.'

'Oh Mr Hawkins.' She puts her hand to his. 'You got through.'

'Just,' he says. 'Wouldn't have given it much longer,'

'I'm glad. So very glad.'

'You're here to find someone,' he says. 'Everyone is here to find someone.'

He gazes a moment along the valley. Looking at ghosts.

'But soon the newspaper will need reporters. George Baker said you were a good one. And he would know. Did he get away?'

'Yes. I think he got away.'

'Hmm. When the British get here, when the hurley burley's done, come and see me.'

'Yes. I will. Thank you.'

She walks to the women's huts. They are miserable, crowded, damp. But the women greet her with smiles. The children fly about. Friends and colleagues offer clothes and open their baskets.

'Jean?' she asks. 'Jean McKenna?'

* * *

The Hearse

Molly calls and beckons with her hand. Li Jun is driving. The car is a hearse used for Japanese funerals. 'All I could get,' Li Jun says, 'at short notice.' He grins. Zahra gets in.

She hasn't been back to the radio station. Yoshida is still in charge. His deputy is Joseph Pillai, reliable, experienced radio journalist. Joseph is the one who has always really run everything whilst Yoshida ate ginger biscuits and got drunk. 'Don't come in,' Joseph had said on the telephone. 'Everything's very unsettled. Yoshida bursts into tears. And he's busy destroying everything. But stay off the streets too. People know who you are.'

They pass the Japanese Central Language School, now the headquarters of the MPAJA. A mass of flags. Red with gold stars. Here and there, like punctuation marks, the blue sky and white sun of the flags of the KMT. Not one Union Jack has appeared. Kangaroo courts. Angry crowds spitting. Accusing.

'When will it stop?' Zahra asks.

'Not yet,' Li Jun says, 'not yet.'

'We only kill our own,' she says. 'Not the Japanese. It's cowardly. The Japanese are to blame.'

He doesn't hear or doesn't care. The streets are a mass of MPAJA trucks and cars. Crowds block the way. Li Jun turns towards the Padang.

She turns to Molly. 'Why is he here? Where are we going?'

'Java asked Li Jun to take all of us to Sime Road. I called the Gardens but couldn't get hold of Simone. I don't know where Jenny is. Or even if she is all right. And Li Jun wouldn't take Anita. He hates them.'

Li Jun nods. 'I do. INA bastards. Hang 'em all.'

'Anyway she couldn't get out of the barracks. They're all in mourning over there. Bose was killed in an air crash. Look.'

Li Jun is on Connaught Drive. They pass the Indian National Army monument to the unknown soldier. It is covered in wreaths and surrounded by wailing men and women.

Li Jun grins and sweeps past. 'Bakaro,' he calls and presses the horn.

* * *

Jean

Simone walks, watching the movement of her feet through the thick grass, one step after the other, on the path that leads to the cemetery.

There is a hut here. Perhaps once it was the greenkeeper's hut for the door handles are golf balls. Inside there is writing scratched onto the wooden walls. Long after the British surrender, before the civilians were moved here, this had been a camp for POWs returning from the Siamese Railway. The writing is a memorial—a record—of those who never returned. Went up four thousand, it says. Came back eighteen hundred. John Arkwright, nineteen, died of cholera. Billy Winter, twenty, died of starvation and malaria. Cholera, beriberi, typhus, septic wounds, malaria, starvation.

She walks past. She can't think of them. Amidst the vastness of the hecatomb, there is only room in a heart for those you know and love.

In July, the Japanese refused permission for the POWs to bury their dead in the town. The cemetery here is for those prisoners who had died since then. A hundred fresh crosses.

Simone looks over the small hillock and sees Sime Road. Down there, not fifty yards away, is the place where once stood the old bamboo and attap hut that was the King George Curry Café. Not a trace remains.

At her feet is a freshly dug mound with a new wooden marker. Jean McKenna died two days ago, the women told her. A bad beating by a Jap kempei. Nasty bastard. The women doctors did their best. The nurses cared for her. But without medicines and on top of malarial fever and starvation, well, the heart just gives out. Even a great heart. She was a Girl Guide, they said. Spoke of it often.

A truck stops. Simone gazes down. Kay looks up and smiles. Behind her a black hearse pulls to a halt. Molly squeals and throws herself at Kay. Zahra looks up at Simone and waves.

* * *

The Imperial Rescript

Tenno Heika moved by a deep concern for humanity's future.

Guy Medoc snorts. The newspaper has finally printed the surrender. 'The troops of the Southern regions have been ordered to cease military activity pending the outcome of armistice negotiations.' He reads this aloud.

'Armistice,' he says and snorts again. 'Not bloody likely. Unconditional surrender. The Yanks won't take anything else. All face-saving bullshit. We should take a flame thrower to the lot of them.'

He throws the newspaper on the table. Simone adds it to the pile she will conceal in the roof. Guy is here to do a job for Mr Guan. One truck a day with two Japanese soldiers on board is permitted to go out of the Maxwell Road Internment Camp to collect food and buy other necessities for the internees.

Guy is bitter about this as well. 'Why are we still there? What the hell is going on?' There is no news still about the British arrival. Rumours of ethnic violence on the mainland. But here, despite the parades, rough justice and loudhailers of the MCP it is localized and limited. It offers no threat to the Japanese who watch it warily but at a distance. What does it matter if they string up their own? The Japanese still control the streets and buildings of the town.

Last night, Dr Haneda's and Dr Ueno's personal and scientific papers were burned, over their objections, by order of the Japanese garrison commander in Tanglin. Mr Guan had rushed over to the Museum and found that it had been stripped of every Japanese notice, map and poster. Guy is here to nail shut every door and window from top to bottom of the Museum and library. Mr Guan moves eight of the Chinese museum staff inside with orders to repel invaders.

Today, none of the scientists are here. They have gone off to a meeting of the newly flung-together Japanese Association. The soldiers are building the Japanese civilians an internment camp in the west of the island to await the British. They will not return to the Museum. They, unsurprisingly, feel that Guy's comment about flamethrowers might actually come to pass.

Simone follows Mr Guan and Guy to the bird gallery. While Guy hammers nails into the floor and doors, Simone approaches the kingfisher exhibit. From a distance the glass case seems filled with yellow paper obscuring the birds. At the case, however, she sees it is not paper but a thousand cicada shells. Mr Guan comes to her side.

'Did Mrs Sugiyama put them here?' Simone asks, 'what does it mean?'

'She collected them. She asked me to have one of the gardeners bring every one he could find. Grief. But also her belief in the good rebirth of her sons. And now herself and her husband. I understood. We spoke of this sometimes. We had a kind of common culture, I suppose. She was not a bad woman, you know. Lost. As tragic as us.'

Simone gazes on the ghostly shells. 'Why here? Why has she put them here?'

'She loved these birds most of all, I suppose.' He points to the yellowing paper. 'The kawasemi and the semi united.'

Simone reads the familiar words.

In the cicada's cry
There is no sign that can foretell
How soon it must die.

Guy stops hammering and in the sudden hush she can hear geta clacking.

'Do you know,' Mr Guan says, 'that the final process of the metamorphosis of the cicada, the stiffening of the cicada shell, is called imagination. The imagination of the cicada shell. Perhaps we may take the cicada shell as a metaphor—the empty shell of Singapore's occupation—and imagine that from it may come, like the soft skin of the new cicada, a reincarnation of this island and its future.'

Simone turns to him. 'Only you can make what has been ugly, something hopeful and lovely.'

'It is neither ugly nor lovely, is it? It is merely a truth. One amongst many doubtless.' He glances at her with a shy smile. 'I have a diary. I kept a diary. My truth.'

Simone grins and puts her hand to his arm. 'Me too. I never told anyone. How little we trusted each other.'

Mr Guan puts his head to one side. 'We wanted to protect each other. Silence was a protection.'

'Yes. Perhaps it was that.'

'I will move the case to the storeroom,' he says. 'It will rot and fade but I should like to keep it for a while.'

Mr Guan turns away. Simone catches her image in the glass. The scar on her cheek. Scrawny. And what a fright, the hair. But now she can bear to look at it.

* * *

The Victory Dress

'What will you do?' Simone asks Kay.

Kay lives with her in this bungalow. Greta simply disappeared so Simone moved into this house with Jumairah, leaving the Guans to have some privacy at last. The third bungalow, the Sugiyama's, is locked. All their personal possessions remain inside. No one wants to deal with them. Their ghosts still haunt the Gardens. It won't last long. Soon the British will be back and they will be a dream.

'I will find Tsuji and kill him.'

Simone nods. She'd thought she would like Tsuji to be dead too. But now, for reasons she couldn't explain, she doesn't care. Vengeance exhaustion. 'He may already be dead.'

'You told me he wasn't amongst the dead Japs at the jail. I'm sure he is alive. I feel it.' Kay touches Simone's cheek. 'He likes to disfigure. He goes for the face first. Leaves his mark.'

A silence falls. It isn't over yet. It won't be over for a long time. Perhaps it will never be over.

Kay points to the pile of Simone's diaries. 'You wrote it down. Dangerous thing to do.'

'I had to, I suppose. Writing is a kind of confession. It offered peace. And if we don't remember this, what was it all about?'

'It was about nothing. A clash of empires. Very little to do with us. A mad, lamentable, occasionally exhilarating, experiment.' Kay laughs. 'Like life I suppose. An interval between birth and death.' She shrugs. 'But you should write it. Leave the evidence so that the dead aren't killed in memory as well as life. But it won't change anything. And it will only be your truth. It won't be mine or anyone else's.'

'It will be a woman's story. There won't be many. The men will write theirs and we shall be invisible. For that alone I must write it. You should write yours too.'

Kay picks up *The Aeneid.* 'God, this old thing. What a rubbish book. We read it in class. All I recalled is that the women are fabulous warriors and queens who suddenly become silly and weak over a man's charms or a dress or some such. Only a man would write such unbearable nonsense. Can't see any women I know in any of it. So maybe you're right. Can't leave men to tell the really big story. But I've no talent for it. I'll leave that to you. Once I have my sweet revenge, I'm all for forgetting.'

She tosses the book. 'Richie Somerville wants me to have a drink with him in the Raffles.' She smiles. 'I need him. He will find Tsuji for me.'

She goes to the mirror. 'God, what a mess. I need a haircut. And I haven't got a thing to wear.'

'I have,' Simone says and drags out the suitcase. 'You might like, my warrior queen, to choose a fitting finery, without, of course, becoming silly or weak.' She holds up the white silk dress with the pearl buttons. 'Isabel von Hoff's victory dress. It deserves to go to Raffles.'

* * *

Radio Malaya

Zahra looks up to the roof of the Cathay Building. The Japanese flag is being taken down. She, like the crowd that has gathered to watch, feels the shivery emotion of this moment. And the mixed feelings of watching the Union Jack raised. Some cheer and clap. She cannot.

'Is there no one else?' the British broadcaster says in clipped tones, staring at Zahra. Two men have parachuted into Singapore to take over the radio station. The broadcaster and an engineer. 'Can't have a woman read out such momentous stuff.'

Mr Pillai stands to one side with the small group of Chinese and Indian language newsreaders, two of them women. A glance passes. 'The Malay people know her,' Mr Pillai says. 'They're used to her voice. She has been their companion. They will believe her.'

Zahra waits. She's glad she didn't clap the raising of the Union Jack. What the hell has changed?

'Read out all the Japanese muck, did you?' He stares at her with barely disguised disgust.

'Read out the British muck, too, when Singapore was falling,' she says. She doesn't care. Let him fire her.

He sways as if she's slapped him. A smile tinkers with Mr Pillai's lips. 'Think you'd better leave all this local business to me,' he says. 'You're a bit too new here.'

The man's jaw clenches. Veins pop at his temples. Zahra can read his mind. How dare they call a British officer in Singapore new? They own it. Have done for over a century. What about Raffles? But here's a bloody woman giving him cheek and a bloody native smiling and calling him a novice. Stiff and bristling, he turns and walks away.

Mr Pillai hands Zahra the paper to translate.

The surrender document has been signed in Tokyo. Tomorrow British troops will land on this island. The days of misery are over. Singapore will be British again.

* * *

Raffles Hotel

People are on the streets of the town. Gathered by the river. Gay, noisy, throwing banana notes around in restaurants and cafes suddenly filled with abundance.

In alleys bodies lie beaten to death. In the river others bloat. But no one wants to be inside. The blackout has been removed from street lamps and buildings. After so long in the dark, everyone seeks the bright lights. They move in groups. Safety in numbers.

Kay walks amongst them. They need a leader to fight for freedom from the British. The communists have the status and the power but they are no good. Too Chinese owned and operated. They can't rally the Malays who would fight them to the death. There is a revolution in the Indies to fight the Dutch. But the Japs organized that at the very end. Here everyone is too tired. Too suspicious. The future is too uncertain. Only live for this day.

She looks to the sky. The moon is new, barely visible. Hiding its light. Ashamed of the earth and the mess we humans make of it. Fanciful. Old moon. New moon. Waxing, waning, gibbous, crescent. She'd contemplated them and this a thousand times from the top of her mountain.

But the hotel doesn't need the moon. It is brilliantly lit. Battered but still beautiful. She had toyed with the idea of marching in in her jungle fatigues. Just to see what would happen. But in the end she couldn't quite resist Isabel van Hoff's beautiful dress. But would they let a Chinese woman in? She had asked Richie not to meet her at the door.

The Sikh doorman saluted her without expression, much as he doubtless saluted the Japanese who used this bastion of British privilege as their playground. Perhaps Richie had told him to let her pass. Or until the British actually got here, things wouldn't settle into the *status quo ante*. This was merely the interval between the acts. She passes through the cool, tiled corridors, feeling the pleasurable swish of the silk against her legs, and into the palm-fringed inner courtyard.

Mrs Guan had produced Chinese slippers and made a handbag out of an old green velvet curtain. Amidst all this vaguely unsettling softness, she feels the reassuring iron of the Webley against her arm.

He gets up as she approaches. The look on his face is worthy of her choice.

'Well, don't you look beautiful?'

She doesn't bother to smile. Of course she looks beautiful compared to jungle-standard. She sits and crosses her legs, examining the slippers, each embroidered with a red peony and a golden phoenix. These are symbols of Straits Chinese marriage. Perhaps they were Mrs Guan's wedding slippers. It was generous of her to lend them.

'What is your real name?' Richie asks, clearly ill at ease at her apparent interest in anything but him.

She looks around. The courtyard is cool. The ceiling fans turn. There is the sound of a fountain. How lovely it is.

'This is nice.'

He hesitates. Then he gives a small shrug and a smile.

'Yes. I have a bloody great room, running water and all the whisky I can drink.' He points to a spot by the fountain. 'A bunch of Japs slit their bellies right there.'

She gazes at the pretty tiles. There should be a trace, shouldn't there? The breeze rills the leaves of the palm trees. She recalls the lines from a play at school decades ago. *Our revels now are ended. Leave not a rack behind.* The Tempest. She'd played Prospero. A tempest has passed through this place yet not a rack—what was a rack?

'Java,' Richie says and she looks up. They are all insubstantial air. But it is good to be alive. Better to be alive. And there's a job unfinished.

Richie offers her a cigarette. She takes it.

'I met Lai Tek. He has agreed to cooperate with us. SEAC forces are already on Penang anyway. Mountbatten has agreed that the MPAJA should be honoured at the surrender ceremony and Commander Chin Peng will get a medal.'

'Really. Order of the Terminally Disappointed? I should think he wanted revolution.'

Richie ignores this. 'Burma Star at least. Possibly an OBE. He and his men saved me. All of us in Malaya. All honours are richly deserved.'

'Did you tell him that Lai Tek is a traitor?'

He shakes his head.

'So Chin Peng will give up all the weapons, will he? Hand them over to you just like that. How many do you think you dropped? How many do you think they've taken from Japanese arsenals all over Malaya these last two weeks?'

'Lai Tek has agreed to a disarmament.'

'Well, good luck with that.'

A group of Englishwomen, thin, but chatting cheerfully, pass across the courtyard. They greet him. One or two glance at her and give a queer look. If Richie notices he makes no reaction. She knows who they are.

'European POWs.'

'Yes. They've been gathered here, waiting for processing and repatriation.'

'Really.' She blows smoke. 'How nice for them. What about the other women in the camp? Chinese, Malays, Eurasians, Jews. Riff-raff married to British men. You know, the others.'

'Well I don't know. Not my remit.' He has the grace to look uncomfortable. 'Gone home I suppose.'

She crushes the cigarette. 'Home to where? With what? God! Nothing has changed. I'm surprised you can bear to be sitting here with me. You'll get hell for it tonight. It'll go round the lot of them like a fly buzzing on meat.'

'Look. I don't care about any of that. It's rubbish. I'll set them straight if they talk about you. Let's get a drink.' He raises his hand. The Indian waiter approaches.

Somehow she believes him. Or, in a vague way, simply doesn't care. What does this British nonsense matter anymore? It may take a few years but soon they will be gone. She lets him order. Pink Gin and Whisky Soda. Why not? She wants something from him.

'Lady Mountbatten wants to meet you.'

She bursts into laughter. 'What on earth? You know everyone on the street calls Mountbatten Linger Longer Louis, don't you? It's been three weeks.'

'I have heard that. It's MacArthur's fault. Anyway, I told Mountbatten about you. He told Lady Mountbatten. She wants to meet you. On the day of the surrender ceremony.'

'Don't be ridiculous. Look, I want you to find someone for me.'

* * *

Status Quo Ante

The Union Jack floats over the Museum roof. The portraits of the King and Queen again adorn the walls. The hensei King Edward VIII, Governor Shenton Thomas, the busts and portraits of Governors of old have been retrieved from the dust of the taxidermy room and brushed anew. Raffles has been restored to his pedestal and now looks down from a lofty height. Soon he will move back to the riverside. Queen Victoria's chips and stains await refurbishment. In the meantime she is shrouded in a white cloth like the Pontianak of Christmas past and the Malays won't go near her.

Simone guards the library, the cat at her feet. A Malay official had turned up demanding a thousand books to start a public library in Johor Bahru. She had simply kicked him out and shut the door.

Uehara and Haneda left for Jurong before the surrender ceremony. Dr Ueno stayed till the last. He thrust his manuscript on Malayan trees into the keeping of a miserable Hatter who offered to appeal to the British. Fat chance, Simone thought. Apparently so did Dr Ueno. He graciously declined. When he bade her farewell in his gentlemanly way, she had bowed to him, the full 45 degrees for three seconds. When she rose her eyes met his and there were tears there. She could find none.

She had no interest in the Surrender Ceremony. Listened to the radio. Big Ben. *This is London calling.* Heard the seventeen-gun salute and, vaguely carried on the wind, Rule Britannia. That was quite enough. Zahra went to the Padang for the ceremony with her radio pals. Said when the Japs arrived only the thick lines of armed sailors prevented them from being torn apart. Being thus thwarted they took to their voices, shouting Bakaro over and over. Ba-ka-ro, Ba-ka-ro, louder and louder. Fifty thousand voices. It rose to a roar. It must have been heard inside. Who can ever forget that insult—stupid bastard—meted out daily to every single man, woman and child for three-and- a-half years? In a few years it will be the only shred of Japanese they remember. That and the horror.

Kay didn't attend, despite the official invitation from Lady Mountbatten. She heard that Lord Mountbatten thanked all the communist guerrillas for their loyalty. Loyalty! She thumped the table and laughed until she had a coughing fit. 'Chin Peng has already changed the MPAJA's name to the Malayan National Liberation Army.' She knows that arms and ammunition sit inside caves throughout the length and breadth of Malaya. Waiting.

Anita is still confined to barracks. The whole INA is being questioned by the British Military Administration, who can't decide whether or not to accuse them of collaboration with the enemy.

Molly is busy with the Shaws, getting the Great World in order for the thousands of British squaddies who will soon be spending their money there.

Jenny's at the General Hospital, treating all the local internees who are trickling in, treating all the poor Javanese romusha, the thousands of orphans, the sick and the starving. She told

Simone that the European internees got a ludicrous pecuniary compensation for their years of imprisonment. The freedom fiver Straits dollar note. The locals got half. She doesn't care about the ceremony. Too much to do in this fallen and faltering island to bother with the show.

Simone's diaries are on the desk. The job at the newspaper lasted only a few weeks. The men came back. She must make way. She was offered the women's page. Hatter and Bertie offered her the library. For the present, it will do.

She can feel the old order tightening around her. But in herself she senses a new fluidity and openness. The war feels as if it has released her and her sisters from the tyranny of tradition. She feels a quickness in her blood. All—women and men—had been blasted by the wrecking ball of violence and humiliation. No one in this long brutal darkness has stayed the same. Perhaps the men might want it to be so, but like the clamouring voices of young nations desperate to throw off the yoke of empire, so too surely was the burgeoning rise of women's wishes to be free: to think, to live, to write. Like the cat I can be blue and green; go anywhere, do anything.

She has kept the faith with George and covered pages with words. Writing as a subversive, even fatal act. What was there to fear now? It could not sit untouched, unexplored. It had to be attempted. If for no one else, then for Teresa—Gray—Ying. And her daughter. How will her daughter know her, what will she call her? She cannot be lost because no one is looking for her. Someday her daughter will come looking for her.

She will not write the pointless glorification of man-made dislocation, hiatus and fragmentation. The fall of Troy was nothing more than Virgil's poetic whining and justification for yet more of the same kind of empire—*sans* women as far as possible—just in another place; the very thing the Japanese so coveted. After all, the English taught this classical nonsense. The fall of Singapore had to be about something more real and substantial. The brief moment of a potential vision for a different world, a world Jean McKenna believed in. She felt an upsurge of exhilaration. To explode and disrupt the cosy image the returned English colonial masters now wished to project. Tell the war as it was. The soldiers and the professors would write their illusionary stories of sterile imperialism. She must contradict. Take the war away from the fathers and give it to the mothers and the daughters. The last page of Miss Woolf is open. *Shakespeare's sister. She lives in you and me. A chance to walk among us. A chance which is now within your power to give her.*

But how to use that power? Her eyes go to her precious shelf of women authors and alight on Pearl S. Buck's *The Good Earth*, a book she has read and re-read throughout the Occupation. A book in which she finds a profound understanding of Teresa and the struggles of her Chinese life. A book where fact and fiction blend because the lives of women, like the poor and dispossessed, are never recorded and can only be brought movingly into existence through the intelligent imagination. Perhaps that is the way to write this story. A different kind of woman. A different set of arms.

In the languor of the heat her pen drifts across the clean white page: Of Arms and the Woman, I sing. She smiles.

'Hello there. You in charge?' The voice has a twang. Soft. Polite. Australian perhaps.

Simone gets up from the desk. Dark-hair flecked with grey, good looking. Dressed in the uniform of a Lieutenant-Colonel. Not Australian she sees from the small flag adorning his jacket. New Zealand. He holds out his hand to her and makes a slight bow. Old-fashioned. Gentlemanly. She likes him instantly.

'No,' she says going towards him. The cat stretches and follows her. Her tail loops lazily around the legs of the newcomer. 'Just being the guard dog. I'm Simone Martel.'

She grasps his hand. 'Roche,' he says with a broad grin. 'Jeremy Roche. Auckland Museum. BMA sent me to find Dr Hatter. I'm the monuments man.'

He reaches down and strokes the cat. 'What an extraordinary cat. *Heterochromia iridis*. Beautiful. What's his name?'

'Her,' Simone says. Jeremy straightens and engages Simone's eyes. 'Of course,' he says. 'And all that's best of dark and bright, meet in her aspect and her eyes.'

Rempang Isand

November 1945

Simone waits for Richie in the lobby of the Goodwood Park Hotel, the offices of the War Crimes Tribunal. He is one of the investigators.

'Hello,' he says. 'Thanks for coming.' His natural politeness has disguised his disappointment. He'd hoped for Kay.

He raises his hand for the car. Upright, impeccable in his starched and ironed uniform—undoubtedly by a woman. She has never cared for him: so typical of his gender and his race. He's filled with confidence and hope for the future. Of course he is. It's always there in the male world. But she remembers what Kay had said about Richie. Makes of men are like makes of cars. Richie was a 1912 model and not quite, but almost superfluous. Poor Richie. But she doesn't really care. His infatuation with Java interests neither of them. Though still vigorous in limb, Kay said, he was already an old fogey. He holds the door for her and climbs in beside her. The driver pulls away.

Simone saw ahead of him only the boredom and disillusion of peacetime. Perhaps there were yet wars to keep him occupied. Men like them so. For the present the power of tradition was desperate to reassert itself. In tradition was the lie of security. It was as if humanity could never progress, doomed to a constant repetition.

The world felt set on the same path. Already the language of the war's ending had become cliché. Singapore is British again. Business as usual. Put it all behind us and get on with it. Despite all the horrors nothing to see here. Back to normal. Normal included getting women back into the box.

Gangs of sweaty Japanese prisoners are filling in trenches and planting grass. Locals crouch nearby watching them. One sends a gob of spit onto the bare back of one of the prisoners. A British squaddie looks on, indifferent.

'When will they be sent back?' she says.

'No ships to send them back yet. A million or more in Southeast Asia. Mountbatten's first task is to repatriate the Javanese labourers, British POWs and all the other poor sods that were shuffled around like a pack of cards. And anyway he wants this lot to clean up the mess they made.'

The car pulls up at Clifford Pier and they alight. Along the length of it more Japanese prisoners repair, clean, unload. They do not look up. They work in this strange limbo—as they did in war—diligently, thorough, impenetrable. A diver sits on the edge of the pier. A crane is pulling up the Governor's Rolls Royce. Water streams from it as it twists and turns. Sunlight catches the cascade, casting rainbows on the surface of the harbour. Nearby stands the Fullerton. Doubtless he watched from his window, pondering defeat, as it slid into the depths. It's a great news story, but no one is here to photograph it or write it. All that ignominy isn't to be remembered. Australian voices call for a Royal Commission or at least an official inquiry. She cannot imagine it will ever happen. The truth will, as always, be governed by interest and blind credulity. Is there ever any truth in war anyway?

A young Japanese man approaches Richie. 'This is Keishi Masamoto,' Richie says. 'He's one of our interpreters.'

Keishi bows. 'I am not a soldier,' he says in a quiet anxious voice. 'I am a clerk at my father's store. I was born here. My father was born here.'

'Keishi's a good man,' Richie says. 'He was just a boy when all this began. Interned in India. Lost his mother on the ship going there.' Richie takes a paper from his coat. He holds it out to Simone who takes it. 'Kay's sketch of Tsuji,' he says.

She contemplates Tsuji's face.

'It's a good likeness.'

'Do you think you'll be able to identify him?'

'How many prisoners are there on Rempang Island?'

'One hundred and forty thousand.'

Simone stares at Richie. 'What? For heaven's sake.'

He shrugs. 'Got to be done. Tsuji isn't just wanted by Java and you, you know. He's a Class B criminal. He's implicated in the murder not only of Jean McKenna and other women in the camp, but was involved in the massacre of Chinese civilians in 1942 and many other deaths. The War Crimes Tribunal want him. He's not here in Singapore. My unit has checked. So we have to go to Rempang.'

'He might have gone anywhere,' Simone says. 'Three weeks of chaos after the surrender. Take off his uniform, get on a boat and sayonara.'

'True. But we still have to check here first. The prisoners without papers were all moved there but the Japanese military have records.'

The motor launch slowly picks its way through the bombed ships and minesweepers clearing the harbour. At Rempang a long jetty sticks like a flimsy tongue into the waters of the Riau Islands. The scarred landscape is visible from afar. All the trees have been cut down in a semicircle around the settlement of flimsy huts and canvas tents.

As they approach the jetty, the stench hits them. The sea is awash with filth sloshing around the heavy piles. 'What's going on here, Corporal?' Richie says to the English soldier watching lines of ragged, emaciated men unloading sheets of corrugated iron.

The man salutes and grins. 'Guess they haven't finished the latrines yet.'

'Good God, man. You'll have cholera.'

The man shrugs. 'It's up to them to sort it out.'

'Do they have a medic?' Simone asks.

The corporal turns to Simone. 'They have their own. We have nothing to do with them.' He indicates the piles of rusty corrugated iron sheets to one side. 'We give them material and tools and they have to get on with it. It's not a holiday camp. Did you see what they did to ours?'

He glares at Keishi who moves away towards a shack. Simone follows. Richie frowns and catches up to Simone. 'You can't write about this, Simone. BMA won't allow it.'

She shrugs. She hasn't bothered to tell him she's no longer with the newspaper.

In the shack Keishi points to an officer. 'This man is Captain Ito. He is in charge here. He says they have not had any rice since they've been here. The island has no food. And no medicine. They're living on insects.' Keishi's voice falters and he swallows. 'He says they have been here two months and seventeen hundred have died.'

'Tell him I'm not here for that. I'm looking for a man named Junichiro Tsuji, a former Captain in the Kempeitai.' He takes out the sketch and puts it on a table.

Keishi translates. The man shakes his head, face impassive.

'Tell him this man is a war criminal.'

Before Keishi can speak Simone puts her hand on Richie's arm. 'Tell him you will speak to the authorities about rice and medical supplies if he can find this man. Otherwise I will be writing this story. And damn the BMA.'

Richie stares at Simone then nods at Keishi who translates. Captain Ito bows curtly and leaves the shack.

'Go with him, Keishi,' Richie says.

'This situation is intolerable. It's pure revenge,' Simone says. 'You must do something about it.'

'Do you not understand the enormity of the job the BMA is doing? Their first priority is the civilians of Malaya. They too are starving and sick. The Japanese refused to sign the Geneva Convention and because it would make their bloody Emperor a POW, they only agreed to be called Surrendered Japanese Personnel. That choice means legally we owe them nothing.'

'I don't care. Whatever they call themselves they need to eat. Have we learned nothing from this damn war? Are we no better than them?'

Keishi returns before Richie can reply. 'Colonel, come please.' Keishi leads the way towards the edge of the destruction that was a forest. 'Captain Ito says to follow him.' A path leads to a small rocky bay. The wind carries a revolting stench and she throws her hand to her nose.

They emerge from the trees. The beach is stacked with bodies. Every body is emaciated and covered in faeces. A man is washing an angular skeleton on the edge of the sea. With a long pole he guides it towards another man who stands on a rock, catches the corpse and pushes it out into the wider ocean. Out there, sharks circle, waiting.

'These are men who died of wounds or hunger and dysentery,' Keishi translates. 'This man washes them clean then sends them into the sea. They cannot bury them. The ground is too hard. They cannot grow food.' Keishi points to a small Buddhist shrine placed in the shelter of a large rock. 'They can do nothing else.'

'Is Tsuji there?'

'He died and was sent into the sea.'

Simone frowns. 'Can we believe him?'

'Captain Ito records every name. Before Captain Tsuji died, he organized building works and helped many sick men. So he also got sick. They wrote his address and keep his belongings to take to his family one day. He was a good man.'

'He was a war criminal,' Richie growls. He points to the silver scar on Simone's cheek. 'He did this to her. He tortured and murdered.'

Keishi lowers his eyes. 'I only translate what Captain Ito says.'

Simone gazes out across the sand and the piles of rotting corpses. Clouds gather and the wind soars. The disposal of bodies is abandoned as waves pound like logs against the shore. Captain Ito leads them back to the hut. All over the island, a dark mass of half-naked, half-starved men huddle for warmth. Ghosts. Husks. Shells. As we once were, they are now. She sighs. A remorseless sense of déjà vu permeates her. But surely they must hope. The war had blown whole places apart, perhaps it might blow new ideas into existence. Women must not conspire with the old order. We, the women, must not be indolent.

Richie looks at Simone. 'We can't be sure then.'

'Maybe we can,' she says. 'Show me his belongings.'

A small bag is placed on the desk. Richie turns out the objects. Beside a slip of paper with Japanese writing is a picture of a pretty woman and three girls. Next to it is an elaborate toothpick.

'It was Tsuji,' Simone says.

Richie takes up the photograph. 'His wife and daughters,' he says. 'He had a family, yet found no compunction in killing women or children.'

Simone's eyes go to the wall of the hut and a picture of a Buddha. Lt. Uehara's face comes to her in a flash, staring at the moon. Then the thousands of dead cicada shells gathered by Mrs Sugiyama. The defunct exhibition and the creed of seishin.

'They are the embodiment of myths and ancient Gods. In a way, even whilst they were our gaolers, they were less free than us. Their myths are so long and deep that we can never truly fathom them. Yamato-damashii.' She looks at Keishi. 'Do you understand it, Keishi?'

Keishi shakes his head. 'I do not. My hope is that this is the end of all that madness.'

'What does this say?' Simone says, picking up the paper.

'It is his family's address in Japan.'

'Where are they?'

Keishi stares at her. 'Hiroshima.'

On the slow journey back to Singapore, the rain falls heavily on the slate-dark sea.